Day *of* Atonement

The Protective DETECTIVE SERIES

A Novel

YOLONDA TONETTE SANDERS

SBI

STREBOR BOOKS

NEW YORK LONDON TORONTO SYDNEY

Strebor Books
P.O. Box 6505
Largo, MD 20792
http://www.streborbooks.com

ISBN 978-1-59309-526-0
ISBN 978-1-4767-4455-1 (ebook)
LCCN 2014936766

First Strebor Books trade paperback edition November 2014

Cover design: www.mariondesigns.com
Cover photograph: © Keith Saunders/Keith Saunders Photos

10 9 8 7 6 5 4 3 2 1

Manufactured in the United States of America

For information regarding special discounts for bulk purchases,
please contact Simon & Schuster Special Sales at 1-866-506-1949
or business@simonandschuster.com

The Simon & Schuster Speakers Bureau can bring authors to your live event.
For more information or to book an event, contact the Simon & Schuster Speakers
Bureau at 1-866-248-3049 or visit our website at www.simonspeakers.com.

This book is dedicated to families with missing loved ones.
I can't begin to understand how you feel.
I pray that you ultimately find healing and peace.

ACKNOWLEDGMENTS

I heard that confession is good for the soul, but bad for the reputation. Yet, I am going to share something with you that may not necessarily win me any cool points. When it came to writing the acknowledgments for this book, I dreaded doing so. Not because I don't want to thank people. Rather, because I put a lot of time (i.e. months) into the acknowledgments for *Wages of Sin* and I thought, "Yolonda, how are you going to top that?" I know some authors copy and paste acknowledgments from book to book, but I didn't want to do it that way. (I'm not knocking the technique. I may very well have to use it in the near future— maybe even for the next book. If I do, don't y'all hold it against me!)

After stressing about the acknowledgments, I had a good long talk with myself. (Yes, literally. Don't worry; I'm okay. No medication is needed. ☺) I realized that I was making this process more difficult than it needed to be. I don't have to "top" anything as it's not about making the acknowledgments of subsequent books better than the previous ones. It's about thanking people from the bottom of my heart for the role they play in my life and/ or their specific contributions to this finished product.

To David Sanders (hubby), Tre (son), Tia (daughter), Wilene (mother), Eddie (father), Janice (mother-in-law) Teresa (friend and Yo Pro team member), Jenn (friend), Regina (favorite officer, friend, and a fabulous promoter of my work), Nancy (business mentor and friend), Angie (friend and possibly # 1 fan lol), Sara (agent), Stephen (Sara's son), everyone at Simon and Schuster (publisher), my family at Strebor Books (imprint), cousins, aunts, uncles, nieces, nephews, in-laws, friends, my hometown supporters in Sandusky and Columbus, churches that have directly impacted my life (Ebenezer, Providence, First Church, and New Hope), Anthony and Nichole Redic (my pastor and his wife), my entire church family at Family Fellowship, Pastor Kenneth Moore at New Birth (an all-around awesome person), Joy Reyes (Director of The Columbus Literacy Council on which I serve as a board member), Twitter followers, Facebook fans, *Yo Notes* members, my students, book clubs, book stores, and you (the reader)—thank you all for EVERYTHING! You are very much appreciated and your support makes a world of difference.

To Bernard Ash of Ash Investigations in Houston, Texas, thank you for responding to my email and indulging me in a phone conversation to answer my questions about P.I. techniques. Our fifteen minute talk gave me the confidence I needed to go forward with the creation of B.K. Ashburn whom I hope will make you proud.

To B.K. Walker, thank you for the use of your initials in creating my private detective. Also, I appreciate your help in promoting my books. I really appreciate your work ethic and integrity.

To anyone who feels that he/she has been overlooked, if you truly know me, you know that it was not intentional and I sincerely ask for your forgiveness.

I have saved the very best for last. To Jesus, the One who knows me better than I know myself. Thank You for being the ultimate sacrifice on the final Day of Atonement. Without You, my entire life would be in vain.

Much Love and Many Blessings,
Yolonda

Website and Social Media Info:
www.yoproductions.net
www.facebook.com/yoproductions
www.twitter.com/ytsanders

Prologue

August, 1982—Houston, Texas

"I'm tellin' Mama that y'all won't let me play," whined eight-year-old Elana, running out the room.

Eleven-year-olds Troy and his best friend, Elvin, had been perched on the olive-green living room carpet since yesterday afternoon, glued to the TV and playing the Atari Elvin had gotten for his birthday.

"Aw, man!" Troy's ship got hit by one of the flying saucers on the *Asteroids* game they were playing. "I almost had it!" He was relieved to have handed the controller to Elvin only moments before Miss Lilly walked into the room wearing plaid shorts and a light-blue shirt. Her short, dark Jheri-curled hair framed perfectly around her light complexion. Troy thought she was pretty despite the gobs of makeup she sometimes wore to cover her bruises.

"Boys, I told you to let Elana play." Her voice was more pleading than it was direct.

"We did," claimed Elvin.

"Nuh-uh. They each keep gettin' like three and four turns and only givin' me one."

Miss Lilly sighed. "I have to run out for a little while and I need to trust that you boys will look after Elana."

"Can she *please* go with you, Mama?"

"I don't wanna stay here!" Elana violently shook her head in protest, causing her pigtails to flop noisily.

"No, she can't. I need to go find your father."

Elvin's bright-yellow skin turned red and he scowled. Mr. Herbert, the man Miss Lilly was referring to, was actually Elvin's stepfather. He and Miss Lilly married last summer and already things were rough. Mr. Herbert was the second stepfather Elvin and Elana had had within the three years that Troy had known them and he was basically a carbon copy of the first. Actually, Mr. Herbert was worse than their first stepfather, Mr. Jeff, who was at least nice. Both Elana and Elvin liked Mr. Jeff. He was an officer who sometimes patrolled the area, and still stopped by occasionally to surprise Elvin and Elana on joy rides in his car. Troy, too, whenever he was around. Mr. Jeff had hit Miss Lilly, but that's not the reason they got divorced. Miss Lilly had told Troy's mom that Mr. Jeff wasn't meeting her physical needs. *Yuck!* Grownups really should watch what they say when children are around!

Mr. Jeff and Miss Lilly were still friends, but now Mr. Herbert was apparently meeting her needs. He hit her a lot more, too, and he was also mean. Mr. Jeff had been kind enough to call Elvin yesterday to wish him a happy birthday. Mr. Herbert lived in the same house and hadn't yet done that. Miss Lilly's attempts to force a loving relationship between Mr. Herbert and her children were not working. "Your husband is *not* my father," was Elvin's reply to her statement. His tone was cold, but respectful. Troy had never seen Elvin's real dad. He thought he would get a chance last night, but Mr. Campbell did not show up as he'd promised.

Miss Lilly looked like she wanted to say something in Mr. Herbert's defense, but changed her mind. Instead, she turned to Elana. "Honey, why don't you play with your baby doll or go outside until I get back? I promise I won't be long."

"It's hot outside and they are gonna be mean to me. Elvin's always meaner when Troy's around. Plus, they won't let me play."

"Troy will be leaving soon, so let the two of them play for now, then you can play with Elvin after Troy leaves, okay?"

"I still don't wanna stay here." She wrapped her tiny arms around her mother's hips. Her skin had more color to it than her brother's and mother's, but she was still considered light-skinned, especially compared to Troy who had a very dark complexion. "They're gonna be mean," Elana moaned.

"No, they won't." Miss Lilly gently pushed her away and knelt down, holding Elana by the shoulders. "Do as I said and leave them be. If you stay and be good, I promise to bring you something back."

"A push pop?" Her voice lightened.

"Sure, I need to stop and get a few things from the store any-how. I'll bring push pops for everyone if y'all promise to behave and get along while I'm gone. I shouldn't be more than an hour."

The solution seemed satisfying enough to Elana who plopped down on the couch behind Elvin and Troy. Within minutes, Miss Lilly was headed out the front door. "Troy, I'm not sure I'll be back before your mom gets here. If not, I promise to make them save your push pop until the next time you come over."

"Okay." He wasn't going to cry if he missed out. It wasn't that big of a deal.

"I'll be back soon. Y'all behave. You boys really should take a break and eat breakfast. There's grits and bacon on the stove," she said before leaving.

Both Elvin and Troy were too engrossed in Atari to attend to their growling stomachs. They continued taking turns while Elana sat on the couch playing with her Strawberry Shortcake doll and giving them evil glares. When the telephone rang, she tried convincing Elvin to answer it so she could take his place. She and Elvin argued about who should answer the phone even after it had stopped ringing.

Elana never got another turn, but things were peaceful for a short while until she got bored with her doll and leaned her head in the middle of them and began singing "Ebony and Ivory" in a really loud and obnoxious tone.

"Shut up!" Elvin nudged her with his elbow. Troy tried scooting over. He had a four-year-old little sister who wasn't quite as good at getting on his nerves the way Elana did. Would this be what he had to look forward to when Tracy got older?

"Come on, y'all. Let's pretend we're on *Soul Train.*" She got right in front of the television and continued her serenade. "Ebony, Ivory, living in perfect harmony. Ebony—"

"*Move!*"

"I wanna play *Soul Train!*"

"That song hasn't even been on *Soul Train* yet, stupid. *Dang!*" Elvin's ship had gotten hit and he angrily tossed the controller to Troy. "See what you did? Get out the way!"

Satisfied that she'd at least ruined her brother's turn, Elana went back to the couch. "Imma tell Mama you cursed."

"Shut up, stupid. I did not. I said '*dang.*'"

"Imma tell her you called me names, too."

"I don't care, you brat." Elvin hurled a pillow at her. "Go upstairs or outside like she told you."

Elana stood up to kick him, but he dodged out of the way of her foot and it ended up connecting with Troy's rib instead.

"Ow! Keep your feet off of me, you rat brat," he teased, firing her up even more.

She swung her foot again, but this time Troy grabbed it and she fell. The boys laughed while she started crying. "I'm tellin' Mama," she screamed, getting up and swinging her arms and her baby doll at them. The doll's stringy red hair flung violently.

They knew better than to hit her back. Instead, both grabbed her arms, laughing and taunting.

"Both of y'all are meanies! I'm tellin' Mama when she gets here. Imma tell her everything you meanies did!" She jerked from their grips and stormed out the front door.

Now that they were rat brat free, Elvin and Troy were able to play the game in peace. They'd gotten so wrapped up in Atari they hadn't realized that hours had passed until Miss Lilly burst through the door shortly after noon, carrying a small grocery bag. "Troy, you're still here?" She did not sound surprised. "I can't believe y'all are still sitting there playing that game." She looked and sounded more distressed than when she had left.

Troy didn't miss the slight relief on his friend's face when Elvin saw that Mr. Herbert wasn't with his mom. Troy guessed that Elvin hated Mr. Herbert, probably to the same extent, if not more, than Troy did his own father who was an unfaithful and abusive drunk. The boys had never talked about their feelings, but Troy understood. He could tell that Elvin wasn't pleased seeing the arguing and fighting that occurred between his mom and Mr. Herbert. It was the same scenario that Troy often witnessed in his household. Troy didn't understand grownups or their crazy relationships. At a young age, he'd already decided that marriage is something he'd never do. The stress of it didn't make sense.

"Where's Elana?"

"Outside," answered Elvin.

"I didn't see her. She's probably around the corner. Turn off the game and get the rest of the bags out the car, then go get her. *Yes,*

I bought push pops," she said before Elvin could speak as she rushed through to the kitchen, "but y'all need to eat *and* clean up first."

The boys didn't move until they heard her yell *"Now!"* along with clanging pots around the kitchen. Not willing to experience her wrath from their disobedience, they grudgingly turned off the game and did as instructed.

After getting the groceries, Elvin and Troy went to find Elana. They'd knocked on the doors of all of her friends' houses and by the time they had circled the block, there was still no sign of her. "I bet she's at home with Mama by now."

More consciously aware of hunger pangs, they'd decided to run back, challenging each other in a race. "I beat you," gloated Troy.

"No you didn't. It was a tie."

"Whatever; you always say that when you lose."

Thirsty, they went into the kitchen for water.

"Where's Elana?"

"We couldn't find her. I thought she might be here by now," Elvin explained.

"Well, she's not. Did you see if she was over Salome's?"

"Yes. We went everywhere. She's probably hiding to get us in trouble."

"In trouble about what?"

Troy was glad that Elvin had been doing all the talking. Elvin explained to Miss Lilly how Elana got in front of the TV and was trying to kick them. He left out the fact that they called her names, of course.

Miss Lilly seemed both irritated and concerned. "I'll find her myself. Stay here and turn off the pot if it starts boiling. *Don't* get back on that game either. Y'all are not playing again until this house is clean."

Still tired from the race that he was sure he'd won, Troy plopped down in one of the kitchen chairs while Elvin stared at the stove. Nerves had settled into the both of them as they heard Miss Lilly yelling for Elana until her voice faded. Troy hadn't been ready to go earlier, but now he wished his mom would come. Maybe Elana was hiding like Elvin said and was waiting for Troy to leave.

Salome's mom was the first to come by to see if Elana had come home. She left immediately when Troy's mom and little sister finally arrived, which was probably best given the circumstances. Troy knew that his mom did not care for Salome's mom. He'd overheard her and Miss Lilly make comments about Salome's mom many times as the two of them suspected that the lady was sleeping with Troy's father after Miss Lilly saw him coming from Salome's house on several occasions. By the time Troy's mom came, whatever feelings she had toward Salome's mom had been put aside as she tried consoling a now frantic Miss Lilly. His mom waited with Miss Lilly for the police while Troy and Elvin went back out to look for Elana, along with several neighbors, relatives, and friends who had joined the search efforts. There was no luck. Hours turned into days and soon it became clear that eight-year-old Elana Campbell disappeared without a trace, never to be seen again.

Chapter 1: The Killing Fields

Thirty years later—Columbus, Ohio

Detective Troy Evans sat in the basement of his large two-story home enjoying the solitude of a nice, quiet Friday evening. He normally didn't get many Friday nights to himself thanks to his rambunctious three-and-a-half-year-old son and his six-months' pregnant wife who, when back pains and stomach cramps kicked in, often reminded him that *he* was the one responsible for her current condition. They were expecting twins—a responsibility that Troy wasn't sure he was prepared to handle, though he had wanted more children. Natalie was out Christmas shopping with one of her friends and Nate was staying overnight with his big sister, Corrine, Natalie's daughter, whom she'd had as a teen. Corrine usually got Nate at least once a month on the weekends. Troy and Natalie often tried to take advantage of those moments by doing something together, but Troy wasn't mad about things working out differently tonight. He'd gone to the gym, showered, and for several hours now, he'd had the house to himself—nothing but pizza, basketball, and peace.

Kevin Durant was going up for a shot when Elvin's call came through. "Yes!" Troy screamed as he answered his cell. "What's up, El? Man, I hope you're watching the game. Durrant just had a swuh-*eet* shot in Kobe's face." Troy had not really had a favorite

team or player since Jordan and the Bulls. He pretty much rooted
for any Texas team, the Heat, and now, maybe Oklahoma City
Thunder.

"They found her, Troy! After all these years, they found her!"
Elvin sounded both frenzied and joyful as he ranted the words
repeatedly.

Troy didn't need to ask questions. There was only one *her* Elvin
could mean. "Elana," he whispered. The knot in his throat pre-
vented him from speaking any louder and he felt like he had been
hypnotized. Though he stared at the screen and saw the crowd
going wild, Troy didn't have any real comprehension of what else
had taken place. He was in a trance. He saw, but didn't see; heard,
but couldn't hear. He cleared his throat, hoping to speak with
more force. "How is she?"

"Mama has been waiting so long for this day. We all have." It
was difficult to make out some of his words through his sobs, but
Troy heard the last words very clearly. "I have always wondered if
we had let her play that stupid game if any of this would have ever
happened."

Those words stung. Troy had always felt the same. For several
months after Elana went missing, neither he nor Elvin played the
Atari much. It wasn't until years later when the first Nintendo
was released that Troy would consider himself actually becoming
a "gamer." Even then, whenever his baby sister wanted to play, he
made allowance for her to do so, fearing she'd get mad, run off, and
disappear. Deep down, Troy knew that had it not been the Atari,
there would have been something else that he and Elvin were
arguing about with Elana. That's the way things went when they
were together. It wasn't the Atari's fault. It had been his...theirs.
After he and Elvin began playing video games together again, neither

talked about what had happened that day. It was a silent under-standing; an unspoken guilt that would bond them forever.

The single tear that trickled down the right side of his face surprised Troy and snapped him out of his catatonic state. Crying was not his mode of operation. He put the TV on mute. The noise from the crowd had become irritating. "Is she okay?"

More sobs from Elvin and then a deep breath. "She's dead."

Troy's heart sank. Over the years there had been some hope that Elana could still be alive. Shawn Hornbeck, Elizabeth Smart, Jaycee Dugard. All were kidnapped as children. All had been found alive. Jaycee, abducted at age eleven, had been kept in captivity for eighteen years until a few years ago. Her case was the one that really helped the candle of hope continue burning for Elana in Troy's heart. The candle that Elvin's words, *"She's dead,"* blew out. "Where was she discovered?" Troy imagined that campers some-where had stumbled upon her remains or perhaps some kids playing near an abandoned railroad.

"This is where things get crazy. No one found bones. They found her body."

"Back up, man, you're not making sense."

"Elana's body, fully grown and developed, was found several weeks ago on I-Forty-five between Houston and Galveston. Some-one shot her and dumped her there."

The Killing Fields, Troy thought to himself, recalling the nickname for the stretch of highway where many bodies of young girls had been discovered. "Several weeks ago? Why are you just now tell-ing me?"

"I didn't know until tonight. I still don't have all the details because Mama is too worked up. From what I gather, there was a news story about a woman's body being found with a heart-shaped birthmark and Mama thought there was a possibility it could be Elana. She'd never stopped hoping that one day we'd find her. I think some people, including the police, think she's been a little psychotic about it because she would always contact them whenever there was a report about a female who might fit Elana's description. She kept this hunch to herself. She told me that when she actually saw the body and the birthmark, she knew it was Elana, but she didn't want me or anyone else to think she was crazy so she kept quiet until the DNA results confirmed her suspicions."

"How is Lilly handling this? How are you?"

"Obviously, Mama's preference would have been for Elana to be alive. Mine, too, but we have her back and that, in and of itself, is important to both of us." Elvin's voice trailed off as he began sniffling. Troy, a nineteen-year police detective, was not used to the mist that continued to form in his own eyes. Crying was not his thing and yet this was the third time this year he had done so! Though all the times seemed warranted, he supposed, together they were more than he could recall doing since being a young child. The first two times happened this past summer when his investigation into several serial killings ventured close to home. Elvin was like family to him, so in a way, Elana's case hit close to home as well. Maybe that's why the plethora of emotions he felt inside was followed by tears. "It's amazing that she has been alive all this time and we never knew."

"Do they have any suspects?"

"No. After thirty years, we now have more questions than answers."

With the television still muted, Troy turned to CNN, expecting to see some kind of headline about her discovery. He got angry when he didn't. "The media better give her story as much attention as they did Etan Patz last spring."

"Who's that?"

"The little boy from New York who went missing in the seventies. I think it was seventy-nine to be exact, but he was the first missing child to appear on a milk carton. Last spring they arrested some dude who admitted killing Etan as a teen."

"Oh, yeah, I vaguely remember that. Man, I doubt the media will care much about Elana. They're still talking about the election results."

"I'm sure they'll keep talking until next year after the inauguration." Last month's presidential race between Obama and Romney had gotten pretty fierce. Though neither claimed to be strictly Republican nor Democrat, Troy and Elvin had found themselves on opposite ends of an intense debate about the two candidates. Obviously, their friendship remained intact, but both adamantly voted for different people for reasons they could not get the other to understand.

"Even if Elana's story doesn't go national, maybe it will generate some attention in Houston. No one ever put her face on a milk carton. Instead, the assumption was that she ran away like that's normal for an eight-year-old. Elana would have never done that."

The older Troy got, the more he wondered if Elana's disappearance was connected with that of other young girls who went missing before and after her. Many of their bodies were also discovered along I-45 between Houston and Galveston. He'd never shared this thought with Elvin, until now.

"I'm sure that's one possibility, but as far as I know those girls all died pretty soon after their disappearances. Elana was kept alive until recently. Mama is convinced that someone in our family could be responsible. Besides Bill, she doesn't want to talk to anyone else about the case until we find answers."

especially as he began thinking about how quickly he left Miss Lilly after everything had taken place.

"I get the impression from Mama that the police are sticking with the initial conclusion. The cops are still going to look into things, but Jeff has hooked us up with a private investigator."

"Your stepfather, Jeff?"

"Technically my ex-stepfather, but yes, him. Believe it or not, he's been a godsend throughout this entire ordeal. He and Mama may have had their issues, but he always looked out for Elana and me even after they divorced. When Elana disappeared, he pulled every string he had on the department to try and find her. Jeff's retired now and has a buddy who works as a private investigator. He talked to the guy about taking Elana's case. I told Mama not to tell anyone that we're hiring a P.I., not even Bill, because he has a tendency to talk too much and if someone in our family is involved, I don't want them to know the steps we are taking to find out what happened. I'm not knocking the police, but I don't feel comfortable solely leaving everything up to them for fear that Elana's case won't be a priority since there is not much to go on."

As a homicide detective, Troy believed that every murder was a priority, despite the lifestyle of the victim. He also understood Elvin's concern. "Man, if y'all need help paying for the investigator, let me know." Troy was aware that Elvin made a pretty decent salary as a graphic designer and his wife, Nikki, had her own catering business, but he also felt responsible for what had happened to Elana. Maybe, subconsciously, that's why he became a cop. What better way to atone for his past guilt than to do good deeds in the future? And a good cop he was. No one could argue about Troy's dedication to his field, but the mysterious disappearance of Elana was something that solving a hundred cases would not let him forget. If he could assist with finding answers, he would do so, no matter the cost.

"I do need you, man, but not your money. I need you to help us find closure. You guys are still going to Houston for Christmas, right?"

"Yep. That's the plan."

"Good. Mama is planning a service for Elana on Christmas Eve and it would mean a lot to us if you would come."

"You don't even have to ask, I'm there."

"There's something else." Elvin paused for a moment as if trying to consider his words carefully. "Will you help look into Elana's disappearance while you're here?"

"I don't have jurisdiction in Texas."

"I know that." Elvin responded as if his intelligence had been insulted. "I was hoping you would meet and work with the investigator. I'm sure he'll want to at least interview you."

"Sure." Troy wasn't sure how helpful he would be seeing how he was only eleven at the time. He had played that day repeatedly in his head and there was nothing he could remember that would provide answers to Elana's disappearance. But, he knew how important his cooperation would be to Elvin and Lilly. Plus, he owed it to Elana.

"I'm not accusing anyone in particular in my family. Until we have answers, I don't know who to trust. I need you, man."

"I'm assuming that since most of your family will be there for the service and the holidays, you want me to see what information I can glean from them." Troy picked up on where his friend was headed.

"You can read people better than anyone else I know. You know as well as I do that there are some shady characters in my family. If Elana's abductor is among us, you can help find him."

Bill was Lilly's older brother. The two of them had always been close as far as Troy could remember. Bill also seemed to be Elvin's and Elana's favorite uncle, filling in as surrogate since their real father was not around and their stepfathers did not need to be. Elana seemed closer to Bill than Elvin since she used to go with him more. The funniest thing Troy could remember about Bill was his use of big words, which were made even more complicated to understand because he stuttered. It wasn't until Troy's vocabulary began expanding thanks to high school literacy classes that he learned that Bill had actually been mispronouncing a lot of the words he used. That made memories of him even funnier. Bill spent a lot of time with Lilly during those early years after Elana went missing. From the sounds of it, he was there for her now, too.

"I feel bad thinking that someone close to us may have been involved," Elvin continued, "but as dysfunctional as my family is, it wouldn't surprise me if one of them knows something. The more Mama shares her thoughts, the more they make sense. You know how Elana was. If a stranger had tried to abduct her, she would have been cutting up so much that someone would have heard something and I'm sure her kidnapper would have given up. We think someone enticed her to go with them willingly and it had to be someone she knew."

"Have you guys shared any of this with the police?"

"Mama has. As far as we know, no one in our family was ever considered a suspect back then and there is even less information to go on now. If I were to suspect anyone, it would be Herbert because he stayed gone for days after Elana disappeared and then he and Mama split up a few months later. I don't think Elana would have gone anywhere with him though. She didn't like him."

Troy wasn't so sure that Herbert should be ruled out just yet,

Troy wondered if the kidnapper and murderer were one and the same. Was it possible that someone abducted her and later released her or she ran away? There were so many questions and little to no answers.

"I know my sister did not run away from home. Somebody took her and if you can at least help figure out the first part of the puzzle, maybe the other pieces will fall into place."

Troy agreed that finding Elana's kidnapper was crucial to solving the overall mystery of her disappearance and subsequent murder. Unfortunately, it would also be the hardest thing to do as the person or persons involved hadn't left a single clue.

Chapter 2: Family Man

$\mathcal{I}$n the days following Elvin's phone call, Troy worked desperately to tie up as many loose ends with his current cases as possible before he and his family headed to Texas. Consequently, he'd been skipping most of his routine workouts. Though his outside physique still looked fit, Troy noticed the toll that lack of exercise was having on his body. He resolved to get back on schedule after the holidays, after he helped close Elana's case.

He hadn't been able to stop thinking about her. The day she disappeared and the recent discovery of her body consumed his thoughts. Troy had done some research on his own and unfortunately, there wasn't much he could find. Not having access to the case files made it even more difficult for Troy to feel like he could be of any help. He was determined to give it his best shot, which is why he'd taken some additional time off in case he needed to stay in Houston longer than the week he and Natalie had planned. It was a very likely scenario and one he hadn't quite gotten around to sharing with Natalie yet.

In his defense, on the day he had intended to speak with her about his plans, a horrible tragedy had taken place. There was a shooting at an elementary school in Connecticut in which six adults and twenty children were killed. His travel plans seemed insignificant at that point as his wife cried like a baby over the lives that were stolen.

Part of her tears was due to hormones; part of her tears was due to her, in general, being soft-hearted. Though Troy did not cry, he did feel a pang unlike any other he'd recalled feeling ever before. That night, he hugged his three-year-old son, Nate, a little tighter, aware that some parents did not have the opportunity to hold their little ones and thankful that God kept his lil' man safe. For someone who had no intentions of marrying or having children when he and Natalie first met, Troy was indeed a family man and loved his wife and son more than anything on Earth. He was proud to be nothing like his abusive, adulterous, alcoholic father. This trip to Houston was going to be a challenge as his parents had reconciled last spring and Troy would not only be spending Christmas with his mom, but his father as well.

His parents had been back together nearly seven months now. This had to be a record for them. Troy had lost track of how many times they had separated and gotten back together over the years. It was a scenario that played itself repeatedly during his entire childhood. Sometimes several times within a single week! During his parents' numerous splits, Troy's dad stayed with his father. Troy's grandmother passed away when Troy was a young child and his grandfather died shortly after he moved to Ohio. Troy's mother called the place a "whore house" since it was no secret that his father took other women there.

Prior to Elvin's call, Troy almost backed out of the trip to Houston, but he did not want to experience the wrath of his mother who was anxious to see her "pumpkin." A generally nice woman, his mom sometimes cursed like a sailor and Troy could only imagine the new words she would invent if he'd said they weren't coming. He was still not sure how he'd let her con him into staying at the house with his father there. His mom claimed that his dad wanted to make amends for being a bad husband and father. As far as Troy was concerned, it was useless trying to rebuild a relationship that never existed in the first place.

"He's changed," his mom had told him.

Troy laughed when she also said that his father had "found Jesus." "Where? Inside his bottle of Jack?"

She didn't think that was too funny. "People can change, Troy. We haven't gotten into any fights or major arguments since he's been back home. That right there is a miracle."

"What about the whore house?"

"He's been steadily cleanin' it out for a few months, bringin' things he had there, over here. His ultimate plan is to remodel and then sell it next spring."

"Don't tell me you've been helping him get the place together."

"Now, I'm not that stupid. I mean, if he really *needed* my help, I suppose I would, but he didn't ask and I didn't offer. I would prefer not to step foot in that house ever again. God only knows how many tramps he took through there. I haven't been in that house since I was pregnant with Tracy."

"I thought he kept Tracy after school at one point."

"He did, but I never went past the front door. I knew if I saw somethin' I didn't like, I might catch a case. The last time I was inside that house, I busted him havin' sex with some heffa. Lord knows if I had not been pregnant, I could be in jail right now for murder. But, I did cuss everybody out." She spoke proudly as though such an action was the key to conflict resolution. "Your daddy, that tramp, and your granddad all got it good. If your grandmother had been livin' that night, I would have cussed her out, too."

"Mama, Granddad had Alzheimer's. Don't you think it was a bit extreme to go off on him?"

"Whatever. He didn't have it then, at least not full-fledged. He kept saying 'Maggie bad,' so I guess that was the woman's name. Trust me, your grandfather knew what was going on."

Troy sighed with disbelief. Only his mother…

"Your grandparents got on my nerves for the way they indulged Reed. I know he was grown and they could not control what he did, but they didn't have to condone it either. If you and Natalie were havin' problems and you stayed with me, I wouldn't let you bring other women into this house."

"I don't see why you have put up with that man all these years."

"That man is your father," she'd said defensively. "You really ought to give him a chance. I may not be into Jesus like you, Natalie, and now your dad, but I do know somewhere the Bible talks about forgiveness. I don't think the Good Lord meant for you to exclude your father."

Troy was not sure if it was his mom, Jesus, or simple curiosity about the new leaf his dad had supposedly turned over that compelled him to agree to be under the same roof with that man, but he was obliged to go to Houston. Now, if for no other reason, than to help find Elana's killer.

As much as Troy disliked his father, he was also thankful because he showed Troy how *not* to treat his wife. Troy could never see himself hitting or cheating on Natalie, despite the fact that she was severely working his nerves right now. "C'mon, Nat! If we miss this flight, we may not be able to get another."

"I'm almost ready!" she yelled down the stairs.

"Zooooom," Nate sang as he ran back and forth from the kitchen to the living room with a model airplane Corrine had gotten him back in the summer. Troy knew he should probably tell him to stop running, but the boy was occupied, which beat him asking a hundred questions about flying like he had done earlier.

Nate was excited. Though he had flown before, this was the first flight he was old enough to actually be aware of what was happening. For a three-year-old, he was pretty smart and inquisitive. They were supposed to have left several hours ago, but a huge snowstorm across the country had delayed their flight. They were fortunate to get the delay seeing how many others had been cancelled. Their 5 p.m. flight was rescheduled to 7:43 p.m. and it was already 6:15 and they were not at the airport yet! This was the last travel weekend before Christmas and that was not good! *"Natalie!"*

"Oh, hold your horses," she said, waddling down the stairs.

Despite being shaped like a letter "P" from the waist down, Troy was still very much attracted to his wife, who had once done some modeling. Her long dark hair was pulled into a ponytail and, even without makeup, her light-honey-colored skin was flawless. Well... *almost.* There was one or two slight creases he'd noticed had formed around her jaw line. She had not complained about them and he was not crazy enough to bring them to her attention. He still remembered the look of death he'd gotten last month when he pointed out a single strand of gray hair in her head. "I can't believe you changed clothes again. That's what was taking you so long?"

"I want to be comfortable in case we get stranded."

Troy liked the maternity jeans and green flannel shirt she had on earlier. It made her look sexy pregnant, like a Hollywood actress. He bit the inside of his lip to prevent from telling her that the red maternity sweat suit she was currently sporting was far from Hollywood style. Red was her favorite color and Troy didn't mind the collage of sexy red outfits she owned, especially those reserved for intimate moments. *Sexy* wasn't the first word that came to mind when he saw her in this one. It was *Elmo.*

"Why are you staring at me?"

He wasn't sure it would be safe to share his feelings. He smiled,

"Because I love you," and leaned in to give her a kiss, which was surprisingly more stimulating than he had imagined considering the *Sesame Street* song had started playing in his head.

"*Yuck!*" Nate stopped zooming long enough to interrupt their moment.

"Oh, hush, and go get your coat so we can go see Gigi."

"Are we still flyin' on 'da big plane?"

"Yes, but I want you to try and go potty first," ordered Natalie.

"Is Sissy comin' wif us?"

"No, remember, I told you Sissy went to Mississippi," she reminded him.

"Dat's anudder state, right, like O-H-I-O?" He actually stopped and did the arm motions along with the chant; something Nate had recently learned while watching an Ohio State football game with his father.

Both parents laughed. "Yes, you silly willy. Now, hurry up and go potty so Daddy doesn't leave us."

"I don't want Daddy to leave. I wanna go on 'da big plane and see Gigi."

"You will. First, do as your mother said."

Nate ran around the corner to the half-bath still zooming. This time with his arms stretched wide instead of with his toy airplane.

"That boy has too much energy for me. I hope Diane can keep up with him." Natalie leaned against the wall and rubbed her belly.

"You know my mama will try for sure. You all right?"

"Yeah. I think your babies are as excited about this trip as Nate because they are bouncing around like crazy."

Troy gently placed his hand on her stomach, feeling the rapid thumps of the little ones moving about. What a miracle. He'd only wanted one more child and now he would have two. Though

Natalie liked to say he must have had an overabundance of testosterone running through his veins during the time she conceived, truth be told, twins ran in her family, not his. Her father had even been a twin. He died when Natalie was only five, but whenever she shared memories about him, Troy could tell how special the relationship was between them. It was something he'd never known with his father, but hoped to give all of his children.

Troy did feel like he'd missed out on some things in childhood by not having a great role model as a father. They never bonded over sports or cars. Troy never received advice about girls nor had anyone with whom he could ask those sensitive questions. In a way, Troy thought it would have been better if he did not know his father at all rather than having one who was presently absent. When he and Natalie married, Troy's father didn't even come to the wedding—something that bothered Troy's mom more than it did him. Troy believed for a fact that people, in general, could change. The real question was, could his father?

In an ideal world, Troy would be going to Houston looking to build some kind of relationship with his dad. However, reconciliation was the least of his concerns. As much as he loved his mom and sister, his focus wasn't even on spending time with them. Ever since Elvin's call two weeks ago, Elana had been at the forefront of his mind. She was his motivation to spend Christmas in Houston. She was the only one who mattered as he finally got Nate and Natalie in the truck, backed out of the garage, and headed to the airport. Destination: H-Town.

Chapter 3: Case Closed

*I*f Troy got any sleep at all, it was only a few minutes. They got to Houston a little after one a.m. central time, but it was at least another hour before they got their bags, rental car, and made it to his parents', and another hour after that before they got to bed. He was sure that he spent the next several hours lying in bed thinking about Elana and the day she disappeared before drifting off. At seven-something in the morning, he was fully awake.

Troy stared at the ceiling. He hadn't occupied this room for more than a couple of weeks at a time since high school and yet he still saw the sticky marks from the posters he'd hung up during his teenage years, mostly posters of models and movie stars in bikinis that he would enjoy looking at every night before falling asleep. He chucked lightly to himself, amazed at how he had matured from a knucklehead teenager who got his jollies from pictures of any attractive woman to a committed husband and father who only had eyes for one woman. No one, picture or in person, could do to his heart or body what Natalie could.

This room had a lot of memories. A few of them good, a lot of them bad. He recalled the time when he, his mom, and little sister locked themselves inside while his dad, drunk and out of control, banged on the door. They all sat huddled on Troy's full-sized bed with Tracy screaming and burying her head in his Chicago Bulls comforter whenever their dad's hits caused things in the room to rattle. Troy was about fifteen at the time and Tracy was eight. They were both downstairs and had witnessed their father slap their mother so hard he'd knocked one of her teeth loose, all because his plate wasn't warm enough. With his mom grimacing in pain and sister screaming, fifteen-year-old Troy took a lamp from one of the living room end tables and hit his father in the head. In the movies people passed out when that happened, but in real life, Troy learned that, not only didn't his father go unconscious, but he also turned his wrath from his wife to his son. Had it not been for one of Tracy's toys in the middle of the floor, causing their father to stumble and fall, Troy was sure he would have gotten one of the beatings meant for his mother that day. Instead, she grabbed Tracy and the three of them darted upstairs and locked themselves in his room.

They were there for hours until his dad finally passed out. When he woke up, he pretended like nothing ever happened and Troy was mad that his mom acted the same way. That was the last time Troy had ever witnessed his father get physically aggressive with his mom, but he knew it wasn't the last time he hit her. Troy was certain that he had startled his father by getting involved. Drunk or not, the man was wise enough to know the older Troy got, the stronger he would become. Troy did not have one positive memory of his dad and yet this was the man his mom had sworn had found Jesus. Thankfully his father was sound asleep when they had arrived from the airport.

The buzz of his cell phone interrupted his thoughts. It was a text from Elvin asking if they had made it safely. Troy responded and the two exchanged several additional messages.

"What are you doing?" Natalie turned his way with a sharp look.

"Texting El. He wants me to meet with him at his mom's around eleven. Is that cool with you?" Troy had already agreed. He was asking simply as a formality.

"Yeah," she mumbled before closing her eyes again.

"You're welcome to come if you want. I know Lilly would like to meet you and she's never seen Nate. Plus Nikki will be there."

"No. I'll see them both on Monday. I'm sure Diane would have a fit if we took Nate somewhere this morning. And anyhow, I want to relax. I didn't sleep well thanks to these overactive twins. When I was finally getting into a good sleep, *someone* woke me up by moving around in the bed."

"My bad." Troy leaned over and kissed her lips lightly. "That same someone will be happy to assist you in going back to sleep if you let him." He seductively twirled his finger around her belly button.

She swatted his hand before he could go any further. "No, thank you. I am not even trying to get down like that with these thin walls and this squeaky bed frame."

"Chicken."

"Whatever. Go to sleep. You'll cool off. I hope you dream about mints because your breath is not nice."

"I hope you don't think you got it going on in there." He lightly poked her bottom lip.

"No, but I'm not trying to be all in your face like you're in mine."

Just to be ornery, Troy got even closer and whispered, "I love you," very slowly blowing the breath of each word in her nostrils.

"Ewe! Stop it!" She playfully hit him and he went down to nibble her neck. He also purposely wiggled the bed with his hips so that there was an abundance of noise coming from their room. "You better cut it out right now," she said between giggles.

"Or else?" Troy made the bed squeak even louder. This time he added a few "Oh, Natalies" for fun and covered her mouth so she could not protest. She looked like she didn't know whether she would die laughing or die from embarrassment when they heard footsteps in the hall.

"I am going to kill you." Natalie swatted him on the head.

"I love you, too, babe."

She rolled her eyes and got out of bed, slipping a robe over her maternity shorts and pajama top. "I'll be back. I have to pee." She peeked out the room to make sure the coast was clear before heading out.

Natalie never did get back to sleep that morning, nor did she give in to Troy's desires for intimacy. She made it very clear that nothing like that would happen all week. He made it very clear that he wished they would have gotten a hotel like they had done last year when they came here for Christmas. At the time, his sister, Tracy, and her husband were separated so she and her kids were living with Diane. Troy's parents were separated this time last year as well, which was the only reason why Troy allowed Nate to stay at the house with Diane and Tracy while the two of them stayed at the hotel. Natalie thought it was sad that this would be the first time her father-in-law had actually seen Nate in person. She had only met him once herself. She knew Troy well enough to know that he didn't necessarily want her and Nate to come with him solely to meet Elvin's mom or to hang out with his wife. She was fully aware of Troy's dislike of his father and he also admitted that he was nervous leaving them at the house with him.

"We'll be all right," she assured him as they finally went downstairs.

The initial encounter with the rest of the family was a little awkward only, because the tension between Troy and his father was evident. Reed gave Natalie a very welcoming embrace, which she didn't mind. He looked as if he wanted to hug Troy as well, but Troy's stiff lawman posture was uninviting. They didn't even exchange a handshake. Rather, Troy gave his father a very dry "hey" and walked right past him to wrap Tracy in a bear hug. He did the same with his fourteen-year-old niece before playfully putting her older brother in a head lock.

Troy's niece and nephew seemed to be a perfect blend between his sister and their father, Al, who, like Natalie, was biracial. It was eerie how divided the rest of their family was by their looks. Troy's mom and sister had the same medium-brown complexion. Also, they weren't the type of women who could easily hide in a crowd due to their height and wide hips. Neither woman was fat; they simply had more than a fair share of voluptuousness from the waist down, a trait that was clearly being passed down to Troy's niece.

On the other hand, it was obvious that Troy had gotten his much darker skin tone and handsomeness from his father. Reed wasn't bad-looking for an older man and if it weren't for traces of life's hardships left on his face through wrinkles and worry lines, he probably would've looked even better. They were roughly the same height, with Troy possibly an inch or so taller, but his six-pack was quite the opposite of Reed's gut.

The oddity of this pre-holiday family gathering was that it was the first time that every member of the Evans family was together. Usually, it was the women, kids, and Troy as Reed and Al had their abusiveness and drunkenness in common and were often missing in action. Al knew better than to lay a hand on Tracy with Troy around. Natalie had heard a story from Troy about the beat-down he'd given Al years before she and Troy met for pushing Tracy in his presence. Troy was not proud of his reaction as he wasn't one to go around fighting people. He was also one who could not stand to see anyone he loved mistreated.

Both Al and Reed seemed to have put their best foot forward for today as they exchanged niceties with Natalie and tried to do the same with Troy. Had Natalie not known their histories, she would not have guessed that these were the men her husband loathed because of their treatment to the women in his life. Diane tried to act like this impromptu breakfast was a routine family occurrence, but the awkwardness on everyone else's face could not be hidden. The only one oblivious to the tension was Nate who was busy counting the boxes under the Christmas tree. Every time he found a present with a tag for him, he'd ask, "Is this mine?"

"Yes," Diane would reply.

"Can I open it?"

"Yes, on Christmas."

"What is it?"

"Nate, get from under the tree and come give your Aunt Tracy a hug," said Troy.

"And say hi to your grandpa, Pumpkin. He's been lookin' forward to meetin' you," added Diane, who avoided a sharp look from Troy by keeping her gaze on her youngest grandchild.

Nate followed both of their directions and Natalie was hoping that she was the only one who saw Troy's jaw lines tighten when Reed picked him up. Natalie was more optimistic about her father-in-law's change than her husband. Though she understood Troy's anger to an extent, she also thought he was unforgiving. Reed did nothing but interact with Nate like a loving grandfather and Troy was getting all bent out of shape.

Apparently, Natalie was not the only one who noticed. It was hard not to with Troy straining his face like he was constipated. The room was silent as everyone watched the interaction between Reed and Nate with glances back and forth between them and Troy. Nate broke the ice and brought a few chuckles when he asked, "How many presents did you get me?"

"Nathaniel!" Natalie looked apologetically around the room. "I'm trying to get him to understand that Christmas is not about what *he* gets."

"He's three. For him, it is," rebutted Diane. "Come on, y'all let's eat."

They gathered around the table and surprisingly, it was Reed who said grace. It nearly brought tears to Natalie's eyes to hear him give such heartfelt thanks for his family. What really got her was when he mentioned regret for having taken them for granted for so many years and prayed that they would one day forgive him. It seemed like Diane and Tracy already had. Reed was, no doubt, referring to Troy. "I know I do not deserve another chance, but I thank You for it anyhow. In the Name of Jesus, I pray. Amen."

"Aaaaaaa-men!" Nate sang ridiculously loud.

"Always the center of attention, huh, man?" Natalie patted his head.

"You ready to do this again?" asked Tracy.

"Girl, I don't know. Ready or not, come March, these babies will be here."

"Are y'all still goin' to wait to find out the sex of the babies like y'all did with Nate?" Diane seemed a bit impatient.

"Yep," answered Troy proudly. "Natalie and I have decided that knowing beforehand isn't important to us. Whether they're boys, girls, or one of each, they will still be a blessing." Guilt rushed over

Natalie as he spoke since Troy had no idea that she'd asked the ob/gyn to verify their babies' genders. With Nate, she wanted to be surprised. With these babies, the pregnancy itself was a surprise. She'd only wanted to be prepared, but in retrospect, finding out behind Troy's back only made her feel paranoid. She was eager to start shopping and yet could not buy any gender-specific things without raising his suspicions. She had shared the info with her best friend, Aneetra, and had stashed some things at her place until it was safe to bring them to their house. Other items were on her Amazon wish list ready to be confirmed immediately after delivery.

"In my day we didn't have a choice but to wait. I don't understand why y'all have to be so difficult. How am I supposed to know what to buy my grandbabies if I don't know what they are goin' to be?"

"What matters most is that they are healthy, right?" Reed affirmed.

"If one of them is a boy, please don't let my brother talk you into having a junior. I think one Troy is enough."

"So was one Al, but you had to jack up my nephew's name, huh, Trace?" Troy fired back. He smiled as if his dig at Al had been a compliment. He must've figured that using "Trace," his pet name for her, would soften the blow. "I told Natalie that she should leave them in the oven until April so they can be my birthday present," he added after Natalie kneed him under the table.

"You know your brother is crazy, right?"

"I've always known it. I'm wondering why you married him."

Natalie made sure to knee Troy again before he could say anything sarcastic about her choice of spouse.

"I think having twins is neat," Tracy continued. "Y'all are lucky."

"Luck had nothing to do with it, baby sis. Your brother happens to be a very skillful man." Everyone laughed, including Nate who was simply copying off of everyone else since he was too young to pick up on his father's innuendos. Instead of kneeing him, this time Natalie chose to kick him for embarrassing her.

Tracy used one of her hands to make the "cuckoo" motion and pointed at Troy.

"Definitely." Natalie nodded and the two of them exchanged an extra laugh, leaving the others at the table wondering what they had missed. Natalie and Tracy were not extremely close, but they had a decent time whenever they were around each other. Their mutual love for Lifetime movies and Troy bonded them. It always warmed Natalie's heart to see Troy interact with his younger sister. His love and protection of her was undeniable. It often made Natalie feel nostalgic about her childhood. Though she didn't have any siblings, she had several male cousins and when she was growing up she had been the youngest grandchild and the only girl. Her cousins looked out for her the way big brothers like Troy had surely done for Tracy.

"What's the game plan for today?" asked Reed.

"Al and I were thinking about going to see a movie. AJ and Alyssa don't want to go, so we were either going to take them home or let them hang out with y'all."

"I want to go to the zoo," said Alyssa.

"Mommy, I wanna go to 'da zoo," pleaded a suggestible Nate.

After such a restless night, Natalie did not want to go anywhere, but a zoo trip seemed fun. "We'll see if we can work that out, okay?"

"Nuh huh," Diane quickly jumped in. "Natalie, you can't go to the zoo. You're pregnant."

"What does that have to do with anything?"

"Girl, don't you know that goin' to the zoo while you're pregnant will mark your babies and they will come out lookin' like monkeys?"

The roar of laughter that came confirmed that Natalie had not misunderstood her mother-in-law. "I have never before heard that in my life." Stunned by this fallacious reasoning, Natalie looked at Tracy, expecting her sister-in-law to make the "cuckoo" motion for Diane as well.

Tracy shrugged. "That's the same thing she told me when I was pregnant."

"Di, you are too superstitious. That is not true, it's an urban legend."

Her mother-in-law could not be swayed. "Some things you're goin' to have to trust me on. We can do somethin' else, but we are not goin' to the zoo."

"I wanna go to 'da zoo and see 'da animals." Nate pouted.

Di looked at him apologetically. "Pumpkin, Gigi will have to take you another time. We don't want your mommy to have monkey babies, okay? I'll take you somewhere else today."

My poor child, Natalie thought, looking at the confusion on Nate's face because he could not comprehend his Gigi's rationale. Natalie had known her mother-in-law was superstitious, but this one defied the usual ones she'd heard like breaking a mirror brings bad luck for seven years. She and Troy both looked amusedly at each other. They would have a good laugh about this later.

"Um, Troy, maybe, we can, uh, go to Bayou Place and hang out for a little while," Reed suggested. "I, uh, know we haven't really done things together, but I would like to change that."

Natalie swallowed her food slowly and held her breath waiting for Troy's response. She still didn't know much about Houston, but she was aware that the Bayou Place was a dining and entertainment center located in Houston's Downtown Theater District. Everyone was looking at Troy. He was looking down at his plate.

"I promised to meet Elvin at eleven so I'm going to have to leave soon." He seemed to speak generally instead of specifically to his father.

"Reed, remember I told you that Lilly's daughter was found. You know how close Elvin and Troy are. I'm sure Elvin needs Troy today." Diane obviously felt it was necessary to explain things further.

"Oh, okay. Maybe later this week?"

Troy didn't respond.

"I'm still amazed that Elana's birthmark helped Lilly identify her after all these years," Diane continued. "The news has said it's heart-shaped, but I would think that there are probably a lot of people with heart-shaped marks."

"Maybe," replied Troy, "but Elana's was very distinctive. If you ever saw it, you would not forget it. I'm pretty sure it's one of a kind." He remembered all too well the unique pattern that branded Elana as though it had been put there by a very skilled tattoo artist.

"I don't watch the news much, but I did see a little bit of her story," Tracy chimed in. "The whole thing seems so bizarre to me."

"Did you know her, Ma?" asked AJ.

"Naw. I was too young when it all happened, but I remember Miss Lilly and Elvin of course. Tell them I said 'hi' for what it's worth," she said to Troy.

"I will. They're having a service for Elana Monday evening. You're welcome to come with Natalie and me if you want to pay your respects in person."

"Why don't we all go?" suggested Diane. "It would be great to show them the support of our entire family."

"I don't think that's a good idea." Reed's voice was stern. "There are too many people here to show up to a funeral unexpected."

"Not to be rude, but I don't know these people at all. I would feel awkward intruding at a moment like this."

"I can understand your point, Al, and yours, too, honey, but I think the rest of us should go. Lilly and I haven't kept in contact much since Troy and Elvin were in school and we were shufflin' them back and forth. I saw her over the summer and we'd talked about gettin' together, but neither of us followed up. I still consider her a friend and I think it's only right that I make an appearance. Maybe Tracy, Natalie, Troy, and I can go. Reed, would you mind keepin' an eye on Nate?"

Troy didn't give his father a chance to answer. "Nate is going with us." Any hint of playfulness had been drained from his voice.

"I don't mind watching him if you guys want him to stay."

"He is young and I don't know if there's goin' to be an open casket or not. It might be better to let him stay with your father." Diane's voice was almost begging Troy to reconsider. It was a sharp contrast from the direct woman known for not holding back and often peppering her words with profanity.

"The issue is not open for discussion. I said he's going with us. Case closed."

Quietness filled the room. The venomous manner in which Troy spoke made Natalie feel sad. She could not recall a time when her husband had been so callous. She was sure she knew what was going on with him, even if he did not. Troy had told her numerous stories about his dad, recalling the tiniest details like they had happened the day before. Troy spent years resenting Reed and could list all the reasons why, but Natalie understood the truth of the matter. Each negative memory equaled an experience of un-processed pain. Together, they culminated into a mountain of hurt, which Troy masked with anger. She knew from experience how cancerous not forgiving another could be and she prayed that God would soften Troy's heart toward Reed.

"What's a casket?" Nate broke the silence.

"It's a bed for dead people."

Content with his father's answer, Nate went about eating his food. Diane began asking Alyssa and AJ questions about school and their sporting activities. Alyssa was a cheerleader. AJ played football and wrestled. He was telling Troy about his stats from his sophomore season last year and how he hoped to break a school record this year when Nate decided that he wanted to join the conversation.

"My mommy and daddy wrestle a *lot*," the three-year-old proudly announced.

Natalie felt her face starting to flush. "Finish eating your food, honey."

"Okay, but I wanna tell my cousin somethin'." He looked at AJ as if he really had valuable information to share. "Every time Mommy and Daddy wrestle, I think he wins 'cuz I hear her yellin' more than him. But 'dis morning me and Gigi heard my daddy yellin'. Does 'dat mean you won this morning, Mommy?"

Natalie, too embarrassed to look in the faces of anyone chortling at her expense, buried her head in her hands.

"Our son asked you a question, sweetheart."

Natalie turned to Troy. Though she wanted to howl, she was too ashamed to say anything, but "I…am…going…to…kill… you!" The only good thing Natalie saw from this was that the joy had returned to her husband's face.

Amused, Troy said to Nate. "Yes, Mommy won this morning because Daddy didn't get to wrestle like he wanted. Mommy didn't want to play."

"Her probably not want you to hurt 'da monkey babies."

Natalie could have gone deaf by the boisterous sounds of cackling that filled the room. She elbowed Troy hard in his side. "I'm going to get you for this," she said before getting up from the table and leaving. Both Diane and Troy called for her, but she kept going up the stairs, finally chuckling to herself while wishing they had used another term besides wrestling to explain to Nate what went on in their bedroom the first time he walked in on them.

Chapter 4: Discovery Green

*N*atalie's phone had stopped ringing as soon as she walked in the room. From the specialized ringtone, she knew it was her best friend, Aneetra. She started to call Aneetra back, but then saw a text she had gotten from Corrine.

Hey, U get 2HOU ok? Lmk. 143.

Natalie was texting long before her twenty-four-year-old daughter, whom she had given up for adoption, came into her life, and she'd considered herself pretty good at it. But, Corrine had introduced her to a form of texting shorthand she'd never seen. The first time Corrine had put "lmk" in a message, Natalie didn't know what in the world the girl was saying. Their relationship was still fairly new then and Natalie didn't want to request a translation, so she Googled it, learning that "lmk" was short for "let me know." The 143 was another brain stumper, but by the time Corrine hipped her to it, they were much closer. When Natalie learned its meaning, she cried.

Yep. Here. Arrived 18. Sorry ddnt text. 1432.

To this day, Natalie only used the number code with Corrine. If it had been Troy, or anyone else, she simply would have written. "I love u 2." Corrine probably used it with multiple people, but Natalie still felt it was something special between them. They exchanged a few more texts, promising that one of them would call the other on Christmas Day so Corrine could talk to Nate.

"You know it's rude to abruptly leave the breakfast table without saying anything." Troy walked in the bedroom with a huge smirk on his face.

"Hush."

He caught the pillow she threw at him and tossed it back on the bed. "What's up with you and all this abusive behavior? You were nearly beating me up at the table and now you're throwing things."

"Correction. I threw *a* single thing, not multiple items, but I can change that." She pretended like she would throw her iPhone and laughed when he flinched.

"You think that's funny?" He jumped on the bed and started bouncing so that it began squeaking again.

"Stahhhp!" She started hitting him with the pillow this time. Thankfully, he listened. The two of them gazed adoringly at each other. "What am I going to do with you, Mr. Evans?"

"Whatever you want. Maybe we can do that thing we did to make those monkey babies in your belly." He put his hands under his armpits and started making animal noises.

Natalie shook her head in disbelief. "Craziness really does run in your family, huh? Don't you have somewhere to be?"

"Oh, shoot! What time is it?"

"A quarter after ten."

"I need to get going."

He'd suddenly lost all the silly bones in his body, like he remembered what he was really in Houston to do. Troy transitioned from a man joking with his wife to a cop ready to protect and serve. Natalie observed him as he hurried to get clothes from the suitcase and other items he needed to shower and dress. He was quiet. Intense. Focused.

She was about to call Aneetra when he left the room, but there was a knock on the door. "Come in."

"Hey, Tracy and Al left and Reed is headed over to his parents' house to clean. Do you want to come with me to take the kids to Discovery Green?"

"What's that?"

Diane explained that it was an attraction in downtown Houston where various events were held throughout the year. According to her, the most current attraction was ice skating, or The Ice at Discovery Green, as it was officially called. "It's a special event they have every winter. I've never been, but I heard it's nice. You comin' or stayin' here?"

"Sure, why not?" Natalie feared Troy would have a fit if she stayed behind. "Will you send Nate in here so I can get him ready?"

"Okay." Diane was nearly out the door when Natalie called her name. "Yes."

"For the record, Troy and I were not doing anything this morning," she felt compelled to say.

Diane grinned. "Girl, what you and your husband do behind closed doors ain't nobody's business. I know you ain't got a belly full of babies by doing *nothin'*." Diane left and Natalie was glad that she hadn't tried to explain herself when they were at the table as Diane's response would have only made the situation even more embarrassing.

Figuring she had a few minutes to herself, she was about to call Aneetra back, but before she could connect, Nate came running into the room.

Chapter 5: Kid 'n Play

Troy tried calling Elvin to let him know he was running late. No answer. It was nearly 11:30 when Troy pulled up to Lilly's house. He hopped out the car and knocked twice on the door before instinctively walking in.

"I'm sorry," he said to Lilly who was walking toward the front. "Old habits die hard."

"Troy! It's so good to see you." She moved even quicker and gave him a long hug. "You should know better than to apologize. My door is always open for you."

"Yes, ma'am." To Troy's knowledge, Lilly never locked her front door again after Elana went missing. She said that she wanted Elana to be able to get in the house if she ever came back and no one was there. "I'm sorry I'm late. My mom sprung a family breakfast on us. Tracy and her kids came over." He conveniently left out Al who wasn't important as far as he was concerned.

"It's not a problem. Elvin's upstairs on the phone with the investigator. He should be down any second. Have a seat."

Lilly's living room had a familiar, yet strange feel to it. Thank God that she had gotten rid of that ugly green carpet. The room now had hardwood floors, but things were pretty much as he remembered in terms of the way the furniture was placed. The consistency, he was sure, was for Elana's sake.

"I was hoping you would bring Natalie and your son. I still

can't believe y'all have been married all this time and I have not met her. I know this isn't the first time she's been to Houston." Lilly gave him a playfully scolding look.

"She really hasn't been here that much. She was here once before we were married, then a few months after Nate was born. She also came for Mama's sixtieth birthday, last Christmas, and now this year."

"Um hmm. Don't try and give me excuses as to why I have yet to meet this lovely lady. She must be something special because, if I remember correctly, you said you never wanted to get married."

"You're right. I did say that and she is something special. You'll see her and Nate Monday at the service. Is it okay if my mom and Tracy come as well?"

"Of course it is! You don't have to ask. I feel bad because I've been meaning to call Diane, but I have had so much on my mind."

"Don't worry. She understands. How are you doing?"

"I'm okay." Lilly had been a very attractive woman in her prime. She had aged much more than only thirty years since Elana had been gone. Her hair, now straight, was completely gray. Her once vibrant high cheek bones like Elvin's did not sit as perky, and her eyes held a sadness that could not be hidden by her smile. It was a sorrow that Troy hoped to never know. "Sometimes I get angry that she's been alive all this time without my knowing. Then other times I'm relieved to finally have some sort of closure. I hope my baby did not suffer too much. I—"

"Troy, my favorite detective of all time. What's up, man?" Elvin came down the stairs and the two of them hugged.

"Sorry I'm late."

"It's cool. We're all running a little behind. Thanks for coming."

"No problem."

"So, Mama, what do you think? Which one of us is more hand-some? Kid," El pointed to himself, "or Play." He pointed to Troy.

Lilly looked as confused this time as she did in the late eighties when Elvin would ask that question. She never did catch on to the fact that Kid 'n Play was a rap duo back in the day. Troy and Elvin got that nickname from their peers because Kid was the really light-skinned rapper and Play was the dark-skinned one. "I should have known that having Troy around would bring out the craziness in you. What was the investigator saying?"

"He wanted to confirm that we're still coming by his office after we leave the funeral home. I told him Troy is here, so he's anxious to get his account of things. Oh, Bill called and said that he may be a little late getting there, but he's on his way."

"Okay. Jeff's already there. Are Nikki and the boys ready?"

"Yep. They should be coming down in a sec. We won't all fit into one vehicle; would you mind driving? Nik and the boys can ride with you and I'll ride with Troy. Or if you don't want to drive, you can ride with Troy." Elvin looked at him for approval.

"Hey, I'm cool with whatever works best for y'all."

"No. I'll drive. I'm sure you boys can use this time together. Let me grab my purse and my hair from upstairs and we can get going."

"Will you send Josh and Caleb down and tell Nicole to hurry up and quit fooling with her hair. She's paranoid about the bald spot in her head, but no one can see it unless she points it out. Maybe you should let her borrow one of your wigs."

"I will tell her you want her, but I will not say anything to her about her hair. I know better than to touch that subject."

"Nikki foolishly mixed two chemicals of some kind and put it in her hair. Now she has a bald spot smack dab in the middle of her scalp," Elvin explained to Troy.

"And she would hurt you if she knew you were telling people," added Lilly on her way up the stairs.

"It's a good thing she won't find out, huh?" Elvin waited until Lilly was out of sight and turned to Troy. His playful demeanor was now serious. "Hey, man, the investigator got a hold of Elana's autopsy report. There were tiny red fibers found on her body." They both looked up as they heard what sounded like a stampede coming down the stairs. "Stop running!" Elvin yelled at his boys.

"Wow! Y'all have gotten big since the last time I saw you." Troy reached out for both of them. Elvin's entire family came in various shades of high yellow. Caleb seemed to be the darkest skinned member of the Campbell family and he was still lighter than Natalie! "Man, what are you feeding these boys. I don't remember us being this tall when we were their ages. How old are y'all now?" Josh answered eleven; Caleb fourteen. Troy engaged them in a little conversation about basketball since he knew both boys played. Caleb, a center, had a stockier build than his slender brother who was a point guard. Basketball was a sport that Elvin and Troy both had a great love for and it was also in the DNA of El's sons. Hopefully it would be in Nate's as well.

Lilly beat Nikki downstairs claiming that Nicole said she'd be ready in five minutes. Troy hoped his face did not display his shock at Lilly's appearance. She had gone from having straight, gray hair to being a curly platinum blonde. *Not a good look*, he thought as they waited at least ten more minutes before Elvin went to get Nikki.

Chapter 6: The Mystery Man

*A*s far as Troy was aware, most families had viewings in the evenings and funerals in the afternoon the next day. El and Lilly had done things differently. Elana's wake was that afternoon and the actual service wouldn't be until the day after tomorrow in the evening. The family decided that a Christmas Eve service would be better than a Sunday service for some reason. Who was Troy to question this? They had waited a long time to find Elana and deserved to do as they very well pleased.

Seeing Elana in the casket as an adult was a little shocking at first. Though Elvin had certainly prepared him, Troy still had the last image of her as a little girl with ponytails in his mind. Overall, her body had been preserved well, considering the amount of time that had passed since she had first been discovered. Troy knew from his occupation that morgues did not like to freeze bodies for extended periods of time. But, Elana's case was unusual, and unusual cases often required special needs such as extra preservation time.

Though others stood behind him waiting, Troy took his time staring at Elana. What kind of life had she led for the last three decades? He wished he could ask her why she did not come home as an adult. Perhaps this was a case of *Stockholm Syndrome*. If Elana had been with her abductor all this time, it is possible that she developed this psychological condition in which victims begin to feel sympathy and empathize with their captors. "I'm sorry," he whispered, placing his hand on hers. She felt clammy. She looked peaceful. He felt all the emotions about things that happened during their last interaction together without producing the tears. If only he could relive that day, he would make sure that he and Elvin treated her fairly as they played the Atari. He would have even played *Soul Train* with her. If he had known how that day would play out, he would have done almost anything Elana wanted to prevent from contributing to Lilly's heartbreak.

There were a lot of people who came and Troy, unsurprisingly, knew many of Elvin's relatives. He'd spent so much time with Elvin's family, from the moment he and Elvin first became friends in third grade, until they both graduated and left for college in Ohio. Many of the people whom Troy did not know had married into the family or were friends of El's and Lilly's. Troy was most surprised to see Elana's childhood friend, Salome. She and her mother had moved from the neighborhood shortly after Elana disappeared. In fact, several families moved within a year. Elana's kidnapping had spooked them all.

Salome looked exactly the same as she did as a child—dark skin, similar to Troy's complexion, and eyes that slanted upward like her mother's had done, hinting at some kind of Asian ancestry in their family. Her afro-styled hair was neatly held in place by a decorative headband that matched her form-fitting outfit. Definitely not the body of the flat-chested eight-year-old he remembered. She'd filled out in all the right places and was letting the world know. He didn't understand why she'd wanted to draw attention to her nose with a ring. It stood out enough on its own.

Salome recognized him, too. Her face lit up when she saw him and Troy wasn't quite sure what to make of her reaction. He remembered the many not-so-nice things his mother and Lilly had said about her and wondered if Salome's smile was a little too friendly for the occasion. "You're Troy, right?"

"Yes," he answered cautiously, bringing his left hand to his chin as a subtle way of making sure she saw his ring in case she had any ideas.

"Hi, you might not remember me, I'm Salome. I used to live around the corner from Elvin and Elana."

"I remember."

Salome began sharing with him her thoughts about Elana's case and how she'd hoped the family could finally get answers. She'd even pulled down the top of her dress to show Troy a tattoo she'd gotten when she'd turned eighteen to match Elana's birthmark. "I did it as a tribute to her. She was the only real friend I had back then."

The gesture seemed a little creepy to Troy, but to each his own.

"When I saw Elana's story on the news, I was both hurt and relieved. It has killed me not knowing what happened to her. I can only imagine how Miss Lilly and Elvin feel. This is so sad." They talked for a few more minutes, filling in the blanks of some details that had taken place in each of their lives over the last thirty years. Her mom died when she was a teen, and for the most part, she lived with her grandmother. She was currently single, no children, and practiced law. If she wore outfits to court like the one she currently had on, Troy bet she could win over a predominantly male jury every time. He, of course, mentioned being *happily* married with one child and two more on the way. "Good for you. I'm glad to hear that you're doing well."

Troy could not help but to wonder about the things his mother would say if she knew that he was conversing with the daughter of one of his father's ex "whores," as she would call them, especially considering how friendly Salome was being to him. "Like mother, like daughter," he could hear his mom say. Troy thought that maybe he should warn her about the possibility of seeing Salome Monday at the service until Salome mentioned that she would not be able to make it. "I'm driving to Dallas as soon as this is over to spend Christmas with my cousins. I don't have family to celebrate with around here since my mom and my grandmother have both passed away and my relationship with my father is strained right now. He's married and has other children. I don't quite fit into his perfect family."

She looked sad. Troy wasn't sure what she expected him to say. He had enough issues with his own father to try and give someone else advice. Plus, this was neither the time nor the place. "Well, have a safe trip. I need to make my rounds. You take care."

"You, too. It was nice seeing you." She surprised him with a hug. "Merry Christmas."

"Same to you."

Despite the many people there of all races, there was one guy that stood out. He was an older white man with a mixture of gray and brown hair and a stocky build who walked around the room like he belonged there. Yet, to Troy, he seemed out of place. It wasn't necessarily the black jeans and polo shirt that made Troy notice this guy. There were people in various attire. But Troy observed him talking and watching others. No one else showed any visible signs that they thought his presence was odd. Maybe he was a former teacher of Elana's? Or, perhaps he was a funeral home employee? Naw, that didn't fit. He was dressed too casually. Could he be the *killer?* Murderers have been known to do twisted things like show up at family events of their victims. Troy looked for Elvin to see if he had any idea about the identity of the mystery guest. He spotted El talking to one of his cousins. Troy was headed toward him when he got stopped by one of Lilly's brothers.

"Troy!"

"Hey, Bill, how's it going?"

"I thought that was you. I ain't seen you in for-for-for-eh-ver." Bill, overly dressed for the occasion in a tuxedo, shook his hand. "You living back he-he-here, now?"

"No, I'm still in Ohio."

"You sa-sa-sa-sa-sa-sound a little citified," he joked.

Troy chuckled to himself, thinking of how people in Ohio would swear he sounded like a Southerner. While Troy would admit to having a slight accent, it was nothing compared to any born and bred Texan he'd encountered since his plane landed. To him, they sounded country. Maybe there's some truth to Bill's statement. "I've been up north for over half my life now; those city folk may have rubbed off on me to some extent, but Houston will always be my home."

"Gawd, bless your heart. Thank you for b-b-b-being here, son." His hand seemed to have found a permanent resting place on Troy's shoulder. "This whole thi-thi-thing about Elana is crazy. It may take a while before we have answers for sure, but I know that the Luh-luh-Lord is going to bring everything to fru-fru-ta-ta-tation."

Older now, Troy would not dare make fun of anyone with a speech impediment. He did, however, expect that Bill would have gotten his vocabulary together by this time. Apparently not so much. "Yes, the Lord will bring everything to *fruition*." Troy tried correcting him as subtly as possible.

"Are you speaking at the sa-sa-sa-service Monday?"

Troy surely hoped not. What would he say? That he hated himself sometimes for partly being responsible for the pain Lilly has suffered the last thirty years? "I don't plan on it."

"I will be speaking. Me and one of my bruh-bruh-bruh-others." Troy didn't ask which one. Lilly had a clan of siblings. Some had the same set of parents, others had the same mom and different dads, or the same dads and different moms. It would take a map and a GPS to navigate Elvin's family tree. "You know I can talk, but my sister doesn't want the sa-sa-sa-service to last too long and I-I-I will respect that. I'm going to try not to be too gra-gralari-ri-ous."

Troy did not feel like correcting Bill about the word garrulous. "Well, I'll see you tomorrow, Bill. I want to find Elvin." What Troy really wanted to do was ask Elvin what in the world he and his mom were thinking when they agreed to let Bill speak. Did they want the service to last *for-for-for-eh-ver!*

By the time Troy did catch up to Elvin, he was consoling Lilly who had started crying and the mystery man was nowhere in sight. Maybe he was a curious passerby. The local news had run Elana's story several times. It still wasn't getting the attention he felt it deserved, but at least it is more than what was aired when she first went missing.

During the remainder of the time, Troy met several people whom he did not know. One was Elvin's biological father. Edgar Campbell had walked out on Miss Lilly and the family when Elvin was only three and Elana was still a baby. According to the stories Troy had been told, Edgar re-emerged occasionally, but was never too dependable. To Troy's knowledge, he never did come see Elvin for his birthday and he wasn't around during those critical early moments when Elana could not be found. Even as a child, Troy knew that was strange.

For a man who had abandoned his responsibilities, he seemed broken up about Elana. Troy found it hard to have sympathy for him. Were these tears of mourning or perhaps guilt for being a deadbeat? Where had he been all this time? How did he hear about Elana? Troy did not recall Elvin saying that he had spoken with Edgar these last several weeks. Then again, neither of their fathers often came up during their conversations. Still, something about Edgar did not sit well with Troy.

"You all right, man?" Troy said to Jeff, Lilly's second husband, who was leaning against a wall with his head down.

Jeff looked up with a glaring stare. "It pisses me off to know that someone here may have done this to Elana. Seeing Lilly cry like that is tearing me apart. She does not deserve this." He looked pretty much the same as Troy remembered—tall, bald, and bulky with a Steve Harvey-like mustache. Troy identified with Jeff's anger. He had the same sentiments. All these family members were in Lilly's face and one of them could be Elana's killer.

"You're right. Let's go outside and get some fresh air." Troy did not want to risk Jeff possibly saying anything that could tip off someone within earshot that Troy was working on the case.

"I'm okay. I need to get back to Lilly." With those words, Jeff took a deep breath and walked away.

Troy caught himself smiling as he watched Elvin move aside so Jeff could take over consoling Lilly. Whatever issues the two of them had had in the past, it was clear that those days were over. Lilly clung to him as if her well-being was dependent on his presence. When Elana's murderer was finally brought to justice, perhaps Jeff would be the silver lining that Lilly needed to live the rest of her life happily ever after.

As Troy scanned the room, he noticed that Herbert Greenfield,

Lilly's third and final ex-husband, was notably missing. He was the man whom she was married to when Elana disappeared. One would assume that he would at least show up and give his respects. Troy was sure that Lilly and Herbert's relationship was nowhere as near as cordial as her and Jeff's. She'd gone from the frying pan to the fire when she married Herbert. Still, if Herbert had any shred of decency, he would have made an appearance. Troy could only think of two reasons why Herbert would not be here: death or guilt for being the one responsible for the circumstances.

Chapter 7: A Date or Two

atalie sat alongside her mother-in-law watching AJ and Alyssa take Nate around the ice rink. Reed was still at home when they left. Natalie got the impression that he was bummed about not being able to spend time with Troy. She felt that Troy really needed to give his father a chance. She, of all people, believed that Jesus could indeed change a person. She was proof. He had changed her.

"Nate is doin' good for this to be his first time," noted Diane.

"I know. I've never been ice skating. Aneetra and her daughters go sometimes."

"Aneetra's Nate's godmother, right?"

"Yep."

"How is she?"

"Fine." Natalie did not feel the necessity to tell Diane about her friend's marital issues.

"Tell her I said hi the next time you speak with her and that she's goin' to have to take my grandbaby ice skatin' with her."

"I'm sure she won't have any problems with that. I figured Nate was too young, but I guess not." Natalie wished she could be out on the rink with him. While she was willing to risk having animal babies by going to the zoo, she wasn't about to attempt a balancing act, though some would probably claim that's what she did anyhow by wearing heels today. "Who would have thought his first time would be in Texas. I didn't even know there was ice skating in the South, let alone outside." The weather in Houston was in the mid-fifties. A slight chill, but nothing like the freezing snow storm she'd left behind in Ohio and certainly not weather she'd imagined suitable for an outdoor ice skating rink. Diane tried to explain to her how the rink was kept frozen, but her mother-in-law didn't quite understand herself, so the explanation was more confusing than it was enlightening. "I guess people with deep pockets can buy the right kind of equipment to make anything possible."

"You got that right. I'm glad that all of my grandbabies are out there havin' fun."

"You can skate with them if you want. Don't feel obligated to sit on the sidelines with me. I'm all right."

"Girl, I'm not gettin' my big a—," she caught herself, "my big *butt* out there on that ice. It would be my luck to fall and split the rink wide open."

Visualizing such an exaggerated scene made Natalie laugh. "I seriously doubt that would happen."

"What? The fall or me breakin' the ice? I can't even walk in heels without bein' afraid of twistin' an ankle." She looked down at Natalie's feet. "You think I'm goin' to be foolish enough to put on ice skates?"

"You are silly." She quickly turned her attention to her son. "Nate, hold Alyssa's hand or you will come sit with me!" He seemed determined to show his independence. "The boy has never been to a skating rink in his entire life and already he's trying to act like a pro."

"He has his daddy's DNA. Troy used to be like that when he

was younger. I remember once he had taken a couple of karate classes, maybe three at the most, and that fool thought he was ready to start choppin' things. He actually got bricks from around my flower bed and tried to break through them."

"Did he get hurt?"

Diane, true to form, could not simply say "yeah" without adding the word "hell" in front of it. "I thought he had broken his hand 'cuz it was all red and swollen."

"He's never shared that story with me before. How old was he?"

"I don't know. I think he was about nine. No, that can't be right because Tracy would have been two and this happened before she was born, so he had to be younger because I think I was pregnant with her at the time, but not as far along as you. And I definitely wasn't as cute bein' pregnant as you. They didn't make maternity clothes back then like they do now. I look at some of the outfits I see in magazines of pregnant movie stars. Some of them look slutty, but there are some cute things, like what you're wearin'. Only you would come dressed to impress to a skatin' rink, but it's cute, though, girl. You are workin' it."

"Thanks." Natalie did not think she had on anything special. Other than the heels, which were only two inches compared to the higher ones she normally wore, she had on maternity jeans and a long-sleeved pattern top. She hadn't felt cute throughout this entire pregnancy. She'd felt uncomfortable, like she'd swallowed a giant exercise ball. Maybe that's why she still tried to spice up her appearance with her attire. It had to be the model in her for sure because the mother in her wanted nothing more than to match Diane's apparel and put on sweats and tennis shoes.

"My son really loves you, you know?"

"And I really love him."

"It's easy to see how much he cares about you and Nate. I can tell by the way he looks at y'all. It's amazin' to see how devoted he is as a husband and father considerin' Reed wasn't the best role model."

Natalie remained quiet, figuring to agree with Diane, despite the accuracy of her statement, would be rude.

"Troy is protective of all the people he loves and he is not one to open his heart easily. Once in, you're in, but once out, the door seems to be closed forever." She turned to face Natalie. "I know you probably think I am a fool for stayin' with Reed all of these years."

"Not necessarily." Natalie hoped she'd sounded sincere. She wouldn't call her mother-in-law a fool, but she did wonder what compelled her to put up with all the crap she had taken from Reed. Diane, a woman who did not bite her tongue, didn't seem like she would tolerate physical abuse.

"I don't even know why I stayed with him. I think it was because of stubbornness more than love. I don't think anyone in my family expected us to make it. We got married because I was knocked up. We stayed married because dysfunction became our norm. I worry about AJ and Alyssa because Al and Tracy's marriage reminds me of how mine used to be. Seein' how much Reed has changed does at least give me hope for the two of them."

"Um-hmm."

"I think Troy blames his father for all of our marital problems, but between you and me, I wasn't perfect either. Reed had more whores than I can count. I know for a fact that he had a woman livin' with him for a while after his father died because Tracy told me about it when she was a teenager. She was mad at me and planned to move in with him. She showed up over there with her bags and he sent her right back home."

"How'd she know another woman was living there?"

"Reed told her he was helpin' a friend and there wasn't enough space for all of them. Plus, Tracy saw the lady when she first got there. I can't remember how it all happened because it's been so long ago, but I think the door was unlocked and Tracy walked in on the two of them in the livin' room watchin' a movie or somethin' like that. She said the woman didn't look much older than her, which didn't surprise me. He had whores of all ages, shapes, and sizes. The young ones liked his money and I supposed the old ones did, too. Anyhow, I called and cussed him out that night. If I had gone over there, I would have left dead or in handcuffs. It wasn't so much that he didn't let her stay that pissed me off, it was that he told her the reason was because of this other woman like that tramp havin' a home was more important than his daughter havin' one."

"Did you want Tracy to leave?"

"Naw, girl. I didn't know she'd pulled that trick until after she came back home cryin'. It was seein' her cry that set me off. Anyhow, that was so long ago. It's not like I've been an angel. I have entertained a date or two myself. Honey, I let Reed know that while he was layin' tricks on their backs, somebody could do the same to me."

"*O*-kay." This was *way* more information than she cared to know about her mother-in-law. "What time does this place close?"

"There was one guy that I was with for about a year. He wanted me to divorce Reed and marry him, but I wasn't about to bring another man around my children."

Natalie's attempt to divert the conversation did no good. Diane stared off in space, continuing to share her thoughts.

"I think Henry would have treated them okay, but I knew no one would provide for them like Reed. Even with all his issues and other women, he took care of us. His parents were well off and Reed benefited from workin' at his dad's construction company. We always had a roof over our heads…food…clothes…we didn't have to worry about anything, except whether or not he would come home drunk."

And if he would beat your butt, Natalie thought. It's a good thing that Troy did not inherit his father's ways. She could feel herself getting worked up at the *thought* of him laying a hand on her. If Troy ever hit her, she would—

"Reed provided financial security, but that's not the reason I stayed with him." Diane continued despite not receiving any verbal feedback from Natalie. "I could have made due on my own if I really wanted. But, like I said, dysfunction was our norm. We were a family and I didn't know any different. At least with Reed, I knew what to expect. I wasn't willin' to take that chance with anyone else, no matter how good the sex was. And honey, let me tell you that Henry has been my best to date."

Diane looked at her blankly for a moment and then started laughing. "Girl, you should see the look on your face. I'm sorry, that was too much info, huh?"

"Uh, yeah."

"I hope you don't think I go around talkin' about this stuff with everyone. My children don't know about Henry or any other man I've been with."

"I won't say anything," Natalie said with certainty. She and Troy talked about a lot of intimate things. She could tell him when she had gas, diarrhea, if her period was heavy or light—when she used to have them before he knocked her up. One thing she would not do was tell her husband about some man named Henry that turned his mama out.

Diane patted Natalie's back. "Thanks for listenin'. I admire the relationship you have with Troy."

"It's not perfect. Nothing ever is. Truth-be-told, I'm surprised at how well things are between us because we had a rocky start." Realizing that she may be opening the door to questions about their relationship she preferred not to answer, she added, "All I can say is that God has been good to us. He has a way of working things out."

"Well, you and God are a lot closer than Him and me, for sure. I ain't crazy enough to think that answerin' my prayers is at the top of His list," she spoke softly, "but I'm hopin' He will hear the one about Reed and Troy's relationship. Troy needs to make peace with his father. Maybe then, we'll finally be a real family."

From the corner of her eye, Natalie saw Diane wipe her cheek. "You have to give it time." She reached over and gently grabbed her mother-in-law's hand.

Diane gave a heavy sigh. "It took over forty years for Reed and me to live peacefully with each other. Let's hope it doesn't take that long for him and Troy to make amends. I doubt we have another forty to spare."

"It won't." Natalie turned her head in time to witness Nate break free from his cousin's hand only to fall hard and start crying. "Oh my goodness!" she shrieked, heading toward the rink.

Chapter 8: A Mental Note

"You know what's crazy, man? This is the first time I've seen my dad in about twenty years," Elvin said to Troy as they were on their way to meet the private investigator.

"How'd he find out?"

"I have no clue. I don't even care at this point. I'm sure he might have an attitude about his name not being in the obituary. Oh well, he'll have to get over it. We didn't know whether he was alive or not until he showed up today. I could have punched him for the way he was crying and carrying on like he really cared about us."

Troy had also noted Mr. Campbell's emotions and planned to take a closer look into him. Something was off. "Do you know why Herbert wasn't there?"

"Nope. I doubt Mama has given him a second thought since they divorced. I don't see why he would have been there."

"Humph. I figured he would at least come show his respects since he was married to Lilly when everything happened. Jeff was there. I assumed Herbert coming would have been common courtesy."

"Elana didn't like him anyhow, so it's no big deal. Besides, you can't compare Jeff and Herbert. Jeff and Mama had their issues, but in the end, he's always been good to us. Jeff genuinely loved us. That has never been Herbert's story. Did anyone in my family stand out to you?"

"No major alarms went off, but there are a few people I would like to follow up on."

"Like who, Jerry?"

Jerry, Lilly's youngest brother, had been in and out of jail ever since Troy could remember. Elvin did not care too much for him and naturally would point the finger his way. Jerry was a hustler in every sense of the word. He lived in Galveston and happened to be in town when Elana's body was discovered. Yet, Troy wasn't deeply disturbed by this, especially considering Jerry's physical limitations. He walked with a heavy limp. Whoever dumped Elana's body had to have strength. It seemed physically impossible for Jerry to have done this. "I need more information before I can point a finger at anyone specific."

"Fair enough," Elvin said as they pulled into the parking lot. The two men finished off the sandwiches they'd picked up on the way before walking into the office of B.K. Ashburn, the private investigator Elvin and his mother had hired to look into Elana's death. It was bigger and much more sophisticated than Troy had imagined. Nothing like the rustic bedroom-sized buildings often seen in the movies. It was structured more like a law office, including a receptionist who called to notify the detective of their arrival.

Moments later, the mystery man whom Troy had seen earlier walked out to greet them. "Elvin, how are you?"

"I'm okay. This is my friend, Troy, the one who was with me that day."

"Ah, you're the fellow who was checking me out at the funeral home. I'm B.K. Ashburn." He extended his hand. The building may have been dressed up, but B.K. wasn't. He still had on the same outfit Troy had seen him in earlier.

"I didn't know it was that obvious. Nice to meet you, Mr. Ashburn."

"The pleasure is mine. Please, call me B.K. I think it was a simple case of cop recognizing cop. Rather, former cop, in my case. I didn't want to introduce myself to you there. Elvin, where's your mom? I thought she was coming."

"She was, but she had a bit of a breakdown at the funeral home after you left and I didn't think she was emotionally stable enough to join us. She is going to call you later to see if she can meet with you next week if that's okay."

"Of course it is. I know this has to be a rough time for her. Please follow me."

As they walked down the corridor, Troy observed B.K.'s demeanor. Even if B.K. hadn't told him that he was a former cop, Troy would have likely guessed after having a clear view of B.K.'s strides. They were assertive and commanding; a manner in which Troy himself had been told he walked.

"Have a seat." B.K. motioned to the dark-brown leather sofa adjacent to his desk. "Troy, Elvin tells me that you are a homicide detective back in Ohio, is it?"

"Yes." The office was structured more like a studio apartment. There was a small sink, electric stove and two other doors. Troy assumed one was a closet and the other maybe a bathroom. "I've been on the force for a little over nineteen years."

"I spent thirty-five years as a detective," he announced, perhaps a bit too presumptuously. "After retirement, I tried to lay low, but it's not in my blood. From what Elvin tells me about you and from what I witnessed at the funeral home, I don't think it's in yours either. Hopefully, we can work together and stay out of each other's way."

"Finding out what happened to Elana is my only priority. As

long as you stay on top of things, I won't have any reason to get in your way."

B.K. smiled. "Spoken like a true cop." Troy sensed admiration from his elder comrade. "Now, let's get down to business. Elvin, how much have you shared with Troy?"

"Everything you told me this morning."

"Good. I won't bother to repeat myself. Troy, Elvin says you will be here until next Saturday, correct?"

"That was the original plan, but I'm prepared to stay as long as needed until we close Elana's case." As he said the words, Troy realized that it was something he still needed to speak with Natalie about. He made a mental note to do it this evening.

B.K. smirked. "*We* may definitely need longer than a week, but I'll do my best to glean whatever I can from you in that time frame. Why don't you start by telling me everything you remember about that day?"

Troy repeated aloud to B.K. the scene that had replayed itself in his mind for the last thirty years. It was so real to him. When he closed his eyes, he could smell the grits and bacon that Lilly had cooked that morning. The heat from the summer sun warmed his body as he recalled how he and Elvin raced back to the house thinking Elana had returned. "His mom told us to eat and clean up then she went to look for her." This was the first time Troy had actually recanted the entire events of that day aloud since initially speaking with the police back then. It drained him, mentally and emotionally, but he did not cry. He didn't even tear up, as some might have expected. It was his upbringing and police training that brought forth his stoic nature, but it was the eleven-year-old boy inside who carefully recalled all the details.

B.K. looked stunned. "As an officer, I'm sure you know that eye-witness accounts are often unreliable because each person sees something different. The truth is often a matter of perception, right?"

"Yeah."

"What amazes me about the both of you is that your stories are nearly identical. Yeah, there's been a little variation here and there about minor details, but that's to be expected."

Troy and Elvin looked at each other. There was an unspoken understanding. Both had relived that day for over three decades. Neither had been able to forget it.

"I still think it will be good for you both to undergo forensic memory recall."

"Hypnosis?" Troy blurted. "Is that really necessary? You said yourself that our stories are similar."

"So, you actually did not share *everything* about our conversation this morning," B.K. said to Elvin who looked apologetically at Troy.

"My bad, man. I don't like the idea either, but it's worth a shot."

"I remember Elana's case. I didn't work it," he quickly added before Troy had a chance to ask, "but I remember it and the way I felt when it wasn't getting the media attention it deserved. I don't have to tell you about racial tensions down here, especially back then. I have a few theories about what could have happened to her, but in order to validate or disprove any of them, we need cold, hard facts. Every detail is important. As good as your memories are about that day, you both were young. There may be things you've seen that can help us out that you may not recall without probing."

Probing? The word itself made Troy feel uncomfortable. He did not want anyone messing around in his head. "I don't see what else I can tell you."

"Okay. Let me ask you a few questions. What color shoes did Elana have on that day?"

"I don't know."

"Did she wear barrettes?"

"Probably."

"What about Lilly? Describe her earrings?"

"Okay! I get the point you are making. I'll do it." Troy agreed warily. *You owe it to Elana*, he told himself

"Good. The first available time my friend can meet with you guys is the day after Christmas, so Wednesday it is." B.K. handed them each a business card.

Troy studied it. *Shauna McCray, Forensic Hypnosis Therapist. Meeting Investigative Needs One Mind at a Time.*

"I took the liberty of telling her you could be there at noon, but please give her a call and confirm. You'll have to leave a message. She's on vacation this week, but she's in the area. I explained to her the nature of the case and that you," he looked at Troy, "won't be in town long and she promised me that she can meet with you anytime next week. The sooner the better."

"Should my mom do this, too?"

"If she's feeling up to it that would be great. Even though she wasn't there when your sister went missing, there could still be details she's suppressing like a strange car lingering about that morning. I was hoping to ask her about it today, but I can wait until she calls me. Though I will be at the service Monday, I want to keep as much distance as possible from y'all. If anyone asks, you don't know me. If your suspicions are true, that someone in your family could have kidnapped Elana, then we have to be sure no one finds out you hired me. Whoever did this thinks he has gotten away with it. He needs to believe that you think so as well. Did you bring the photographs?"

"Yes." Elvin handed over the manila folder with pictures and names of his family members. "We found the most current ones possible. Some I got off of Facebook, but as you see, some of them are still pretty old. I drew a diagram to help you keep track of our family tree. It gets pretty wild because my grandfather had children outside of his marriage with my grandmother and she had others before and after him."

"I've seen worse." B.K. quickly scanned the material. "Looks like I'll have some homework tonight."

"What about Herbert Greenfield?" asked Troy. "I thought it was strange for him not to be there."

"That's the stepfather, right? Oh, don't worry. I'm checking up on him. As a matter of fact, I'm going to Hitchcock to meet with him next week."

"Hitchcock…" Troy thought aloud, searching his mind for its location. Then it finally registered. "That's a small city between here and Galveston off of I-Forty-five, right?" The same interstate where Elana's body was found!

"I know." B.K. leered.

"That's a strange coincidence," Troy said more to Elvin as confirmation that his inquiry into Herbert's presence wasn't too far-fetched. He turned his attention back to B.K. "You think he's connected to Elana's disappearance?"

"Maybe. In my book, everyone is a suspect until proven otherwise. I can't make connections where there are none, but I promise to leave no stone uncovered."

Everyone is a suspect until proven otherwise. What was that supposed to mean? Was B.K. implying that he would look closer into him? Is that what all this hypnosis crap is about? Troy could not get offended. He understood the process of eliminating suspects. "Fair enough," he responded.

"If there's nothing else, we'll touch base after I get Shauna's report. Elvin, please be sure to have your mom call me. I would prefer to be the one to ask her about undergoing forensic memory recall, if you don't mind."

"Sure, that's not a problem."

"The sooner I'm able to meet with her, the better. Maybe she can come on Wednesday while y'all are with Shauna."

"I don't want her to come by herself. I'll see if my wife will ride with her. The boys can stay at the house alone." Elvin seemed to be thinking out loud more so than responding to B.K.

"I can always ask my mom to come with Lilly. I'm sure she won't mind."

"Y'all figure it out and have Lilly call me. If I don't hear from her by Wednesday morning, I'll contact her."

"Okay," replied Elvin.

"Well, I think we're done for right now. Elvin already has my card; let me give you one, too, Troy. If you can think of anything else or you have any questions, give me a call day or night."

"I would like a copy of the autopsy report, if you don't mind," Troy stated, taking B.K.'s card and putting it in his jacket pocket without looking at it. "And any photographs of Elana's body when she was found. Basically, I want a copy of everything you have. Not to step on your toes, but to analyze the evidence for myself."

B.K. smirked and paused a moment before responding. "Give me a few minutes." He grabbed a file from his desk and left the office.

"What do you think of him?"

"I think he is a bit smug."

"So you're basically meeting an older version of yourself, huh?" Elvin teased.

"Aww, whatever. I actually like him. It shows me that he's confident in his ability to help with the case. I believe this dude is going to finally help us find answers. Is he expensive?"

"Thanks to Jeff, he's cutting us a break, but even with the discount, he's not cheap."

"I told you I would help. Let me know what you need."

"I have what I need right here, man…you. Thanks for being here."

Normally, Troy would have teased Elvin for being too sentimental, but this was not the time. He nodded and gave El a reassuring pat on the knee. Then B.K. returned.

Chapter 9: The Curse

*U*nfortunately, Nate's first ice skating adventure involved an injury. Though she knew her boy was rough as he'd gotten many scrapes and bruises along the way, Natalie's heart still ached for him and his protruding lip. Seeing him tumble to the ground and then get up a screaming, bloody mess, kicked her mommy instincts into full gear. Diane had to hold her back from going to get him and let Alyssa bring him to her. "Girl, you will fall and hurt yourself out there tryin' to walk on ice with those heels," she had said.

Natalie knew that Nate's injury looked much worse than it actually was, and though she, too, was crying inside, she managed to hold her emotions together as Troy had told her many times to do in front of him. *"You are going to make him soft by overreacting every time he gets hurt. He's a boy. He'll be all right."* And Nate was. Big-lipped and all, he stopped crying after a few reassurances from his mom and grandmother that he was a big boy and all would be okay.

Alyssa was very apologetic.

"It's not your fault, honey," Natalie had said to her. She'd seen exactly how Nate's fall had happened and after the crying and bleeding stopped, she scolded him for his actions.

"Can I go back out there?"

If Natalie had been the one to fall, she would have been done skating for the day, maybe even for life, but Nate's persistence did not surprise her. She reluctantly agreed, despite the urge to continue coddling him. Troy would be proud. She did issue a very stern warning that his skating days would be over if he did not follow the rules.

Nate's accident ended the heart-to-heart she and Diane had been having. Natalie was willing to talk about God all day long with her mother-in-law, but sex was one topic that was strictly off-limits. They engaged in small talk...the weather...what they would do later in the week. While Natalie kept a close eye on Nate, ready to yell at him for the slightest act of defiance, Diane's thoughts ventured to the game plan for Christmas dinner.

"I think we should start on the desserts tomorrow or first thing Monday mornin'. There's no tellin' how long the funeral will last that evenin' and I ain't tryin' to be up all night. My heart really goes out to Lilly. I can't imagine losin' one of my children, not like that."

"Me either. I'm a little nervous about meeting her. I don't know what to say. I wish it was under different circumstances, but I know being there is important to Troy."

"Both he and Elvin had a hard time when Elana first disappeared. I kept Elvin a lot at first because Lilly had a nervous breakdown after a few weeks. Reed and I were separated at the time, so bein' able to help someone else kept me from dealin' with my drama. Those boys had a tough time. They blamed themselves."

"I know. Troy has shared some of his feelings with me. I've tried to tell him that it wasn't his fault."

"He blamed everyone, even me for not pickin' him up. To this day, Troy thinks that I got busy and lost track of time. I never had the heart to tell him that I'd called Reed the day before at work and left word for his father to get him. Troy already had enough animosity for his dad. I didn't want to add fuel to the fire. I tried callin' Lilly's to see if Reed had come, but no one answered."

"Why didn't Reed pick him up?"

"He never got the message. This was long before the days of voicemail and answerin' machines. We depended on people to write things down with pencil and paper. Unfortunately, one of the workers never gave him the message. I think back on the day Elana went missin' and I do blame myself. Even if Reed had gotten my message, deep down I knew he likely wouldn't follow through. Reed was good at givin' us money, but he was never reliable when it came to gettin' the kids and it was always because of one or both of the two b's, booze or a bi—"

"I got the point."

Diane laughed. "Girl, you crack me up actin' like you're allergic to certain words. That's good, though. You are settin' a good example for Nate. Troy and Tracy heard it all when they were comin' up. They still do. Anyhow, Reed was messin' around with this lady who lived near Lilly. I figured since he would likely be over that way, he could get Troy this one time. I do feel like I partly contributed to Elana's disappearance. Maybe she would have never left had I not neglected my parental responsibilities. I'd taken Tracy to my sisters and I was at a hotel with Henry. I'm sure you know we weren't havin' a prayer meetin'."

Natalie remained quiet, hoping to keep the conversation from once again venturing down that path.

"There was only one time when I depended on Reed for childcare and that was when Tracy was in kindergarten. I had started a new job and it would take a few months to get my schedule straightened out. I told Reed that if he did not agree to pick her up, I would go down to the courthouse and sign over custody of the kids and they could live with him at his parents' house. I wouldn't have really done that, but it was the only thing I could think of. I needed his help until I could get my schedule together. For about five months, he got Tracy from school and kept her until I got off of work and to his credit, he never missed a day. The thing with Elana spooked us both and I felt better knowin' he had her than for the bus to drop her off and she be at home alone. Troy was always stayin' after school for somethin'. Sometimes it was for detention. That boy can be so bullheaded when he wants to be."

"Tell me something I don't know."

"The crazy thing is that the night before Elana disappeared, a black cat had crossed my path and I had a feelin' somethin' bad was goin' to happen."

Natalie rolled her eyes unaware if Diane saw or not.

"Although my heart really does go out to Lilly, I'm glad it wasn't Tracy. I feel horrible sayin' that out loud."

"Don't beat yourself up. I think that's a normal feeling. I'm sure many parents would say the same." Natalie could relate. She reflected on her own feelings regarding the recent school shooting. As much as she cried about those babies, there's not a minute she didn't thank God for keeping Nate safe.

"I think part of the reason Troy treated Tracy so good was to make up for how they picked on Elana that day. Troy has always been protective of Tracy. He's protective of everyone he loves. You have a good husband, girl. Hang on to him."

"I have no intentions of letting him go anywhere."

It was around seven or so when Diane, Natalie, and Nate made it back to the house. Diane had dropped Alyssa and AJ off first, but not before taking them all to get fast-food. Natalie avoided the temptation of getting a greasy burger and fries by reminding herself that, although she was eating for three, only one of them would have to worry about the pounds from those extra calories setting in. Lord knows she did not want her hips to be like her mother-in-law's. Diane didn't seem the least bit concerned about the effects of a high-caloric value meal.

Natalie hadn't heard from Troy all day and expected him to be there. But, as Diane pulled into her driveway, the rented vehicle they'd gotten from the airport was notably missing.

"Troy must still be with Elvin."

"I guess." Natalie tried not to sound disappointed. She turned to the backseat. The long day and absence of his usual daily nap had finally caught up with her son on their way back to the house. "Nate," she said, shaking his legs. "Wake up, honey. We're at Gigi's."

He let out a shrill that sounded as if he were irritated about being disturbed, but his eyes did not open.

"*Nate.*" Natalie tried again.

"Leave him alone. Here, take my purse and I'll carry him in."

As soon as Natalie stepped through the door, the urge to pee hit her like lightning. She threw both of their purses aside and sprinted—as fast as a pregnant woman could—to the downstairs restroom.

After conducting her business, Natalie went back out to the living room to find Nate was still asleep and had been laid on the couch and Diane was swearing as she dumped the contents out of her purse onto the coffee table. "What's wrong?"

"I need to get everything out of this bag," she said frantically.

"Here." Diane flung Natalie's purse to her. Luckily she managed to catch it before it collided with her belly. "You can put your stuff in the armchair for now so it doesn't get mixed up with mine. I have a purse you can use."

The confusion must have been all over Natalie's face as Diane further explained. "You had our purses on the floor."

"Sorry. I had to go to the bathroom. Did they get dirty or something?" Instinctively, she began wiping the bottom of hers.

"No, silly, they didn't get dirty. But we can't carry these anymore. Don't you know it's bad luck to put your purse on the floor? You'll always be broke."

"What!" Natalie laughed, but Diane was not amused. "So, what now? Do you have to wash your purse to break the curse?" Her obvious sarcasm was either missed or ignored.

"No. We have to throw them away." She balled her purse like it was trash and headed toward the kitchen.

"Are you seriously getting rid of that?"

"Yeah. What else am I goin' do with it? I can't carry it anymore."

"Come on, Di, it can't be that deep. That's a Gucci, much too valuable to discard because of some crazy superstition."

Diane stared at her for a moment and Natalie braced herself for one of those decorative tongue-lashings that Troy had gotten from time-to-time. "It's a material, replaceable item to me, but if you think it's precious, take it. I ain't got no more use for it."

The last thing Natalie needed was another purse, but she took it anyhow, hoping Diane would come to her senses later. The purse, a simple black tote, was cute, but it really wasn't her style. It was too plain. She was tired and her nerves were a little thin with all the superstition craziness. First it was the zoo thing, then downtown Natalie got fussed at for splitting a few poles, and now this. It was too much for one day. "I'm going to lie down. You want me to take Nate upstairs?"

"No, he's fine down here. I'll get him dressed and ready for bed."

"All right. Thanks. Good night."

Diane did not respond. She was too busy repeating some mantra to herself about not being broke.

Natalie shook her head and went up the stairs. Upon further examination, she understood why Diane was so quick to discard the purse. It was a fake. Natalie could tell from the stitching pattern that looked a lot different from the Guccis she owned. It felt different as well. "I bet you wouldn't have been so quick to throw it out if it were real," she said to herself and then threw the purse in the can in Troy's room. *Troy*…she wondered what was up with him. She tried calling. No answer. She sent a text. *What's up?*

It was a few minutes before she got his response. *Is everything ok?*

Yes. All is well. Wanted 2c what was up w/u?

Not a good time 2talk rgt now. Sorry.

That was a lot of words to explain nothing!

Realizing that she hadn't yet called Aneetra back from this morning, Natalie changed into her pajamas, washed her face, and dialed her best friend.

Chapter 10: Every Foul Word

*T*roy was mentally and emotionally drained after leaving Lilly's. He knew he would have some explaining to do to Natalie about why he didn't answer her phone calls. She called again, *twice*, even after he texted and told her it was a bad time. She finally left a message, which he listened to on the way back to his parents'. Her attitude was apparent as she explained that she was "bored" like it was his job to entertain her.

He pulled into his parents' driveway a little after ten, expecting to walk in and find his mom, hopefully accompanied by his wife, in the living room watching some typical chick flick on Lifetime. With any luck, it would be the distraction Troy needed to calm Natalie's nerves. She'd always been a tad bit high-maintenance thanks to her inner model diva, but the degree of her neediness seemed to have been turned up with this current pregnancy. He didn't recall her being so moody with Nate. Maybe she was and he didn't remember.

There were two people in the living room when Troy walked in. Instead of his mom and wife, it was his father and Nate!

"Daa-dee!" Nate jumped off his grandfather's lap and ran and gave Troy a big hug. His son was the only reason why the lid had not come off of the boiling rage inside of him.

"Hey, lil' man. Why are you still up? Where's Gigi and your mommy?"

"Upstairs."

"I think Natalie is sleep, but your mom will be right back. She went to change into her nightclothes." The voice of his father felt like needle pricks in his ears.

"Hey, man, let's go upstairs with Mommy, okay?"

"But I wanna stay down here wif Grandpa. He was tellin' me funny stories about Santa Claus."

"You know Santa isn't real, right?" He and Natalie had agreed that they would not make the fictitious philanthropist part of their tradition. They wanted Nate to know the true meaning of why their family celebrated Christmas.

"Yes, but Grandpa still has stories about him."

"Why don't you come upstairs and tell me the funny stories." He took Nate's hand and the two of them proceeded up the steps—Nate, rambling; Troy, fuming!

"Troy!" He was startled and stopped in his tracks by his mother's sharp tone. "Let him go. You're hurtin' the poor baby."

Troy looked down and saw that he did not have hold of Nate's hand. It was his arm, and Nate was being dragged along like a rag doll. What Troy thought were "ramblings" of Santa Claus stories, were actually cries from Nate that he was going too fast. "I'm so sorry, lil' man."

"'Dat's okay."

Troy's mom looked like she was about to pick up Nate. Troy beat her to it. There was no way his son was going back down there without him. Without saying anything else to his mom, Troy burst into the bedroom where he found Natalie lying on the bed playing Candy Crush Saga on her iPad.

"Nice of you to finally come back."

"Why weren't you downstairs with him?"

"Because he was with your parents."

"No, my *parents* were not with him. I came in and found him alone with my dad."

"And?"

"How could you be so careless with my son!"

"He's not only *your* son. And if you cared that much, then why weren't you here with us?"

"Don't start with that. I asked you to come with me and you wouldn't."

"I didn't think you would be gone all day."

"Can I go back downstairs wif Grandpa?"

Both Natalie and Troy answered at the same time. She said yes; he said no.

"Get dressed. We're going to a hotel," he demanded.

"You can go wherever you want, but Nate and I are staying here. You're being ridiculous."

"What's ridiculous is that everyone seems to forget all the crap that man put our family through."

"It's called forgiveness. Try it!"

"I wanna go downstairs!" This time Nate was crying.

Natalie tried to appease him by giving him her iPad so he could take over her game. That didn't work. Neither did her suggestion of Angry Birds, which Nate generally liked to play. He shoved the iPad aside and kept crying.

Troy knew being here with his dad was a bad idea. No, it was beyond a bad idea. It was a horrible one. The stupidest thing he had ever let his mom talk him into doing. He wanted out of the house. He needed out of there. Too many negative memories of his mom swollen and bruised and his sister screaming her head off. The stress of those occurrences and the emotional buildup from witnessing Lilly have two meltdowns, plus the guilt he felt about Elana and the determination he had to find the person responsible for her death, all seemed to be colliding at once. Like a Boa constrictor wrapped around its prey, the pressure of these things were squeezing the life out of him. He needed to get out of this house, away from his dad, and get some fresh air. And he was taking his family with him!

"Get up and let's go now!" Troy screamed at the top of his lungs and kicked the trash can across the room. Natalie gasped and Nate clung to her crying frantically in a manner that Troy had never seen before.

His mom ran into the room. "What's goin' on in here?"

Troy stood frozen, in shock that he had put that look of fear on his son's face. He knew that look all too well. He'd seen it on Tracy's face when their father went into his rages. And the anger in Natalie's eyes toward him, he was sure resembled the way his eyes had bore into his father. Troy always felt that his father was wrong for coming home and yelling so viciously at his mom in front of him and Tracy. Yet, Troy had barged into the room exhibiting that same abusive-like behavior. Behavior he now deeply regretted and hoped would not be seared into the mind of his young son.

Troy's mom grabbed a screaming Nate from the bed and left the room. Troy didn't catch everything she said on her way out, but in so many words, she colorfully told him what she thought of his behavior.

Natalie continued to glare at him. He read her expression effortlessly. Confusion…anger…hurt. Of the three, it was the hurt that bothered him the most. The intensity of her gaze was only softened by the tears he saw filling her big brown eyes. He genuinely loved her and pain was the last thing he ever wanted to cause her. His mom was right. He was a dumb butt. He deserved every foul word she'd said to him. He couldn't even get upset that she'd said them in front of Nate. He'd done worse. "Natalie," he said softly, walking gently toward her, "I'm sorry, babe."

She remained quiet. Tears spoke in her place.

He sat next to her and pulled her into his arms. Her body was tense. "I'm sorry," he repeated. "I have a lot on my mind, but that's no excuse for the way I talked to you. I should have never done that at all and I definitely should not have done that in front of Nate."

She cried into his shoulder. Whether this was her natural response to his behavior or her hormones, he didn't care. He'd caused a deep wound to her heart and it was his responsibility to repair it. He would hold her until it healed. No matter how long the process would take.

Chapter 11: Current Movement

*N*atalie and Troy stayed up half the night talking. There was no arguing, simply a good heart-to-heart between husband and wife about what had taken place between them. Without making excuses for his behavior, Troy explained to her what had been going through his mind and how concerned he was about Lilly.

"I'm worried about how she's going to handle the service," he told her and then described her two meltdowns. The first was at the funeral home. The second, after he and Elvin had come from meeting with the private investigator. "Lilly had gotten herself stirred up again by thinking about all the things that Elana possibly went through. She'd worked herself into an emotional frenzy to the point where Elvin and I had to stronghold her until she calmed down. That happened right before you called and I could not tell you what was going on at the time."

Natalie felt bad. "I'm sorry. I'm sure I didn't make the situation any easier for you by calling like I did."

"You're cool. You have to remember that when I am working, I'm not always going to be able to answer your phone calls."

Natalie wanted to remind him that he wasn't working. He was on vacation, but she thought it might sound callous. She told him about her day and how his mama worked her nerves about the purse thing. "Has she always been like this?"

"As long as I can remember. I never gave it much thought."

Natalie had been struggling with how to approach Troy about his relationship with Reed. He helped her segue into it when he mentioned having to talk to Nate first thing in the morning.

"How do I explain to a three-year-old what happened? I feel like I have shattered his trust."

"Oh, I don't think it's that deep. You scared him half to death for sure, but you guys will be all right. Tell him that his daddy had a big temper tantrum, apologize, and ask for his forgiveness. Then show him that Daddy is a changed man through your actions."

"It's that simple, huh?'

"It can be. The best way to teach your son forgiveness is to demonstrate it for him." She ignored the tension in his jaw line and chose her words carefully. "You're angry about how Reed treated Diane and I absolutely agree with you that it was wrong. Troy, it could have been much worse. There are fathers who beat and sexually abuse their own children. He never laid a hand on you guys. That's at least something to be thankful for. You blame him for everything, but your mom has to bear some of the responsibility. She's the one who continually allowed you and Tracy to be subjected to his behavior by staying with him."

"So, now you're trying to make me mad at my mama?"

He was joking. Perhaps a sign that Natalie was getting through to him. "No, silly. My point is that you need to consider all sides of the story. Reed was not perfect, but I'm sure your mother wasn't either." Natalie was uncomfortable by Troy's blank stare. She had to look away, afraid that somehow he would read her mind and uncover the secret Diane had shared with her about Henry. "No one is perfect. You proved that tonight by coming in here acting like a lunatic."

"It's called forgiveness. Try it," he teased, repeating the words she'd thrown at him hours earlier.

She chuckled. "I do forgive you. How would you feel if you sincerely asked and I wouldn't give you the time of day?"

"My dad has not asked me."

"You haven't given him the chance. Besides, didn't you hear that prayer this morning? He wasn't only asking Jesus, he was asking you. Will you do your mom and me a favor and please talk to him?"

"Do I have to?" He pouted like their son when being instructed to do something against his will.

"Do it for Nate. He needs to see you positively interact with his grandfather. Like it or not, Reed is all he has."

"What about Richard?"

Richard was a friend of Troy's and had also been Natalie's mom's boyfriend at one time. He was the one who introduced them to each other, initially oblivious of the sparks that ignited between them. Richard was now married to Natalie's godmother and the two of them did act as surrogate grandparents to Nate, which Natalie appreciated. "You and I both know that Richard and Sylvia will always be there for Nate. There's room in his heart for your dad as well. So, will you talk to him?"

"Sure, Natalie." Troy seemed as enthusiastic as someone signing a contract with a gun pointed to his head.

She smiled warmly at him, rubbing his thigh as reassurance that all would be okay. The way she saw it, Troy should be thankful he still had a father. She'd give anything for a chance to talk to her daddy again. He was only in her life for five years before he died. He lived in her heart forever.

"Can we stop talking about my dad now? I'm tired."

Natalie glanced at the clock. It was almost two in the morning!

"I didn't realize it was so late. I know this sounds bad, but I'm so glad we get to attend Bedside Baptist in the morning. I don't think I would have the strength to get up for church. I am pooped."

Before moving to the other side of the bed, Troy once again pulled Natalie into him. He hugged her tight. She felt at ease in the arms of the man whose desire to protect his family was so strong that it sometimes got in the way of good judgment. "My protective detective," she whispered.

"I love you, babe. Again, I'm sorry about tonight."

"Shh. It's over. Let's move on."

He lifted her chin and greedily took her mouth into his. She matched his fervor. After four-and-a-half years of marriage, almost three kids, and a little bit of drama, Troy's kisses still had the power to flutter her stomach. Wait…the current movement was due more to her active incubating twins than his kiss. Maybe a combination of both.

"There's only one thing left to do to make this argument mirror the others we have had," he said once they stopped devouring each other's lips and paused for air.

"What's that?"

"Make-up sex." He smiled cunningly.

"Good night, Troy."

Chapter 12: The Umpteenth Time

*M*orning came quicker than Troy anticipated or wanted. He hadn't really slept amidst the tossing and turning during the night, wondering exactly what he would say to Nate…to his father. As much as he loathed his dad, it seemed it would be easier to talk to him than with his son. The memory of the look in Nate's eyes pained him in the same manner, maybe even worse, than Natalie's. Troy always prided himself on being a better father than his own. Last night he'd failed miserably and that would be sure to bother him for quite some time.

Troy had been devoting more time to learning the Bible ever since coming head-to-head this past summer with a serial killer who had used scriptures to justify murder. Of course, Troy knew that the killer's rationalizations were erroneous. Still, he learned the importance of studying the Word for himself so he could correctly apply its principles to his life as Paul instructed in 2 Timothy 2:15. Last night he'd neglected to practice any of the many scriptures that warned against out-of-control anger such as Proverbs 29:22. *An angry man stirs up strife, and a furious man abounds in transgression.* Troy had done both.

For all of these years, Troy had felt justified in his disdain toward his father. Natalie did make a good point in saying that his dad had never laid a hand on him or his sister. Except for the time when Troy jumped in to help his mom, his father had never even threatened him. Still, that didn't excuse his overall behavior and yet Natalie's words, *"The best way to teach your son forgiveness is to demonstrate it for him,"* weighed on his heart. Even though Troy knew forgiveness was something Jesus demanded, it was the desire to be a good example for Nate that motivated Troy to at least try and let the past go.

Might as well get this over with, Troy said to himself after hearing heavy footsteps descending the stairs. He had promised Natalie that he would talk to his father and Troy knew she would not relent until he kept it. And he had to do it now. It could not hang over his head as Elana was depending on him. He needed a clear mind in order to find the evidence needed to put away her killer.

Troy slid his arm from underneath Natalie, who did not stir, threw on some pants, and made a pit stop at the bathroom. Before heading to the kitchen, he peeked in on Nate who had slept in Tracy's old room. Like his mama, lil' man did not stir. Troy stared at him for a few moments as a flood of emotions filled him. Nate deserved better and from here on out, he would get it.

Closing the door, Troy walked down the stairs. The closer he got to the kitchen, the slower his pace. *Why?* That was the one question he would ask his father. The one question he *had* to ask his dad, even knowing that there would never be a satisfying answer. Nothing the man said would adequately explain why his father had treated his mom in such a horrible manner.

Troy stepped into the kitchen, realizing that he would have to wait to interrogate his dad because it was his mom who he had heard that morning. "Hey," Troy said, walking over to assist her in putting up dishes from the dishwasher.

She looked up at him without Christmas season jollies running through her veins. She happened to be holding a knife at that time as well. "Don't 'hey' me. I'm so pissed at you right now; I don't know what to do."

"Please don't stab me." He smiled, hoping his charm would calm her nerves. It didn't.

"You think you did somethin' cute last night comin' in here actin' like a fool?" The force with which she continued to unload the dishwasher intensified as she continued talking. "You need to get over the issues you have with your father. You have a lot of nerve comin' into this house, *his* house, bein' disrespectful."

This coming from the woman who's proud to say she went off on a man with Alzheimer's?

"I was tellin' Natalie yesterday how proud of you I am because you're a good husband and father and then you come in and show you're a—"

"*Mama!*" Troy was sure she was about to throw the plate in her hand. "Watch what you're doing."

She put it on the counter and slammed the dishwasher shut without emptying it further. She stood with her arms folded staring at him. There was that look again. The look of disappointment from someone he loved.

"Mama, I'm sorry." He reached out for her. Despite her resistance, he held her anyhow, feeling her body relax ever so slightly. "I did not mean to upset you."

After taking several deep breaths in his arms, she broke away.

"I'm sorry," Troy repeated, hating the glossiness coming from her eyes. This was unusual as his mom was a long way from his sensitive, sometimes overly emotional wife. Both her inner and outer toughness were often portrayed through her eyes. Hardened eyes that had likely seen the unimaginable, witnessed the unforgiveable, and yet still held hope for the impossible. "Why?" Troy found himself asking his mom the question he had intended for his dad.

"Why what?"

"Why did you stay with him after all he'd put you through? I don't understand why you kept Tracy and me in this environment."

She shook her head, sighing as she walked past him to sit at the small kitchen table. "The one thing I do regret—that your father and I both regret—is not settin' better examples for you and your sister. I often wonder if you went to Ohio after high school to get as far away from here as possible."

Troy wouldn't doubt that subconsciously he might have been running away, but he also recalled how bad he'd felt leaving Tracy behind. He went to Ohio because that was the best opportunity for him at the time. He would have never made such a drastic move simply to escape knowing his baby sister would be left behind.

"Last night I realized that part of the reason you hate your dad so much is because of me and my big mouth." Her voice was soft, speaking like she was having this conversation with herself and he happened to be nearby. "I know I couldn't shield you from everything he did, but there was a lot that you wouldn't have known had I not told you. The most important thing is that I'm with him now because I love him and I truly believe he has changed. He's been livin' here since last spring. I swear I think this is the longest we have ever gone without separatin' for at least a few weeks."

"What kind of marriage is that? Why do you still want to be with someone with whom you have more bad memories than you have good ones? All he's ever done is cheat on and beat you. You have been such a good wife to him."

She smirked. "Have a seat, son. I have wrongly allowed you to put me on a pedestal all these years. You only know about your dad's wrongs, but I have not been perfect. Your father is not the only one who has been unfaithful."

"Stop, Mama. You don't have to make yourself look bad in order to make him appear better. I'm sure he drove you to it."

"There you go vilifyin' him without all the facts. I am not in the mood to sugarcoat things for you, so I'm goin' to tell it like it is. Throughout our entire relationship we both have cheated on each other, even before we were married. In fact, he married me not knowin' for sure you were his child."

"What are you saying?" Troy had wished for many years that Reed Evans was not his father. Yet, now faced with the possibility, he didn't feel relief. He felt empty…lost, like his entire identity would be stripped from him.

"Relax, he's your father. It was confirmed a long time ago through a blood test. What I'm tryin' to tell you is that he took care of you even before he was legally obligated to do so. That right there should tell you that he's not all that bad. Yeah, he was a drunk, but he still took care of business. When I told the other guy I was seein' that I was pregnant, he all but left town. He wasn't tryin' to marry me. Back then, that's what a girl had to do when she got knocked up. Even knowin' the circumstances, Reed refused to leave me hangin'. Sort of like Joseph stepped up when Mary was pregnant, except in my case I can't quite claim Immaculate Conception."

It came as no surprise to Troy that his mom had a shot gun wedding. He pretty much figured that out as a child through simple mathematics of calculating their wedding date and his birthday. The other details, though, were shocking.

"I have stayed with your dad because I always knew he was a good man. True, we have never had a perfect relationship. We have fought like cats and dogs, and have both done things to hurt each other, but we're older now. It's high time that we both grow up and your dad has done that. He has stopped drinkin' and I see the changes in him. He is really tryin' and the last thing he needs is for you to come in here actin' crazy because he was playin' with Nate. Give him a chance. *Please*."

"I'm sorry," he said for what seemed like the umpteenth time.

"You need to say that to your father."

Apologizing to him hadn't been in Troy's script, but he wasn't about to argue with her on the issue. If anything, the man owed him an apology for being such a crappy role model. "Believe it or not, I came down here because I thought you were him. As soon as he gets up, I promise to speak with him."

There was a brief glow in her face before it turned solemn again. "You won't be doin' it here. He left after all the ruckus last night and said he would stay at the other house until you leave because he did not want his presence to ruin Christmas for everyone. I think it would mean a lot to him if you go over there and talk to him."

"I don't know about that, Mama. I really need to talk to Nate. Plus, I'd planned to spend most of the day working on Elana's case." He hadn't had a chance to look at any of the information B.K. had given him. "Before I forget, would you mind picking up Lilly on Wednesday and taking her to meet the private investigator?"

"Sure, what time?"

"I think he wants her there around noon. I'll get her number from Elvin so you can call and verify."

"That's not necessary. We exchanged numbers when I saw her last summer. I still have hers."

"Okay. Elvin and I have another appointment that day and he doesn't want her to be by herself. Nicole's here, but I thought it might be good if you went with her since you guys used to be close and you witnessed firsthand what she experienced. I think she would appreciate having you there."

"Oh, I definitely don't mind. But, don't think that by changin' the subject, I'm done talkin' to you about your dad. I know you have a lot on your mind with what's goin' on right now. I also think you are makin' excuses. If you are really serious about talkin' to him, it shouldn't matter if you do it here or elsewhere. I'm not goin' to try and press you, but I will say this: I would like your dad to spend Christmas with us. I think the only one who can make that happen is you. You messed things up, now fix them," she said before getting up and walking away.

Troy continued to sit for a few moments, reflecting on the conversation with his mom. After praying for guidance on how to handle the situation with his father, Troy got up and finished putting away the dishes.

Chapter 13: Sentimental Value

fter the conversation with his mom, Troy took care of his ultimate priority and that was making things right with Nate. Talking with his son wasn't as awkward as he had anticipated. He did as Natalie had suggested and said that he had had a temper tantrum. Nate made him laugh when he asked if Mommy had spanked him or put him in time-out.

"No, son. Mommy was very disappointed with me though."

"What does disappointed mean?"

"It means unhappy." Troy explained how he was disappointed with himself and that he would understand if Nate had been disappointed as well. It jabbed his heart when Nate told Troy that he had scared him. Troy asked for his forgiveness. Nate gave it. The two hugged and began play boxing until Nate ultimately "won."

Afterward, Troy was really eager to review the things B.K. had given him, but he knew he would not be able to do so in peace if he did not make the trip to his grandparents' home to talk to his father. Both Natalie and his mom would be on his case until he did.

"I'll be back," he said and headed out.

Troy could not remember the last time he was at his grandparents' house. His mom wasn't very close to them. Consequently, neither was he. The last time Troy could recall being there was when he was taking karate classes. If his memory served correctly, that was before Tracy was born. It had been so long since Troy had been there that if it weren't for his father's pickup in the driveway, he would not have known exactly which house it was.

Troy pulled up behind the pickup, trying not to talk himself out of it as it could go wrong in so many ways. If Troy were to unleash nearly forty-two years of rage on his father, no one would be there to stop him and either he or his father would end up dead. Troy's father owned several guns and Troy was carrying a piece himself. Emotions could easily spin the situation out of control. With the two of them being alone, it could get ugly. There was too much baggage...too many bad memories. Troy vividly remembered how his dad had threatened to blow his mom's brains out with one of his guns. Troy was only about four or five when this happened, maybe even younger. They had gotten into a fight about something, most likely another woman, and his dad pulled the gun out on his mom. She didn't flinch. She walked right up to him and said that if he shot her, he had better be prepared to kill her because if not, she would surely kill him.

Abuser? Yes. Killer? No. Troy was sure his father was only using the gun as a scare tactic. It probably wasn't even loaded. His dad had been unsuccessful in scaring his mom that night, but his mom had surely scared his father. Troy wholeheartedly believed that his mother would have been crazy enough to follow through with her threat if she had been shot. His dad put the gun away and left, getting cursed out by his mom all the way back to his car.

That was the first and only time a gun had ever been involved, but it still disturbed Troy that his father did such a thing in front of him. He would never do that to Natalie, whether Nate was around or not. Husbands were supposed to love their wives. They were supposed to love and protect them, not beat them. *Husbands, love your wives, even as Christ also loved the church, and gave himself for it. Ephesians 5:25.*

Troy turned off the rented car and took several deep breaths. *Jesus, please give me strength.* He continued to sit with his eyes closed. Praying...breathing...thinking about all the stuff this man had put their family through...getting angry again...praying harder!

Man, forget this! Troy was about to restart the car and go back to the house. He'd make up something to tell Natalie and his mom. He opened his eyes and was startled by the figure standing next to the driver's window staring at him. Instinctively, Troy reached for his gun, withdrawing when he realized it was his dad. His heart raced, but surprisingly he wasn't as angry as he had been earlier.

The two Evans men stared at each other through the cracked window, neither knowing quite how to initiate a conversation. It was the elder Evans who spoke first.

"Your mom told me you would be coming by."

"Yeah, she seems to think we need to talk."

"What do you think?"

Troy took a deep breath before responding. He wanted to say that he didn't see any use for them talking. It was too late, but Natalie's words rang powerfully in his head. *The best way to teach your son forgiveness is to demonstrate it for him.* "I don't think one heart-to-heart conversation will undo so many years of hatred, but I guess it's a start." Troy nodded for his father to move back so he could open the door and they could go inside to get this talk over with. Elana was waiting on him. The more time he spent here, the less time he was devoting to her.

"The house is a mess. I've been gutting it and redoing everything. I don't know if your mom told you or not, but I'm going to

sell it," he said a little too excitedly for Troy's sake. Was he expecting to be congratulated for finally getting rid of the house
where he routinely committed acts of adultery? "Let me lock up
and maybe we can go get a bite to eat."

Troy didn't have much of an appetite, but he agreed that being
in a public place would probably be best. While waiting for his
dad, Troy looked on the passenger's side and noticed that Elvin
had left his fast-food bag there yesterday. Troy's first thought
was to simply throw it in the backseat. Instead, he saw the trash
can on the side of the house and took it there.

He immediately regretted the decision as the contents of his
father's cleaning efforts were apparent and contained reminders
of how low-down and dirty he had been. There were many items
of women's clothing inside. Troy shuffled through them, finding
himself getting angry all over again. Not even the school drawing
of Tracy's or one of her old red-haired dolls could calm him. If
anything, it infuriated him even more. So what that the freckled
doll was nearly hairless, or that the picture was torn. Those things
should have held sentimental value and not been something that
their father discarded with the junk of his whores!

"What are you doing!" His father came running from around
the house in a panic.

"I'll be waiting in the car." Troy angrily dropped his own trash
to the ground. He fought every instinct to take off. Instead, he
found himself once again calling on Jesus, repeating the prayer
that he'd said only moments ago. *Please give me strength!* Without
the help of a supernatural power, Troy knew he would never make
it through.

Chapter 14: The Million Dollar Question

"I should have gone with him," a nervous Diane said to Natalie as they were in the kitchen, cleaning up the mess they had made from baking desserts for Christmas.

"I'm sure everything is okay." Natalie tried her best to sound confident. Troy had been gone for hours. She, too, was a bit anxious.

"I have tried Reed's cell phone at least a half-dozen times and he didn't answer. Maybe I should ride over to the house."

"No. Give it some more time. If you go over there, I'm sure it won't help the situation."

"I'm done, Mommy," said Nate, who enjoyed licking the cake batter out the bowl.

"Wow, you're a mess! C'mon, let's get cleaned up and then I want you to take a nap." Chances are, Nate would not go to sleep now that he was filled with the sugar from the cake batter, but she'd give it a shot anyhow.

"Gigi said I could sweep 'da floor."

Natalie sighed, amused by the naïveté of her three-and-a-half-year-old who still thought chores like washing dishes and sweeping the floor were fun. "Okay, but after you do that, you're going to take a nap, you hear me?"

"Yes, ma'am."

As she and Nate headed to the bathroom, she heard Diane's cell phone ring and wondered, *hoped*, it would be Troy or Reed letting them know that everything was fine. While Nate was drying off, Natalie took a peek at her cell phone. Nothing. After last night, she did not want to call him and risk interrupting a crucial moment. It was a little after one p.m. now. If Troy wasn't back by three, four at the latest, then she would give the green light for Diane to go over there!

"Can I go sweep the floor now?"

"*Yes*, Nate." He ran out the restroom while she waddled behind him. Her body ached from the long day yesterday, particularly her back and feet. Troy's old bed was comfortable because of the size, but the mattress was a long way from their Tempur-Pedic that Natalie always appreciated a little more after a few days away from it.

Diane, still on her phone, had stepped out the kitchen when she and Nate returned. Natalie sat at the table and watched her son make a mess of the small pile of trash that Diane had neatly gathered to make sweeping easier for him. Nate did everything with the collection except get it in the dustpan. Natalie let him do it his way. After she put him down for a nap, she would do it correctly.

"Was that Reed?" she asked when Diane came back into the kitchen, trying to sound casual as not to further worry her.

"No. That was Lilly returnin' my call. This mornin' Troy asked me to go somewhere with her on Wednesday since he and Elvin have an appointment. She was confirmin' the time with me."

"Oh." Natalie wondered when her husband had planned to fill her in on his appointment.

Diane sat across from her at the table and they talked a little more about Lilly and tomorrow night's service. Tracy was planning to ride with them. Al and the kids were staying behind. Diane had been able to talk Reed into coming, but with the latest blowup with Troy, his attendance was now up in the air. While Natalie and Diane were talking, Nate had ventured away from the spot Diane had designated for him to sweep. He was skipping all around the kitchen with the broom. Natalie let him go, figuring he was getting the sugar out of his system and tiring himself for his nap.

"Even if Reed decides not to come tomorrow, I really hope he spends Christmas with us Tuesday. This will be the first time ever that we will have everyone together. For all we know, it could be the very last time we get the chance."

Natalie didn't think it was that dramatic. "I'm sure as time goes on, we'll look back several years from now and it will seem like these family gatherings have been a long-time tradition."

"I hope you're right. Natalie, I have what will probably seem like a stupid question, but I feel like I can trust you to tell me the truth." She'd piqued Natalie's interest. "Do you think Jesus permanently changes people or is the change temporary?"

Caught off guard, Natalie took a moment before responding. "I think it depends on the individual," she said, drawing from her own experience. "If a person really opens his or heart to Him, that person can't help but to be permanently changed. Does this have something to do with Reed?"

"No, not really. I mean, of course I wondered about him initially, but the more time goes on, the more I believe he has changed. I have only seen him cry one time and that was last night after Troy's outburst. He said, 'Di, there are some mistakes in my past that I will never be able to fix.' Then he took off and I assumed he was about to relapse and go into one of his drinkin' binges. I thought for sure it would ruin all the progress we have made in our marriage. But, he called me and told me that he went straight to the other house and would stay there until y'all leave. I asked you about Jesus because I'm curious. I didn't think much about dyin' when I was younger. I even foolishly walked right up to the barrel of a gun before, but now that I am gettin' older, I'm wonderin' if it's too late for me."

"Why would you think that? Reed's older than you and look at how he has changed. You said so yourself."

"I guess I see Reed and me differently. People say that when children grow up bein' taught about God, even if they stray away, they come back. Reed's parents weren't the most holy examples, but from what I understand his grandparents were and he used to go to church with them all the time. My case is different. I never had a church upbringin'. We didn't even go on the holidays. I'm guessin' my parents believed in God, at least my mother, because she did make us say grace and sometimes prayers at night, which is more than I can say I did with my kids. I always thought of God, in general, as bein' this higher power, but I never really thought much about this whole salvation thing until you and Troy got together. My son doesn't talk to me about God, but I can tell he has changed."

"Why is it that you see change happening with people around you, but you have a hard time believing it can happen *for* you?"

"That would be the million-dollar question, wouldn't it? I honestly don't know. I've never known how to be any other way except what I am. I may be that one person God cannot fix."

"Excuse me, Mommy." Nate, still amusing himself with the broom, began sweeping under Natalie's side of the table. She lifted her feet to accommodate him while Diane stared into space.

"Maybe on some level I'm scared of change, even if it's good."

Natalie's best friend would know exactly what to say to Diane right now. Aneetra was one of the first people to inspire Natalie to seek Christ and she did it without being preachy or judgmental while also not wavering from biblical truths. Natalie understood Diane's feelings more than she could relate with words. She searched her mind for the right thing to say. Finally, she reached over to hold Diane's hand and said, "I agree that change can be scary because of the uncertainty that comes along with it. You're not the only one with a past." Natalie quickly glanced at Nate, who, at the moment, was a perfect reminder of how far she had come from being a conniving, man-stealing woman who had given her body away more times than she could count. She felt herself tearing as the before and after snapshots of her old self compared to her new creation in Christ flashed through her head. Natalie turned her attention back to Diane. "The one thing I am certain of is that no one is beyond Jesus' grasp. All you have to do is let him into your heart."

"Excuse me, Gigi."

"You make it sound so simple. I—" Their intimate moment was abruptly interrupted when Diane jerked from Natalie and stood up swearing because Nate had swept her feet with the broom. She wasn't swearing directly at Nate, but in general. Still, he started crying, especially after she snatched the broom from him and spat on it.

The whole thing happened so fast that Natalie sat frozen for a few moments while she processed the chain of events. A crying Nate running into her arms forced a reaction from her. "What is wrong with you, Diane!"

Immediately, remorse filled Diane's expression. "I'm sorry. I did not mean to scare him. It's bad luck for a person's feet to get swept."

"Oh my gosh, are you for real?" Natalie didn't wait for a response. She gathered her son and stormed out. Diane tried to stop her by apologizing, but Natalie waved her off. "He needs to take a nap anyhow." Stomping up the stairs, she coddled Nate, trying to assure him that he didn't do anything wrong. The last thing her big pregnant butt needed was to be toting a toddler around, especially in light of the aches and pains as a result of yesterday, but she was mad. This was the second time within twenty-four hours that her son had been scared because of someone else's craziness. "And they think Reed is the one with issues," she mumbled to herself when she'd finally made it to the room. She lay down with Nate, eventually drifting off to sleep herself.

Chapter 15: A Happy Medium

It was around 2:30 when Troy dropped his dad back off at his grandparents' house. "I guess I'll see you later tonight. Are you going to the service tomorrow?"

"I don't want to. I haven't seen Elvin or his mom for decades. I would feel awkward because this is such an emotional time for them."

Troy understood. As a detective, he'd seen more dead bodies than he cared to recount. He tried to stay away from funerals as much as possible unless it was a fellow officer or someone with whom he had a special connection. In Elana's case, it was the latter, combined with the drive to help find the person responsible for her circumstances. "All right. I need to get out of here." His father stared at him for a moment. Troy wasn't sure if he was expecting a goodbye hug, but Troy extended his hand instead. "See you later."

He shook it. "Thanks, son. You will never know how much our time together has meant to me."

Once his dad got out of the car, Troy backed out of the driveway and headed to his mom's. Though he and his father had broken bread, there were still many feelings that Troy needed to work through. One afternoon of intense conversation wasn't going to immediately repair the full extent of their damaged relationship, but as Troy had said to his father earlier, it was a start. That should at least mean something and appease his mom and Natalie. It also helped him because his anger toward his dad had been distracting him from his current mission. Troy still had yet to go over information that B.K. had given him. At least now he could do so without increasing resentment for his father clouding his mind.

For the first time ever, Troy had actually felt sorry for his dad. That in and of itself was a miracle, considering how angry he'd been after seeing the items in his trash can. Troy did not waste any time laying into him either. They hadn't even made it down the street when Troy started about how horrible of a father, a *person*, he had been while giving plenty of examples to make his case.

"Tell me something I don't know!" Reed shouted back before breaking down, an act that stunned Troy into silence. "Son, have you ever made a mistake so bad that you feel there's nothing you can do to recover from it? I'm sorry. I don't know what else to tell you except that I am really sorry for everything and everyone I have hurt."

Anyone crying made Troy uncomfortable, but he was especially so when it was another man and that man happened to be his father. He couldn't exactly wrap his arm around him and console him the way he had done to Natalie last night and with his mom this morning. He'd felt bad for them because he'd felt responsible for their tears. However, Troy did not take any responsibility for the outpouring of emotion displayed by his father. His sympathy came from wondering what it would be like to be in his shoes, to have his son hate him so much that nothing he said or did would make a difference. Troy, who was definitely not a crier, could only imagine the depth of such pain. That, combined with the words spoken by both his mother and his wife, caused him to be slow to speak and simply listen as his dad spoke of his remorse. It's difficult to verbally beat a person up when they are doing it to themselves. When all was said and done, the men had found what seemed like a happy medium. His father would not try and force the two of them to build a relationship and Troy would not aggressively resist any efforts to do so. They would let it happen gradually and naturally over time.

Troy never did get around to asking the burning question of "why" as he had planned. It was pointless. No answer would be satisfactory. If they were going to move forward, Troy knew he had to bury the past and let forgiveness work itself into his heart one day at a time.

Troy got back to his mom's shortly after 2:00. The house, smelling quite pleasant, was quieter than he'd expected. Natalie and his mom had been baking when he'd left. Troy followed the smell into the kitchen to get a sneak peek, and perhaps even a taste, of what they had been whipping up. He was surprised to find his mom sitting at the table, starting into space. "What did I do now?"

She smiled. "Nothin'. Thanks for makin' an effort to talk to your dad. He told me that y'all worked out your relationship issues."

Troy would not have exactly worded it that way, but he let it roll. "So why are you sitting here looking like you lost your best friend? Where are Natalie and Nate?"

"They're upstairs. Natalie's mad at me and Nate probably thinks I'm crazy."

She filled him in on the broom incident and got mad when he started laughing at her. "It's not funny! It's bad luck to get your feet swept."

"Why? What supposedly happens?"

"I don't know."

"But you know that spitting on the broom cancels the curse? *Humph*...yeah, that makes sense."

"I'm not crazy, I'm cautious. Bad things happen in life, you know?

We don't have to invite them into our lives. Superstitions have some truth to them, otherwise they would not have told us about them."

"I don't know who *they* are, but all of y'all are crazy," he said, grabbing a sugar cookie off the tray. "Is it okay for me to walk and eat this at the same time or will I have bad luck?"

She tried swatting a kitchen towel at him but he dodged out the way, laughing as he headed out and went upstairs to check on his wife and son.

They were both knocked out with Natalie's arm wrapped lovingly around Nate's young body. It was a Kodak moment for sure. Troy snapped a picture with his phone with the intentions of sending it to Natalie later to do whatever she wanted with it. Ever since a serial killer whom Troy was after last summer sent a friend request to Natalie's daughter after searching his friends' list to find her, Troy had all but deactivated his Facebook account. Everything was now set to private and no one could post to his page unless they were replying to something he wrote. Though he was not one to regularly post updates, this was a picture he would have shared. Nowadays, he stayed clear of sharing anything personal as not to inadvertently put his family in jeopardy.

Troy could have stood there staring at Natalie, Nate and the twins until they woke up, but he wanted to take advantage of the few moments he would have to review Elana's case. He kissed Natalie gently on her cheek and lightly patted Nate's head before grabbing Elana's case file and heading into his sister's old room.

He stared at several photos that had been taken of Elana's adult body. Instantly, her birthmark stood out. It was indeed very distinctive. Located immediately below her left collar bone, it was heart-shaped, but not symmetrical by any means. The right half was nearly twice the size of the left. When the two halves met, they fish-tailed to the right with a tiny spiral curl at the end. To Troy's understanding, pictures of her birthmark had not been circulated in the media per the request of Lilly. Troy understood her desire to keep a piece of Elana private, but Elana's birthmark was so unique that if anyone had ever seen it, they would have certainly remembered it. Maybe it could help generate some leads. Perhaps he would run it by B.K., he thought, as he glanced through the rest of the autopsy report.

The autopsy started at 8:30 a.m. on…body presented in a black body bag…victim is wearing a white tank top and navy blue shorts…

Troy would be the first to remark that December in Texas is nothing like December in Ohio, but still he wondered why Elana wore a tank top and shorts. He continued skimming the report.

The body is that of a normally developed African American female measuring 67 inches, 165 pounds…Cause of death: craniocerebral trauma due to a gunshot wound to the head…semen found…further examination of the pelvic area indicates that the victim has given birth some time within the last year.

Troy did a double-take to make sure he'd read that correctly.

After reading for a third time, there was no denying the information. It was there. Immediately, he pulled out B.K.'s business card and dialed him. "Why didn't you tell me that Elana had a baby?"

"Ah, Detective Evans, I've been awaiting your phone call," he said cunningly. Troy could imagine the smirk on his face. "That's a bit of information that investigators do not want to be leaked to the public. I didn't think it was something I needed to mention at this time in front of Elvin. The family has enough unanswered questions about Elana. The last thing they need right now is to compound those questions with more about a baby who could have been stillborn for all we know. My first step is to help find out what happened to Elana. In the meantime, I do have someone looking into whether any babies mysteriously showed up on doorsteps or at hospitals."

As a friend, Troy didn't like keeping this information from Elvin or Lilly, but as a fellow detective, he fully understood B.K.'s reasoning. "Do you think it's weird that Elana had on a tank top and shorts?"

"Not necessarily. Some people wear shorts all year long. I'm more concerned with finding the primary crime scene. We know that Elana's body was moved after she died. Personally, I believe that whoever took Elana thirty years ago is the same person who placed her body alongside I-Forty-five. He could have easily taken her deeper into the field, but he didn't. Assuming it was his semen inside of her, I think he wanted her to be found and he is also confident that any DNA on her can't be linked to him. Maybe he's finally feeling some remorse about what he'd done to her."

"So, do we check out the person who is crying harder than anyone else tomorrow night?"

"We look at everyone. Her abductor may not even be there. If he is remorseful, I'm guessing it would be hard for him to see all the hearts he'd broken. I could be way off base since I'm not a profiler."

"I want to go with you to Hitchcock when you see Herbert. He wasn't at the wake yesterday and if he's not there tomorrow, based on what you said, he could be the number one suspect."

"I was only speculating and we both know that speculation is not fact. From what I understand Mr. Greenfield is not in good health. Why don't you finish looking through everything I gave you and we'll touch base after your meeting with Shauna."

"When are you going to Hitchcock?" Troy was determined to get a straight answer from B.K. "I'm not trying to get in your way, but this case is personal to me."

"All the more reason why you need to step back. I appreciate your desire to help, but you're too close. You're going to miss something."

"Then it's a good thing that we are working this case together. I'm sure you'll find whatever it is I overlook. Now, when are we going to visit Herbert?"

Chapter 16: Running Scared

*A*fter his phone call with B.K. and establishing a time they would hook up, Troy continued looking through the file and B.K.'s notes. Elana had been shot with a .22 revolver. With the lax gun registration laws in Texas, it would not be easy to determine which of the suspicious characters owned one.

The case file did not yield much in terms of evidence. With the exception of learning that Elana had given birth, nothing else stood out. Everything else was consistent with what he'd already been told—red fibers that were found on her, angle of the gunshot wound, position and location of the body. With such little information, finding who kidnapped Elana would be like searching for a needle in a haystack, but Troy had closed cases with fewer leads before. He would not return home until this mystery was solved.

The ringing of his cell phone startled him. It was Natalie. "Hey, sorry to bother you, I figured you'd be back by now. Is everything okay?"

"Yes, everything is fine."

"How'd things go with your dad?'

Troy gave her a quick synopsis of his conversation with his father while gathering all of his stuff together, still not letting on that he was down the hall. "He's coming back tonight and he will be with us for Christmas, so all is right in Mama's world now."

As soon as he walked into the bedroom, Nate ran and jumped in his arms. "*Da-dee!*"

"Hey, what's up, lil' man?"

"Did you just get here?" asked Natalie.

"Naw. I've been here for a minute. You guys were asleep so I went in Tracy's room to do some work. Mama told me what happened."

"Gigi spit on 'da broom," blurted Nate.

"I know. Gigi is a little cuckoo like that, but she did not mean to scare you, okay? What about you?" He looked at Natalie.

"She didn't scare me." Her tone indicated that she still had an obvious attitude about the incident. "She's tripping me out with all of her super-titions."

"What are super-titions?"

Natalie looked at Troy. "I'm going to let you handle this one since it has to do with your mother. Plus, I need to pee."

After giving him a quick peck on the cheek, she left.

"*Daa-dee*, what are super-titions?" Nate repeated impatiently.

Troy looked at his son and chuckled, wondering how best to explain the concept.

On Christmas Eve, the church was packed with relatives and friends from near and far who came to show Elana her last respects. There were even more people today than there were on Saturday. Troy was certain that the building's maximum capacity limit had been exceeded. There were news crews present, but they were not allowed to come inside. Elana's case had started generating some buzz as pictures of her as a child had started circulating. People seemed more intrigued with the mystery surrounding her disappearance and resurfacing three decades later than the emotional turmoil this had on Elvin and Lilly. Still, any media attention given to the case meant the possibility that a witness would come forth. Someone had to know something.

Troy and his family sat behind Lilly and her blonde wig, Jeff, Elvin, Nicole, and their boys. It was him, Natalie, Nate, and his mom. Tracy had decided not to come after all, telling their mom that she had to finish Christmas shopping. It was a pretty lame excuse in Troy's opinion, but in Tracy's defense, she wasn't as close to Elvin and his family as he was. She was only four when Elana went missing, and other than the first few months after Elana disappeared when their mom was at Lilly's consoling her, Tracy did not spend much time there. Troy wondered if shopping was an excuse she'd made up simply not to go. Either that or she and Al had gotten into it and she was maybe a little too bruised to make an appearance. That had been known to happen before. Troy did not let his mind linger too long on that possibility as not to get himself worked up.

Troy scanned the crowd of others coming in, looking for anyone who seemed suspicious. B.K. had his theory that Elana's abductor might not show up, but Troy didn't want to put too much stock into that possibility. Why wouldn't the guy show up? He hadn't been suspected of anything for the last thirty years. Why feel bad now?

Why now? That was the burning question in Troy's mind. Why, after all this time, did he kill Elana? If she had access to the gun, why didn't she shoot her abductor? There were so many aspects of this case that did not make sense.

During the service, Troy's emotions toggled between guilt and anger. Both vied equally for attention and surprisingly, Troy held it together. He didn't exactly anticipate crying a river, but he would not have been embarrassed if he had shed a tear or two. The man in him wanted to cry, but the cop in him was on duty.

Lilly handled the service very well. She did cry, but nothing like the breakdown she'd had Saturday. While Elvin and Jeff consoled her, Troy found himself sitting in the middle of his own mother and Natalie, holding Nate, and also patting their backs as tears trickled down both of their faces. His mother he expected, but Natalie? Then again he should have known she would empathize with Lilly. Natalie could be soft-hearted, especially when it came to a parent who lost a child.

Bill eventually took the podium and Troy watched warily as he began his speech. "The family and I want to thank all of you fuh-fuh-fuhor coming out today. My sister and nephew nuh-nuh-need your prayers. W-w-w-we all do. This is a tuh-tuh-tuh-tough time for our family." He loosened the jacket to his lime-green tux, an outfit that Troy found disturbing on so many levels. "S-s-s-s-s-s-someone else bears the re-re-re-responsibility for my niece lying in this c-c-c-casket."

Shouts of "amen" were hurled his way from the crowd. This was the wrong thing to do if people ever wanted to go home because it only fired Bill up. He went on and on about how God was going to bring all things to "frutation," rather "fru-fru-fru-tation," which Troy was beginning to think was his favorite word, and how whoever dumped Elana on the side of the road off of the back of his truck like she was garbage would eventually pay.

Bill talked so much that the pastor giving the eulogy came and politely stood beside him, subtly encouraging him to wrap things up. At one point the pastor even placed his hand on top of Bill's around the mic. That was when Bill finally got the message and apologized for being "lequocious."

"What does that mean?" Natalie leaned and whispered.

"I have no clue." Troy was simply glad Bill was able to get the word out on the first try. Chances are, he had mispronounced it.

The rest of the service continued without a hitch. Other family members expressed much shorter words of thanks and memories of Elana. As they were proceeding out, Troy noticed that several strands of Nicole's hair had come out of place and revealed the shiny half-dollar-like bald spot in her head. Natalie must have seen it, too, because she nudged him for staring. Unlike him who didn't know the proper protocol for such a scenario, Natalie tapped Nicole on the shoulder and whispered something in her ear. Nicole's hand immediately shot up to her head to correct the error and then she looked back at Natalie for assurance.

Instead of following the family to the cemetery, Troy stayed behind to help set up tables at the church since this was where the family would come back for dinner. More than Bill's ridiculously long speech, or Herbert Greenfield's still not making an appearance, Troy was disturbed by the absence of Elana and Elvin's biological father. Troy did not notice Mr. Campbell wasn't there until he overheard some of Elvin's relatives who had also stayed behind talk about how odd it was for Mr. Campbell not to be there. "If she was my daughter, there is nothing that could keep me away," one older lady said.

"I know that's right. I think it was so tacky that his wife came without him," another woman with a gray wig that sat a little too crooked chimed in. "I heard her tell someone that Edgar was having a hard time handling this. That man probably ain't spoken to Lilly since that chile went missing and now all of a sudden, he's too broken up to come to the service. Sumthin' don't sound right to me."

Troy would have agreed though he thought it shameful that these two ladies were sitting in their Sunday bests gossiping at a time like this. Yet, he placed the chairs up against the banquet tables as slowly as he could, taking it all in, deciphering between information that might be useful and useless information such as how disgusted one of the women were that Mr. Campbell's wife did not wear a longer skirt.

"The chile ain't but in her early thirties and you know they say she didn't have a good upbringing," the wig lady said in her defense. "She might not know any better. I heard she used to be a stripper."

"Oh, I think she got more sense than you think. Ain't no way she's in love with Edgar as old as he is. I bet she married him for the insurance money and that baby they adopted last spring will ensure that she gets paid social security for a long time to come if something happens to him."

Troy recalled the words of the autopsy report. "*...The victim has given birth some time within the last year,*" as well as B.K.'s theory, "*I'm guessing it would hard for him to see all the hearts he'd broken.*" Could it be? Could Edgar Campbell have kidnapped and impregnated his own child? Crazy things had been known to happen. There was a similar case of the Austrian man who imprisoned and fathered children with his daughter, so it wasn't a complete stretch to think the same thing couldn't have happened here.

Troy ran outside where the reception was to better send B.K. a text. They'd agreed to share any information either of them uncovered and this lead was too hot for Troy to sit on. He didn't necessarily like taking the back seat on this investigation and he was certain that B.K. would not practice full disclosure with him, but like it or not, Troy needed B.K. He had no jurisdiction or connections with law enforcement down here. If it weren't for B.K., he wouldn't have any information at all.

Troy waited a few minutes to see if there would be a response. When none came, he headed back inside. Something caught his attention right before he entered the church doors. A man was walking alongside a fence when he was scared by a barking dog. The man yelped and ran a few paces until realizing that he wasn't in danger. The man was Jerry, one of Elvin's uncles, and for those few seconds when he was running scared from the dog, he did not have a limp.

Chapter 17: Turning Point

*T*roy was the first one up on Christmas morning. After coming home from the service yesterday, he'd secluded himself in Tracy's bedroom yet again, searching the Internet for any tidbits of information he could find about his three primary suspects: Edgar Campbell, Herbert Greenfield, and now Jerry.

B.K. never responded to his text message about Edgar and that irritated him. Not having connections down there made investigating this situation difficult. Troy did not bother to share with him what he'd learned about Jerry. He'd wait until they got together tomorrow after the mind-searching appointment with Shauna that Troy was not looking forward to. Unfortunately, his Internet search yielded no results. Nothing but their names and addresses, which is information he could have likely gotten from Elvin. Frustrated by the lack of progress, Troy awoke this morning and slipped on some sweats to go for a run.

Troy liked jogging, though he did not get out much during the winters in Ohio. Spring and fall were when he would run the most often. The winter and summer months were when he got the most use out of his gym membership. This Christmas Day run in Texas felt good as the conditions seemed perfect. No snow to crunch through or ice to worry about slipping on, there was only the cool breeze of the air as he struggled to keep up with his normal pace—a reminder that he had not worked out in several weeks.

Troy could not remember the last time he'd jogged around his old neighborhood. His run was interrupted briefly on two occasions when he stopped to speak with several familiar faces and offer season's greetings. In a way, it felt good to be home. He wished the circumstances were different, of course. It would be nice if parts of the last thirty-plus years could be rewritten. Elana would be living her life happily ever after instead of being buried six feet under. When she ran out of the door all those years ago, there was a peace within Troy that had left with her. Natalie would argue that he was insanely protective of her and Nate. To some extent, she might be right. Troy would not know what to do if something ever happened to either of them, especially something as malicious as had been done to Elana. He worried about his family's safety and oftentimes that anxiety ate away at his peace. He had to learn to have healthy concern without it leading to unreasonable fear before he drove both his wife and himself crazy.

It was about fifty minutes later when Troy returned to the house and found his parents in the living room playing a game with Nate. Troy fought against the residual bitterness that tried to linger toward his father. Forgiveness was definitely a process. He swallowed his negativity and greeted them all by saying "Merry Christmas" and Nate excitedly showed him what "Gigi and Grandpa" had gotten him.

"It was only *one* present," his mom said, responding to the look he'd given her after seeing the torn wrapping paper strewn on the floor. "I told him he can't open the rest until you and Natalie were up."

When Troy got to the room, he found Natalie dressed and on

the bed FaceTiming Corrine on her iPad. "Hey, Merry Christmas." She greeted him with such a huge smile that he couldn't resist giving those luscious lips a warm welcome.

"Ex-*cuse* me. I really don't care to see y'all make out," Corrine announced via video.

"Merry Christmas, Corrine. Here, I'll give you a kiss, too." Troy puckered and put his lips on the screen.

"Ewe!" She shrieked while Natalie fussed at him for putting his mouth on her iPad.

Troy laughed as Corrine called him crazy. As expected, she was wearing a locket with Nate's baby picture inside. She never took that thing off, an indication of how strong her feelings for Nate were. Corrine's adoptive parents had other children, but Nate was her only biological sibling. Troy could imagine the depth of the bond she felt for him, and for Natalie.

Corrine was nearly the spitting image of his wife. She, too, was tall with long, dark, satin-like hair. Corrine also had big brown eyes like Natalie. The major difference between them was that Corrine had a lighter skin complexion than Natalie's honey-colored one. Though he and Corrine were nowhere near as close as she and Natalie, Troy loved her. He was actually surprised at how much he loved her, but then again, he loved Natalie so much that he could not help but deeply care about those who were important to her. Troy talked to Corrine for a few seconds about how her visit was going in Jackson. After telling her to say hi to the family for him, Troy got his things together and hopped in the shower.

Natalie was making the bed when he returned to the room. "Your phone has been blowing up."

Immediately, Troy checked, hoping there was a message from B.K. He scrolled through the eleven text messages, not finding a single one from the investigator. He did find three very disturbing ones.

Hi Troy. It's been a while. I miss u.

Just want 2 say Merry Christmas.

Hope u & fam r having a good time in TX.

The third one bothered him most of all. How did *she* know that they were in Texas? He hadn't spoken to her since the summer and though she would leave voice or text messages periodically, he'd never responded or returned a call. He'd hoped that ignoring her would make her go away. So far that hadn't worked. She kept popping up like a cold sore at the most inconvenient times.

"Everything okay?'

"Uh, yeah. You know how people like to send mass holiday texts," he said, deleting the ones from her first.

"I know what you mean. Well, hurry and finish getting dressed. You know Nate is bursting out of his skin to open presents."

"Mama already let him open one." Since Natalie seemed to still be keeping his mom at an arm's length after the broom fiasco Saturday, Troy thought he should warn her.

"Why am I not surprised?" she said before leaving the room, rolling her eyes.

Christmas morning went perfectly without any hitches. Troy, his family, and his parents opened their presents for each other while setting aside the ones for Tracy, Al and the kids for later. Of course, Nate was the center of attention. Whatever attitude Natalie had had earlier about his mom, she had gotten past it by the time Troy made his way back to the living room. The joy on her face as she watched Nate "ooh and ahh" about his things was priceless. She FaceTimed Corrine again and also Aneetra, so they could both talk to Nate and at least see him open the things that they had bought for him.

By this time next year, Troy and Natalie would have two additional little ones to the mix and he looked forward to it. This would make the second year in a row that they had traveled to Texas for Christmas. Next year, they would be at home. Everyone would be welcome to join them and by "everyone," Troy was not yet sure if he would include his father. Things had been cordial between them since their talk yesterday, but a father-son relationship was still unchartered territory. Troy had to be certain that this change in his father was real. Time would tell.

After opening presents, Troy grabbed a bowl of cereal and a banana. Apparently, the others had gotten something to eat before he had come down. His mom did not make a big to-do about breakfast this morning like she had done Saturday, which was not surprising. Christmas dinner would be the extravaganza and that wasn't taking place until Tracy got there, which, from what he was told, would be around 3:00.

The rest of Christmas morning went much faster than Troy had anticipated. His wife and mother spent most of their time in the kitchen putting finishing touches on things and he forced himself to stay in the living room with his father while Nate played with his toys. Troy would like to have been working on Elana's case, but with no leads and no communication from B.K., his efforts were useless at this point.

At first, the silence between him and his father was awkward. They sat opposite one another and stared at Nate who toggled back and forth between his toys as though they would disappear if he did not play with them all in the same day. It was Troy's father who broke the silence.

"Do you want to watch the games today?"

Troy had been so occupied with Elana that he'd totally forgotten about the Christmas Day headliner games. "Uh, yeah, who's playing?"

His father knew the entire day's lineup. "There are five games today. Celtics and the Nets first play first, then the Lakers and Knicks. At four-thirty it's the Heat against Oklahoma City Thunder. The last lineups are Rockets and Bulls, and Nuggets versus the Clippers."

Troy had no idea how into basketball his father was. It was nice to discover that they had something in common and Troy was eager to see the matches as his favorite teams were playing. He was usually on top of the game schedules. How'd he let today's slip? *Elana...*

Basketball became the activity over which Troy and his dad began to bond. They watched the first while also engaging in conversation. They talked about last season's playoffs, who they thought would make it to the finals this year, injured players, rookies, and about everything else one could think of when it came to basketball.

When Tracy and her family arrived, Troy and his father were both engrossed in the pulse-pounding competition between the Lakers and the Knicks, which went back and forth in one possession leads. In order to get their undivided attention so they could open the remaining presents, his mom turned off the TV after several attempts to get the guys to focus since Al and AJ had gotten distracted by the game as well. Though her action almost got her mauled, she stood firm. To appease her, and perhaps to prevent the Christmas spirit from being interrupted by tongue whipping meant for sailors, the men obliged her request, ripping through presents without any small talk. Both Tracy and Al seemed to be in good moods and there were no signs that any type of altercation had recently taken place between them. Maybe she was telling the truth about having to finish shopping yesterday, Troy figured.

Troy's mom may have won the battle about the television while opening presents, but she lost the war when it came to Christmas dinner. She had wanted everyone to sit around the dining room table like they had done Saturday morning at breakfast, but in the midst of an intense basketball game, none of the males were having it. They stood around the table for grace, but simultaneously, got their plates and resumed their positions in the living room.

His mom protested, stating how this was their first Christmas dinner as a family and they should all be eating together. "Basketball should not be more important than family." She tried manipulating them into complying with her wishes.

Natalie, knowing how much Troy enjoys the game, stepped in. "Di, it's okay. You know how men are about their sports. I'd rather them watch it instead of sitting here talking about it the whole time."

His mom huffed without further protest and Troy gave Natalie a best-wife-ever kiss on the cheek. It wasn't long before the females and Nate joined them in the living room. Immediately, Alyssa began playing with Nate and his toys. Tracy and his mom each took a seat next to their husband's. Troy liked the way Natalie nestled next to him on the couch and into his arms. It reminded him of the times when she did so in their home when he was in the basement watching games. He had to remind himself that they were *not* at home or alone and that he needed to keep his hands in public-friendly places on her body. He gently rubbed her belly, admiring the two growing miracles inside.

"How was the service last night?" Tracy had the decency to wait until a commercial break before asking.

"Sad, but good because, in many ways, it provided closure. At least partially. There were pages of pictures of Elana from the time she was a baby until when she went missin'. The one Lilly chose for the front of the obituary was so heartbreakin' because it showed Elana's birthmark. She could not have been more than six or seven, but she's smilin' like there is no tomorrow. The front read, 'Rest in Peace. You are Loved Forever.' Oh, you have to see it. Reed, what did you do with the obituary I showed you last night?"

Though the game had not yet resumed, he continued staring at the screen. All the men did. They were waiting on edge to see how things would play out in the final quarter.

"*Reed*," his mother said with more force. "What did you do with the obituary?"

"Oh, uh, I don't know. I thought I gave it back to you."

"You did not. That's a lie and you know it."

"Whoa, someone is turning into the Grinch who stole Christmas." Troy hoped to fan the flames of her burning fire as he could tell that she was getting worked up by her tone.

"Oh, shut up."

"I'm sorry, Di," his father pleaded. "It's an obituary, for goodness' sake. You act like it's a photo album."

"It had pictures like one. You're sittin' up here tellin' that lie that you gave it back to me when you could not have done so because I went upstairs and you didn't come up until later."

"Again, I'm sorry. I don't know what I did with it."

Troy did not think he would ever see the day when he would take his father's side in an argument with his mother. Such a day had arrived. "Mama, chill. It's not that serious," he said when the game had come back on. "If you can't find it, get another one from Lilly when you see her tomorrow."

"But I want to show your sister."

"You can have ours. I'll go upstairs to get it before Tracy leaves, if that's okay," offered Natalie.

Her suggestion seemed to satisfy his mom and Troy was able to fully concentrate on the exhilarating fourth quarter of the game without his mother's crabbiness interfering. Cheers went up around as the Lakers scored. Troy gently turned Natalie's head and gave her a quick, but soft, kiss on her lips.

"What was that for?"

He smiled while again thinking, *best wife ever.*

Chapter 18: The Usual Suspects

*T*roy and Elvin had driven separately to Shauna's office since Troy had a meeting with B.K. scheduled for later. He decided to take his turn with the mind explorer first so that more anxiety would not build while sitting in the waiting room.

In retrospect, it really did not matter if he and Elvin had ridden together because Troy would still have time to drop off Elvin and make it to his meeting. In all honesty, Troy was trying to keep as much distance between him and Elvin as possible. There was a war between cop and friend battling within him. The cop had no problems withholding information about potential suspects and the fact that Elana had given birth until there was something concrete to share. The friend, who had been there when Elana disappeared…who had witnessed the pain that Elvin and his mother had endured…who felt partly responsible for the circumstances, that friend, felt like every piece of information he withheld was betrayal.

"You can relax, Troy; I'm not going to hypnotize you today," Shauna said with a warm smile. He sighed with relief. "The purpose of having you come in today is to do a pre-hypnosis interview." Her name did not match her appearance. Shauna seemed like a sexy name. Like it should belong to a woman with long legs, curvy hips, and a pair of forty double-D twins. Instead, a short, fat, flat-chested redhead with glasses and gapped teeth claimed ownership to the name. The one thing sexy about her was her voice. If she wasn't a hypnotic, she could probably make a good living as a 1-900 phone operator. "B.K. tells me that you're a detective, correct?"

"Yes."

"Our session today will be similar to how you conduct interviews with witnesses. The purpose is to find out what you already know and give me a framework for which I will use to ask questions during the hypnosis sessions."

Sessions? "How many do you think it will take?"

"It varies. Sometimes it takes a few trials to complete a successful therapy session. Other times it can happen on the first try. It all depends on you and your comfort level. B.K. tells me that you will only be in town a few days, so I am hoping your first session will go well."

Troy thought about telling her that he'd planned to be there for a while, but decided against it. If she knew she had more time to play around in his head, she might have found it necessary to have multiple sessions. He'd rather spend his time actually working Elana's case than seeing a head shrink.

After confirming his understanding that this and any future sessions with her would be recorded, Shauna began. "Why don't you start by telling me everything you remember about the day Elana disappeared?"

Troy recanted the story without skipping a beat.

"Did either you or Elvin go outside to see which direction she may have gone?"

"No. We didn't go out until his mom came home and asked us to look for her."

"What about her doll? Did she take it with her?"

"I…" Troy paused for a moment. He was puzzled. As many times as he had replayed the day in his mind, that detail had escaped him. "I honestly don't know," he said with a sense of disappointment. How could he not remember? Recalling barrettes were one thing; remembering a stringy red-haired doll that she used to play with seemed like a bigger deal.

Shauna grinned, rather smirked. "Don't beat yourself up. That's something I can possibly help you remember." She sounded as if she had been waiting to find the right moment to say something to that effect. "Also, I don't want you to worry about being in a trance and doing crazy things that you won't remember like is often depicted on TV. You will be able to remember everything we talk about."

Her last statement actually made him feel a little better about the whole thing.

"Is there anything else that you would like to add before we end today's session?"

"No, nothing I can think of."

"Okay." She turned off the recorder. "Normally, I like to give myself a week to review the tapes and interview notes, but I understand the urgency in this case. Can you come back either tomorrow or Friday so we can start?"

"Sure. Tomorrow's fine," he answered, eager to get it over.

"Good. One o'clock okay?"

"Yep."

"Here is some information you can read through to help you understand the process better." She handed him some pamphlets. "If you have any questions, give me a call. Otherwise I'll see you tomorrow."

They exchanged "nice-to-meet-yous" and Troy followed her

out to the waiting room where he double-checked with Elvin to see if he wanted him to stay during his session.

"Naw, man, you're cool. I'll touch base with you later."

Since he had some time to kill before meeting B.K., Troy grabbed a bite to eat and did a little joyriding while he gathered his thoughts. It had been a long time since he'd roamed the streets of Houston for the heck of it. He had lived in Columbus longer than the eighteen years he'd spent in Texas, and his current navigational skills proved as much. At first he found himself forgetting what streets led to where and certain shortcuts. But, the more he drove, the more familiar things started to become. He wandered aimlessly like the car was on autopilot without much thought and attention being given to where he went since his mind was elsewhere.

The major problem with Elana's case, besides him not having any jurisdiction, was that there was no evidence. Nothing that he could use to single out any of the persons he found suspicious.

First, there was Edgar Campbell. What father would not show up to the funeral service of his daughter? He seemed so grief-stricken at the wake. Yet, he hadn't been in touch with Elvin or Lilly in years. If the funeral was too much for anyone to handle, it should have been Lilly. Edgar never showed up the day of Elvin's birthday. Could he have come by the next day? If Elana went with someone willingly, who could be more trustworthy in the mind of an eight-year-old than her father? And what about the baby? Most men in their sixties would not think of adopting a baby despite having a young wife. Could this be a cover-up to conceal the fact that Edgar and his wife have Elana's child? Adoption records could easily prove or disprove this theory. Even in this day and age of electronic transactions, there still had to be a paper trail.

Another suspect, in Troy's mind, was Herbert Greenfield. Technically Herbert did not *have* to be at the service. He and Lilly were currently divorced and likely had not been in contact since separating. Still, common courtesy would have been to make an appearance or at least call since they were married at the time Elana went missing. Only a man with something to hide would not have the decency to give his condolences. Plus, he didn't stay around to comfort Lilly in the immediate aftermath of Elana's disappearance. Herbert left Lilly within a few months, another uncompassionate act that possibly pointed to his guilt.

Then there was Jerry, who was obviously faking an injury, but for what purpose? Was he trying to make it seem as if he was physically incapable of committing this crime? Jerry was no friend to the law and held a frequent visitor's pass to confined spaces. Could this be a real-life reenactment of *The Usual Suspects*, a movie in which the bad guy turns out to be the one everyone least expects since he was assumed to be physically impaired?

Elvin and Lilly thought someone from the family was involved. If not Herbert, Edgar, or Jerry, then who? Frustrated, Troy finally made his way to B.K.'s office. As he pulled into a space, he immediately knew that something was wrong.

Chapter 19: Damsel in Distress

atalie peeked in on Nate, napping in Tracy's old room, before making her way back to Troy's. To say she had an attitude would have been putting it mildly. Troy was gone, so was Diane, and Reed was at his other house doing some work.

Natalie wondered if she was being selfish by expecting Troy to be around more than he had since they'd been in Texas. She understood the importance of Elana's case. Then again, *every* case was important to Troy. She honestly did not mind him working so hard to find answers about Elana's disappearance because she knew he felt a sense of responsibility. She did not understand why he had to drag her and Nate down there with him if he had not planned to spend any time with them. If she was going to be by herself, she'd rather do so in the comfort of her own home! When Aneetra called to see how things were going, Natalie gave her an earful.

"You only have a few more days, and then you will be coming home. Try not to give Diane a heart attack in the meantime. Have her write down all of her superstitions so you'll know what not to do while you're there," Aneetra teased.

"Girl, Saturday can't get here fast enough. I might take Nate to the zoo Monday since I'm not *allowed* to go down here. You and the girls want to come?"

"If you do, let me know. I'll go, but they will be with Marcus."

There was a sadness in her voice that Natalie wasn't quite sure how to address. Aneetra and Marcus had separated over the summer. Natalie still wasn't sure about the final direction their marriage was taking, but she knew the separation was a lot harder than Aneetra had anticipated.

"How's the communication been between you and Marcus?"

"It's been okay. He stayed over last night."

"Wow. That's a good sign, isn't it?"

"I wouldn't say all of that. I think we both got caught up in enjoying Christmas with the girls and I let my hormones get in the way. I haven't been taken care of since he moved. I can't say the same for him."

"Stop it. Don't think like that."

"I'm being real."

"Okay, Miss Real. You're also being sarcastic."

"Whatever you say, Miss Know-It-All. I bet you wish you knew Diane would spit on that broom so you could have stopped Nate from sweeping her feet."

Natalie couldn't help but laugh. "She should be put in a strait-jacket for that. At the very least, given meds. Anyone who spits on a broom for no good reason has to have a psychological disorder." She and Aneetra shared several more humorous moments talking about Diane's crazy beliefs before another call came in. "Hey, I need to take this. It's Corrine."

"Okay, tell her I said hi. I'll talk to you later."

Natalie quickly answered the incoming call. "Hello?"

"Hey, what are y'all doing today?'

She decided to be more politically correct with her daughter about her discontentment than she had been with Aneetra. "Nothing much. Both Troy and his mom had some appointments. Nate's taking a nap and I'm hanging out at the house. What are you guys up to?"

"Mama and Dorrinda went shopping. I don't know where Dad and the boys are. I'm getting ready to go help Uncle Tommy at the center. I don't know exactly what's going on, but I told him I would be there."

Natalie was only thirteen when she had Corrine and was forced to give her up for adoption. Soon thereafter she and her mother moved to Ohio and it was a long time before Natalie had learned that her father's sister had been the one to adopt her child. Sometimes tensions arose between Natalie and her aunt Toni, but for the most part they have been able to coexist in Corrine's life.

"Do you and Troy have plans for New Year's Eve?"

"I was thinking about taking him to the zoo and then we may go to church that night, but nothing's set in stone. Why, what's up?"

"I want Nate to stay overnight."

"That's fine." Suddenly, Natalie had an idea to plan a romantic evening for her and Troy on New Year's Eve. "Y'all can hang out and I'll take him to the zoo another time."

"If that's what he wants to do, I have no problems with that. We can all go."

"I don't think that boy is worried about the zoo." Natalie filled Corrine in on Diane's monkey baby theory.

"Wow. Your mother-in-law can be special."

"If you only knew," replied Natalie, beginning to feel bad about only focusing on Diane's negative attributes. "She does have a good heart though. I only brought up going to the zoo because she got on my nerves at the time. Nate has probably forgotten."

"Well, if he does mention it, I don't mind taking him. We'll figure it out later because I need to get going. Give Nate a kiss for me."

"Will do. Tell Tommy hi. I love you, honey."

"Love you, too."

Natalie continued to hold the phone after Corrine hung up. In her wildest imagination she could not have fathomed having such a close relationship with her daughter. It was an atypical mother-daughter relationship for sure. Her role in Corrine's life seemed to toggle between mother and big sister with the latter being more prevalent. Natalie was fine with that. Simply being a part of Corrine's life was a blessing in and of itself.

Natalie was still under the impression that she was at the house alone until the screams she heard coming from downstairs startled her. She jumped up and ran in the hall, standing at the top of the stairwell. There, she witnessed Tracy standing face-to-face with Reed, yelling at him.

"You are a monster!" Tracy stood with her fists clenched and visibly shaking as a result of her anger.

"Calm down, Tracy. It's not what you think."

In a form similar to Diane's nature, Tracy not-so-kindly told Reed that he was full of crap. It caught Natalie off guard because she had never seen her sister-in-law like that before. Because of how protective Troy was of Tracy, Natalie had always pictured her as this quiet damsel in distress who never spoke up for herself. Natalie was fully aware that, for Diane, swearing came as natural as breathing. Though she'd heard the words Tracy said many times, and, in the past, had even said them herself, it came as a shock to see a side of her younger sister-in-law that she had never known existed. "If I'm wrong, then why won't you tell me who she was?"

Natalie crept backward with the intention of getting as far away from the drama as possible. When she did, the floor creaked, causing them to shift their attention in her direction. "Um, hi…"

She waved, giving what had to be the fakest smile she'd ever contrived in her entire life.

Reed looked embarrassed. No, worried would have been a more accurate description of his expression. Tracy glanced fiercely her way and then turned back to Reed. "I'm not crazy. I know what I saw. She was at the house!" She stormed away with Reed yelling *"wait!"* and running after her.

Natalie waited a few minutes and then went down the stairs with the sole purpose of looking out the front window to see what was happening with Reed and Tracy. They were in the driveway. Tracy sat on her front bumper bawling and Reed was trying to console her. Whenever he touched her, she would jerk his hand away. He finally gave up trying to make physical contact, instead kneeling next to her, apparently trying to reassure her that whatever she had thought wasn't what happened. Natalie couldn't clearly make out everything he was saying, but some key phrases like, "There's a big misunderstanding," and "Trust me. I'll explain everything later," stood out.

Hearing only bits and pieces of their conversation was frustrating. Natalie decided to open the front window slight enough to assist in her eavesdropping. Desperately trying not to make any noise, she did so slowly and when she finally got it open enough to hear with clarity, Tracy got in her car and left.

So much for that! Natalie thought and was about to shut it until she saw Reed on his cell phone. "Hey, please call me when you get this message. Something has come up and I need to talk to you," he said.

Natalie had pretty much pieced together the gist of what had happened. Tracy must have gone by the other house this morning when Reed was there working and saw him with another woman.

Feeling like she already knew much more than she needed, Natalie closed the window and headed back upstairs. She hoped...*prayed* that Diane would not find out about this before she and her family hopped on the plane back to Ohio Saturday. Tracy's anger would be nothing compared to Troy's and God only knew what her husband would do if he learned of his father's affair. *Poor Diane.* She really believed that Reed had changed. This was going to destroy her.

Chapter 20: Back Burner

The second Troy realized he was sitting in an empty parking lot, he knew it was a waste of time to get out of the vehicle, but he did anyhow, hoping for the best. As suspected, the building was locked and despite Troy's persistent ringing of the buzzer, no one responded.

He practiced great restraint not to allow the foul words in his mind to come out of his mouth as he headed back to the rental. Had B.K. gone to Hitchcock without him? B.K.'s lack of communication angered Troy most of all. He had yet to return Troy's phone call from Monday and if B.K. had gone to see Herbert without him, at the very least, he should have notified him.

"Hopefully, we can work together and stay out of each other's way," B.K. had said to him the first time Troy was at his office like Troy was trying to steal his thunder. Elana's case was getting increased media attention and Troy figured that B.K. wanted to solve it in order to bring more notoriety to his business. Though, from the looks of his building, he wasn't doing too badly. What would it take for the man to understand that Troy didn't care about his name being in the closing credits? His only concern was finding closure for Lilly and Elvin. He didn't have time for this territorial nonsense.

Troy grabbed his cell phone with the intention of calling and letting B.K. have it as professionally as he could, but when he noticed that his screen was completely black, Troy could only blame himself. He had forgotten to turn his phone back on after his session with Shauna. Upon doing so, he discovered that he had several voicemail messages.

12:31 p.m. "This is Tracy. Call me as soon as you get this. I need to tell you something."

12:57 p.m. "Troy, this is B.K. I need to delay our meeting about an hour or two. I'm following your mom and Lilly to Shauna's office. We're going to see if Shauna can do Lilly's assessment today. If so, I'm going to take your mom to lunch so she doesn't have to sit in the waiting room by herself. We should be back around three o'clock. Meet me at Shauna's office instead. If I don't hear from you, I'll go on to Hitchcock and touch base with you later. Oh, and thanks for the tip about Edgar. I have my assistant looking into those adoption records. I'm thinking about making a surprise visit to Edgar's after we come from Hitchcock if it's not too late."

Having heard B.K.'s message, Troy now felt better about his communication skills. He was slightly annoyed that B.K. chose to have lunch at a time when they should have been working. *Why is he so concerned about her being alone?* Troy wondered.

12:59 p.m. "Troy, please call me back. I'm about to lose my mind. I need to talk to you. It's important."

1:24 p.m. "I'm on my way to the house. I hope you're there."

2:03 p.m. "Hey man, where are you? B.K said he tried to call to let you know that he wouldn't be at the office. My mom is meeting with Shauna as I speak. I'm headed back to her house to pick up Nikki and the boys and take them to lunch. If you want to join us, holla at me."

2:11 p.m. "It's me again. I don't know what to think or do. I need you."

Concerned about how distressed Tracy sounded in her messages, Troy tried calling her back immediately.

Voicemail.

He called Natalie. "Hey, babe, is Tracy over there?"

"She was outside talking to your dad earlier, but they are both gone now."

"She left me four messages about needing to talk to me. I tried to call her back and she's not answering. You know what's going on?"

"Uh, not really."

"It was a yes or no question," he said irritably. "Was Al with her?"

"Nope. She was by herself."

"Man, if that fool put his hands on her—"

"Don't jump to conclusions. I don't think it's anything like that."

"Then what is it like, Natalie? Is there something you're not telling me?"

"Don't get an attitude with me. I'm not the one who called you. All I know is that Tracy was talking to your dad and she was upset about something. If you want details, you will need to talk to her."

Troy sighed. Nothing seemed to be going right today. "If she comes back, call me."

He and Natalie hung up without any I-love-you pleasantries being exchanged between them and Troy tried his sister one more time.

"Trace, I got all of your voice messages and I'm trying to get in touch with you. You got me worried and now you're not answering. I don't like that. Call and let me know what's up."

Troy tried his dad. His voicemail kicked in, too. He didn't bother leaving a message. He started the rental and headed back to Shauna's office. He would be early, but at least he would be there.

"What's on your mind, Troy?" B.K. announced as they hopped onto I-45 and headed south to Hitchcock.

A lot! When Troy went back to Shauna's office, he was forced to wait in the parking lot because her building was also locked. He understood the safety precautions since Shauna was in session with Lilly and there were no other personnel around. Still, all this waiting around seemed futile. Troy sat in the parking lot stewing after several additional failed attempts to get ahold of Tracy before B.K. and his mother arrived. He got out of the vehicle without saying much to either of them and got into B.K.'s sedan while B.K. walked his mom to the building door, which had been miraculously unlocked.

Troy watched in the rearview mirror as his mom and B.K. embraced for what seemed like a little too long in his opinion. So, when B.K. asked what was on his mind, Troy decided to take heed to the New King James Version of Proverbs 29:11, "A fool vents all his feelings, but a wise man holds them back." He had a lot he wanted to say to B.K. right now, especially regarding whatever game the man was playing with his mom. Instead of taking the foolish route and lashing out at him with everything that was going through his head, Troy simply said, "Where did you and my mom go?"

"To a little spot not far from Shauna's office. I enjoyed talking to your mom. She seems like a very nice lady. She's also funny."

"Since when did socializing with my mother become more important than working on Elana's case?" Perhaps he wasn't doing so well with the whole Proverbs thing.

"Rest assured, I'm always working. If you think I'm trying to hit on your mom, relax. I've been happily married to the same woman for nearly thirty-five years. Since Diane and Lilly were close during the time Elana went missing, I wanted to see if she could provide any insight."

"She was nowhere around that day." Troy shared his new revelation about Jerry.

"I already knew he was faking. Insurance fraud. He got into a car accident and it was the other person's fault so now he's trying to get money."

"But he was in town about the time Elana's body was discovered."

"I know. He had a meeting with the insurance company. As far as being a suspect in Elana's case, he's been eliminated through DNA."

"When and how did you get his DNA?"

"Jerry is a convicted felon. Under Texas law, he had to submit a sample to be kept in CODIS."

CODIS stood for Combined DNA Index System, which was a nationwide FBI database that matches DNA from known criminal offenders with biological evidence from crime scenes. "When were you going to tell me? I can't help solve the case if you are constantly withholding information."

"You and I have never had a chance to sit down and discuss things. Besides, the day I met you, I didn't have the results of Jerry's DNA. We're discussing everything now, to some extent, and I'm telling you what I know. But, for the record, I'm not going to detail every single step I make. I will keep you informed as best as possible. However, there are some things I'm going to keep to myself whether you like it or not. You're too emotionally involved in this case. You're going to miss something. You already have."

"Like what?" Troy asked. There was a venomous tinge to his tone, and he didn't hide his distaste for B.K. at that moment.

"You've told me about Jerry and Edgar, but you have yet to

mention Bill's statement at the service. I'm assuming it's because you didn't catch the oddity of his words."

Confused, yet concerned by B.K.'s accusation, Troy softened his tone. "What did he say?" He felt completely incompetent when B.K. brought back to his remembrance Bill's words about someone having dumped Elana off the back of his truck.

"How could he possibly know this unless he was the one who put her there?"

"If you suspect him, why are we on our way to Herbert's instead of his place?"

"I can't say for sure that Bill is the one, despite his odd statement. Remember what I told you when we met? I consider everyone a suspect until proven otherwise. The more suspects we eliminate, the easier it will be to focus on those who are left," he spoke condescendingly and Troy felt like even more of an idiot. He knew how investigations worked. This wasn't his first case and yet, he felt like a novice compared to the veteran investigator. Maybe B.K. was right about his emotions being in the way.

"We have to tread with caution when it comes to Bill," B.K. continued. "I'm sure you know how close he and Lilly are. I was under the impression that she and Elvin weren't going to tell anyone in the family that they'd hired me, but he knows. I tried to talk to him casually and he immediately referred me to his attorney. I got a message from his attorney this morning requesting a meeting. There's obviously something weird going on with him, but until we know for sure what it is, we have to keep digging everywhere there's a possible lead, hence why we are still paying Mr. Greenfield a visit."

Troy stared out the window, feeling useless. He wanted to ask if he could sit in on the meeting with Bill, but at this point, he thought it best to let B.K. fill him in as needed. He was angry with himself. How could he have not been alarmed by Bill's statement?

"I get why you want to be involved with this case. If it were someone close to me, I would feel the same way. I have no doubt that you're a good cop, Troy. You have to put guilt on the back burner and treat this case like you would any other."

"This is not any other case. I am partly responsible for the chain of events. I owe it to Elana to find out what happened and somehow try to make things right."

"Yom Kippur," B.K. mumbled.

Troy looked away from the window and at B.K. "What?"

"Yom Kippur. It's a Jewish holiday, which means Day of Atonement. It's first mentioned in Leviticus 16 when Aaron was instructed that he would have to make yearly sacrifices, known as the sin offering. It was the priest's responsibility to atone for the sins of the people. Nowadays, Jews typically fast for twenty-four hours and they also pray and have special synagogue services, all for the purpose of repenting and making amends for their sins. That's what I feel you're trying to do. Don't take offense, but your motive for wanting to solve this case is all wrong. It's not about you and easing the burden of whatever guilt you may have. It's about finding justice for Elana. The sooner you realize that, the more effective you will be."

"Are you Jewish?"

"Nope. I happened to know a lot about various religions because a long time ago, I attended seminary." B.K. laughed as the shock on Troy's face must have been evident. "What, you can't see me standing in a pulpit with a robe?"

"Now that you brought it up, it doesn't seem that far-fetched." From the moment he and B.K. first met, Troy had taken note of his commanding presence. "So, were you studying to be a pastor?"

"I can't really say what I would have done because I dropped out. Of course, my parents were not pleased, particularly my father because he wanted me to be a preacher, but I feel that I have made more of a difference in people's lives by working in law enforcement than I ever could have done in a pulpit. Nothing against those who serve in official capacities. I don't think it was my calling."

"A buddy of mine had a similar experience except he did pastor a church for several years until he was forced to step down. I didn't know him at that time," Troy explained. "We met a few years back when I worked on a case involving his daughter. Now he's working in a totally different field and feels the same as you, that preaching was never his purpose. He did it because he'd been expected to follow in his father's footsteps."

"Yeah, sometimes fathers can put a lot of pressure on their kids, especially their sons. I guess that's why the good Lord gave me four daughters. None of them work in law enforcement. What's your relationship like with your dad?"

"Complicated," Troy replied humorously as B.K.'s GPS instructed them to get off at the next exit.

Chapter 21: Legal Authority

*H*itchcock was an extremely small town only about forty miles from Houston, located in Galveston County. Troy was willing to bet that the population hadn't yet reached 10,000. Its serene residential environment combined with the ease of travel between Houston and Galveston made it an attractive place to live. In fact, Troy had heard once before that many workers from the Johnson Space Center commuted from Hitchcock. Named after the thirty-sixth U.S. president, Lyndon B. Johnson, the Houston-located center was *the* place NASA educated its astronauts. It's also a really neat attraction because visitors could actually watch space explorers train for missions and participate in a bunch of other out-of-this world activities. The space center was a place Nate would likely enjoy and Troy felt bad that he probably would not have a chance to take him there or anywhere else this week.

"Your destination is on the right," announced the GPS as they pulled in front of a one-story, mustard-yellow house.

Troy trailed slightly behind B.K. as they headed up to the front door. A petite Caucasian woman dressed in scrubs answered. "May I help you?"

"Hi, I'm B.K. Ashburn, an investigator with the Texas Department of Public Safety. I called last week about seeing Herbert Greenfield."

"And you are?" She eyed Troy suspiciously.

"He's a detective. Now may we speak to Mr. Greenfield, please?"

"I tried to tell you that he's in no condition for company." She stepped aside and let them in. "Have a seat. I'll go get him."

As soon as the unnamed lady and Herbert came around the corner, Troy knew that this trip had been a waste of time.

Neither B.K. nor Troy said a word for the first ten minutes or so after leaving Herbert's.

"I had been told that he wasn't in good health, but I wasn't expecting to see him like that." B.K. finally spoke.

"Yeah, that was shocking. Am I wrong not to have sympathy for him?"

"I'm not the one you should ask because I feel the same way. Perhaps life has paid him back for his misdoings."

Those were Troy's exact sentiments. The lady, who was Herbert's full-time caregiver, rolled him out in a wheelchair. Herbert appeared before them as a partially blind double amputee, paralyzed from the chest down, all courtesy of a drunk driving accident from years ago. He had some cognitive difficulties as well and was unable to form complete sentences or comprehendible words at times. When B.K. showed him pictures of Elana, he kept saying, "Maggie hurt her," which made no sense. There was no one, family member or otherwise, with the name Maggie connected to this case. Herbert denied any personal involvement with Elana's abduction.

The thing that angered Troy the most and rid him of any compassion he may have had for Herbert under different circumstances was when he admitted to molesting Elana. When B.K. asked if he'd ever touched her inappropriately, he nodded yes. He continued nodding as B.K.'s prodding became more descriptive, adding the words, "I'm sorry," each time and becoming increasingly agitated with each question.

"Fellas, I think your time is up. Clearly, he doesn't know anything about a kidnapping or murder. This other stuff is irrelevant. I trust that you will see yourselves out." The caregiver then got up and rolled a sobbing Herbert away, swiftly ending the interrogation.

Troy was curious about what prompted B.K. to venture into that line of questioning and asked.

"A little birdie told me that Herbert was a pervert," he'd replied lightheartedly. "We couldn't find any criminal records, but there were enough collaborating stories to at least ask him. I'm surprised he was truthful, but then again, what does he have to lose at this point?"

Troy didn't bother getting all bent out of shape about B.K. not telling him about this before. He had come to accept the fact that he would not be in the driver's seat during this investigation. Considering his emotional connection, that was probably for the best. At least justice had been served in some capacity and Herbert would never get a chance to hurt another child.

"You want me to take you back to your car or are you coming with me to speak with Edgar?"

Troy opted to go with B.K. and from Hitchcock, they ended up in Katy, a small city about thirty or so minutes west of Houston, located within the Houston-The Woodlands-Sugar Land metropolitan area. They rode in silence, listening to the turn-by-turn instructions being given by B.K.'s GPS and soon pulled up to a luxurious, two-story, multicolored brick home.

"Looks like the computer software business has been good to him."

Troy never knew what Elvin's dad did for a living. "You think he's here?" he asked.

"There's only one way to find out."

Once again Troy followed behind as B.K. led the way to the front door of another suspect.

The current Mrs. Campbell answered the door wearing a red see-through dress with a black, fitted extremely low-cut shirt underneath and skin-tight leggings. Her heels were higher than any that Troy had ever seen in his life and she was holding a martini. She looked like she'd been expecting someone else. "May I help you?"

"Uh, hi, ma'am. My name is B.K. Ashburn. I'm an investigator with the Texas Department of Public Safety. Is Edgar Campbell home? I would like to talk to him about his daughter, Elana."

"Yes, but this isn't a good time because we're on our way out. The only reason I answered the door is because I thought you were the babysitter."

"Everything okay, honey?" Mr. Campbell walked up behind her.

"Edgar," she whined, "These people want to talk to you about Elana. Tell them we have to go. I don't want to be late to the party."

"We won't be. I promise. Finish getting the baby ready. I'll handle this." After his child-like wife walked away, he turned to them. "Gentlemen, what can I do for you?"

Again, B.K. spoke. "I'm investigating your daughter's disappearance and death. I have a few questions I'd like to ask you."

For a father so distraught at his daughter's wake and supposedly too torn up to attend her funeral, he had bounced back pretty quickly. "As you can see this isn't the best time. My wife and I are due at a holiday party in less than an hour."

"This will only take a few moments. May we please come in?"

Reluctantly, Edgar agreed and they followed him inside to a huge family room with a ceiling so high it could almost reach heaven. "Have a seat. I'll be right back." Though it was hard to make out the words that he and his wife exchanged in another room, it didn't seem like a pleasant conversation.

"Let's hope he's asking the missus to put on more clothes," whispered B.K. jokingly.

Troy admired B.K.'s laid-back and calm demeanor. He, himself, was fuming. What kind of father would find an investigator's visit inconvenient because of a party? *A guilty one.* He realized that B.K. was right: he was too emotionally involved. His best bet was to keep quiet.

"I'm sorry about that," Edgar said when he returned. "Like I said, we have plans this evening, so can we make this quick? Have you found the person who killed my daughter?"

"Not yet. I was wondering if you could answer a few questions for me. Where were you on the afternoon Elana disappeared?"

Edgar rolled his eyes. "How many times must I go over this? I'm not going through the details again. I told the other investigators. You guys really need to compare notes."

"I hear you and your wife adopted a baby earlier this year?"

"Yes. A little girl we named April because that's the month she was born. What does she have to do with anything?"

"Did you have any contact with April's birth mother?"

Immediately, Edgar's disposition changed from annoyance to nervousness. He fumbled over his next words before spitting them out. "Why do you ask?"

"Because I'm curious. Some people find it peculiar for you to adopt a child in your seasoned years."

"Did either of you bother to show my wife or me identification?"

B.K. pulled out his ID, while Troy sat still. He didn't see any reason to show his ID since he was out of his jurisdiction.

"I thought you said you were a police officer."

"No, I used to be on the force. What I said was that I'm with the Texas Department of Public Safety. I'm a private investigator hired to look into the abduction and killing of your daughter. I would think you would be more cooperative."

The doorbell rang.

"Looks like that could not have come at a more perfect time. I'll see you two to the door." They had no choice but to follow him. Mrs. Campbell could be heard giving instructions to the baby-sitter. For someone so immature, she seemed very responsible when it came to the care of their child—a child that could possibly be Elana's.

"Is it possible for us to continue our conversation another day?" B.K. held out a card to give to Edgar.

He didn't take it. "No. If I answer any more questions, it will be with those who have the legal authority to make arrests."

"Is there some reason why you should be taken into custody?"

"Goodbye, gentlemen." Edgar slammed the door in their faces and B.K. slid his business card through a crack.

"He's definitely hiding something," B.K. said to Troy once they were in the car. "The question is what?"

Chapter 22: The Unknowns

*T*hree more days, Natalie thought to herself as she lay in bed wondering when her husband would get back. It was after ten o'clock at night. Nate was sound asleep and she had no idea whether her parents-in-law were still up or not. She'd pretty much tried to stay clear of both of them after what had happened earlier today.

Natalie felt bad that she hadn't told Troy everything. After Tracy left, Reed had come and knocked on her door.

"May I speak with you for a moment?"

"Sure." Natalie felt a little uncomfortable when he shut the door and sat down on the bed opposite of her. She didn't mind his warm embrace on Christmas Eve in front of the rest of the family, but this—being alone behind a closed door in a bedroom with her father-in-law, a man she had only met once before this trip—was awkward. Despite Troy's attempt to let go of negative feelings about his dad, Natalie knew he would not appreciate this scenario. Granted, there was no other place for him to sit since the room was empty besides the bed and dresser, but standing seemed like a nice option. Since he didn't, she did. "What would you like to talk about?"

"I'm not going to hurt you, Natalie." Apparently her change in stance had come across as fear rather than discomfort. He stood up, opened the bedroom door and leaned against it, motioning for her to sit back down. "Is this better?"

"I'm sorry, I—"

"No, it's okay. I get that I invaded your personal space. I'm sorry. I want to know how much you overheard, but I can tell by your actions." He blew a heavy sigh and put his head in his hands. "I think I've been able to calm Tracy down. She's not going to say anything to Troy or her mother, at least I hope she doesn't. I know I can't ask the same of you, but because you heard her accusations, I at least want to explain who it was that Tracy saw at the house. Given all the pressure Troy is under because of this case, I don't think he would understand and I also don't want to mess up the little progress we have made in our relationship."

"Reed, I honestly don't want to be involved so the less you tell me the better. It's not my place to tell Diane that you're seeing another woman and I would prefer that Troy not find out while we're here."

Reed looked confused. "So, you heard Tracy accuse me of being with another woman?"

"Yes." Natalie was unsure why his expression changed from confusion to relief. Suddenly she found her anger flaring. It wasn't only because she hurt for what Reed's current affair would do to Diane. It was also the fear of this being a setback for her husband. This could really be spiritually and emotionally damaging for him and the fact that Reed was hurting the person whom she loved most infuriated her. Before she could think about her actions, she was on the other side of the bed, standing face-to-face with him. "Personally, I find your actions disgraceful. You should be ashamed of yourself. Diane really has a lot of faith in believing that you have changed and Troy is doing his best to get over things from the past. For both of their sakes, I hope Tracy doesn't tell and that you get right, especially with God."

"Understood," Reed said and walked out.

Now, Natalie lay in bed wondering if telling him that she did not want to get involved had been the right course of action. She already felt bad about keeping the sex of their babies from Troy. Did she have the right to withhold this information? *Yes!* Yes, she did. It was not her business to share. Besides, she didn't know all the facts. Troy had enough on his mind with Elana's case and hopefully Tracy would take that into consideration.

Natalie could not get over how relieved Reed looked knowing that his secret was safe with her. She felt like a co-conspirator. He soon left, likely for his clandestine meeting with his mistress, whom Natalie suspected was the recipient of the voice message she'd overheard him leaving. When Diane got home, Natalie thought it best to stay out of sight. She allowed Nate to hang out with his "Gigi" while she stayed in the room with her heart aching about the false sense of security her mother-in-law had in Reed. If Diane knew that he was still cheating, that would destroy her and up-root any spiritual seeds about Jesus that had been planted in her life. That was the part that angered Natalie the most—that Reed was using Jesus as a cover-up. Somehow Natalie would find the way to resume her heart-to-heart with Diane that they were having a couple of days ago in the kitchen before the crazy broom thing happened. Diane asked once before if Jesus could really save some-one like her. Natalie knew the answer was yes, but she did not know how she would ever be able to convince Diane that people can and really do change if her mother-in-law ever learned about Reed's façade.

"Hey, you…," Troy said when he came in the room.

"Hey, yourself." She smiled, relieved to find him in a decent mood. He leaned over to give her a kiss and she held him tight.

"You okay?'

"Yes. You?" She tried to sound casual, but what she really wanted to know was if he had spoken with Tracy.

He blew a deep breath. "Tired. We went to see two of Lilly's ex-husbands today."

"How'd things go?"

"Okay. If the person who kidnapped Elana and later left her on the highway are one and the same, then Lilly's last husband is crossed off the list." Troy informed her about Herbert's condition. "There's no way Herbert could have been involved with disposing of Elana's body. Now we're thinking it was either El's uncle Bill or their father. I thought it might be a different uncle, but he's been eliminated through DNA. After tonight, my bet is on the father."

"What makes you think that?"

"Oh, babe, it's a long story and I really don't feel like getting into it right now. I'm just happy to see you." He kissed her again. "I know we haven't spent much quality time together since we've been here. Thanks for understanding how important Elana's case is to me and not complaining."

Why would she complain? In three more days she would have her husband and life back.

"I have an appointment tomorrow, but how about on Friday, we all do something together?"

"I'm cool with that. You'll have to check with your mom. I'm sure she'll be thrilled to be one big happy family." Natalie spoke with bitterness as Reed's affair crossed her mind, but luckily it came across to Troy as humorous.

"Actually, I was thinking that it should be the five of us—you, Nate, me, and the unknowns." He frowned. "That doesn't sound right, does it? Sounds like they were made in a petri dish." He lifted her shirt and began kissing her belly. "I can't wait to meet them. I do wonder what they are, but I am so glad that we are waiting to be surprised."

The knowledge of her deception was too much to bear in light of her now keeping Reed's secret. "Honey, I have to tell you something." Natalie remembered how irate Troy got when he'd learned that she hadn't stopped taking birth control pills prior to this pregnancy. Hopefully, what she was about to disclose would not cause a repeat of that behavior. "I found out what we're having."

Troy froze, looking up at her from her stomach. "Seriously?" He got up and paced back and forth. "You know how I feel about you keeping things from me. I thought we agreed we would wait until they were born. How could you go behind my back?"

"I'm sorry, honey. At first I wanted to wait, too, but then I started freaking out. I know you say you'll be more involved, but we both know how you are when you are working on a case. I was scared that I would be overwhelmed and wanted to be as prepared as possible. I'm so sorry, Troy." She walked to him. "I should have told you when I found out. No, I shouldn't have found out without talking to you first."

"Yes, you should have talked to me *first* instead of being deceitful. You have violated my trust and I don't know if I can get over this." He looked at her and then away from her quickly and covered his eyes with his hands. His tone and actions were a little too over the top. When her generally stoic husband started sniffling and asking questions in a voice a few octaves higher than his norm, that's when she caught on.

"You idiot!" She playfully punched him in the arm. "How long have you known?"

"How dare you physically assault me after shattering my trust in your ability to communicate honestly with me?" He continued his antics.

Natalie rolled her eyes and got back in bed. "You suck at acting. How'd you find out? Did Aneetra tell you?"

He followed her back to the bed, resuming his position on her mid-section. "Oh, so the BFF is in on this, too? What about Corrine?"

"No. I didn't think she would be able to keep it a secret. Seriously, how did you find out?"

"Babe, did you forget that you're married to a detective? I discover things for a living. The next time you want to add items to your Amazon wish list without my knowledge, it will help if you changed the setting to private."

She laughed. "I can't believe I did that. Talk about having baby brain. So, you aren't mad?"

"No. At first I was disappointed because I would have liked to have been there with you, but I understand your reasoning. I figured as much. Then I found it hilarious that you were pretending like it was still a surprise. I was curious to see how long you would keep up the charade. I wanted to bust you out the other morning at breakfast so bad, but I couldn't bring myself to do it in front of everyone."

Natalie hoped Troy would be as understanding if he ever found out that she knew his dad was still cheating on his mom. She motioned for him to move closer to her face. "I love you," she said before giving him a kiss that was sure to wake up his extremity.

He smiled. "If I say I'm mad, will we get to make up?"

Instead of answering him, she pulled him in for another kiss.

Chapter 23: A Good Night's Sleep

"Okay, Troy, I need you to take slow deep breaths." The soft, soothing sound of Shauna's voice helped calm his nerves as he lay back in the chair, closed his eyes, and followed her instructions. "As you breathe, you will feel yourself relax more and more every time you exhale. Your body is light, like a feather, and you're gently floating through the air. I want you to think of a happy place and stay there."

Happy place? Besides home, his wasn't a particular location. It was a condition, anywhere that included Natalie, Nate, and peace. His happy place involved seeing the smile on his wife's face when she looked at him or hearing the excitement in lil' man's voice when he walked into the room. The peace he felt when he lay down next to Natalie at night, knowing she's safe in his arms… smelling her hair…sometimes watching her sleep, the pride he cannot contain when hugging his son…their growing family…these were the things that made up his place of happiness.

"You should feel very calm right now. I want you to stay there and focus solely on the sound of my voice. I'm going to count down and as I do, you will go deeper into a relaxed state of mind. Ten…," she began softly, "nine…eight…seven…"

As she continued, his nerves about the process began to dissipate and Troy found himself at ease as the tranquilizing sound of

Shauna's voice walked him down the road to serenity. There, he separated from himself and followed all of her instructions, uninhibited, answering all of her questions unrestrained.

"Let's go back to the day Elana disappeared. How old were you then?"

"Eleven."

"Troy, you are now an observer to the events that took place that day. I want you to look around and tell me everything you see and hear. Tell me where you are and what you are doing."

Troy watched the eleven-year-old version of himself sitting alongside Elvin in the living room. It was the day after Elvin's birthday. He'd turned eleven. They'd been up all night playing the Atari Elvin's mom had given him. Both boys still had on the same clothes they'd worn yesterday—Troy, a pair of black shorts with a white crewneck T-shirt; Elvin, denim jean shorts and a red-striped T-shirt. Details that had previously escaped him had now become clear—the crumbs from all the junk food they'd eaten overnight as well as the stain from the soda that Elvin had spilled that he had not yet gotten up. To keep Miss Lilly from seeing it, he had placed a pillow over it while pretending it was being used for cushion for his knees.

"Where's Elana while you and Elvin are playing the game?"

At first she was upstairs. Elana had asked if her friend, Salome, could stay overnight, but Miss Lilly had said no because Salome was too "fast" and she didn't want that little girl staying all night when boys were around. If Miss Lilly thought that Troy or Elvin would take a second look at an eight-year-old, she was really out of touch with the minds of preteen boys. There was no way Salome could compare to the girl who played Thelma on Good Times. *That show had been off the air now for several years and yet Troy was still stunned by her beauty. Once he heard his aunt's boyfriend say that Thelma had curves in all the right places. Troy hadn't known what that meant back then, but now, at age eleven, he was starting to comprehend. Salome could not compete no matter how "fast" she was.*

Upset that Salome could not come over, Elana spent most of the evening in her room pouting. Miss Lilly would not let her hang out downstairs with Elvin and Troy because it was a given that there would be a fight. There always was. If Elana wasn't picking on them, they were picking on her. The next morning Elana came down in her Strawberry Short-cake pajamas before Miss Lilly or Mr. Herbert had gotten up.

"What are y'all playing?" she asked, sitting on the couch behind them. She didn't have her doll.

Elvin explained the game and the concept.

"Will you show me how to play?"

"Maybe later when Troy leaves."

"When is he leaving?"

"I don't know. Later."

"Then I wanna watch cartoons."

"No. Go back upstairs. Mama said that we can have the TV." Elvin's family only had two televisions. One in Miss Lilly's room and the "good" one down in the living room.

Elvin and Elana continued arguing back and forth until footsteps descended the stairs. It was Mr. Herbert. No one spoke. As soon as he rounded the corner, Elana got up and ran up the stairs. Soon her bedroom door slammed.

Mr. Herbert belched loudly as he went into the kitchen. Moments later he returned, headed out the front door. "I'll be back."

Elvin didn't respond. Last night, the night of his eleventh birthday, there had been another fight. This one wasn't as bad as it could have gotten, but the kids did hear yelling and a few slaps being exchanged as they sat in the kitchen eating cake and ice cream. Elana was with them and they were all getting along. Actually, they were quiet, purposely focusing on the treats while pretending not to hear what was happening upstairs in the master bedroom.

"Tell me what was happening in the moments immediately prior to Elana's disappearance," Shauna prodded.

Troy and Elvin had been playing Asteroids at that time. Troy's butt was numb. The heel of his right foot had left an imprint in his left thigh from him sitting Indian style for so long. The soda stain was no longer wet and had become even darker after it dried. Miss Lilly was in the kitchen making several phone calls, worried about Mr. Herbert who hadn't been seen since leaving that morning.

The boys had not moved. Still clothed in yesterday's attire, they continued playing the game. Due to her whining that she was "bored," Miss Lilly had told them to let Elana play. They did. Kind of. She wasn't that good so her turn would be over within a few minutes of her having the controller. Instead of making allowances for her being a novice, they took advantage of the situation. They made up a rule that anyone who scored a certain number of points would get an extra turn, maximum of three, knowing that the conditions would never apply to Elana. Consequently, both Elvin and Troy could be playing for up to thirty or forty minutes each while Elana waited. At first she was patient, going upstairs to retrieve that ugly doll to keep her occupied. After a while, her patience started to wear thin and she began arguing with them. That's when Miss Lilly got involved. As a compromise, she promised to buy them all treats if they would behave while she was gone. That did not work too well. Before long, Elana and the boys were at it again and she ran out crying.

"Did Elana take the doll with her when she left?"

"Yes." She had been holding it by one arm. Her braided ponytails flopped as she took off. She did not have barrettes in her hair.

"I want you to really concentrate now, Troy. Did you hear anything after she left?"

Crying! Troy could faintly recall hearing sobs coming from the front porch.

"Very good. Now think really hard. Is there anything else you can tell me about that day?"

Troy heard Elana crying. He was sure Elvin heard it, too, but neither of them paid her any attention. They were both too engrossed in the game and happy to have her out of their way. Troy knew that if Elana was still on the porch when Miss Lilly got back, he and Elvin would get a good fussing out. Knowing Elana, she would cry even harder when her mom returned. Now Troy wished his mom would hurry because he didn't want Miss Lilly being upset with him about anything. She was pretty. He didn't like seeing her mad. Plus, she had enough troubles with Mr. Herbert. Troy wasn't sure how long Elana sat out there sobbing. After a while he heard a car door.

"When you say you heard a car door, was this right before Miss Lilly came into the house?"

"No. It was way before Miss Lilly came home."

Shauna asked him a series of other questions about whether or not he'd seen anything when they went out to look for Elana such as if they found her doll or any trace of her having left the front porch. Troy answered them all.

"Good job. I am going to count down again and when I do, you will be fully functional and alert, able to remember everything that happened here today." When she finished, Troy came to himself. "How do you feel?"

There was still a calm feeling over him, but there was more edginess to it. "Weird. Sort of like I took a nap, but watched myself do it."

"You did great. I was a little concerned after meeting you yesterday. What did you do between last night and today to become so relaxed?"

Flashbacks of his last encounter with Natalie raced through his mind and Troy felt his insides tingle. "Uh, I got a good night's sleep." He smiled to himself.

"Good for you. Most people would be surprised at how much sleep or lack thereof can impact these sessions. Anyhow, I'm going to give B.K. your recording and he will go over it with you. I don't think we'll have to do this again, so do you have any questions for me?"

"No."

"Well, nice to meet you. Best of luck in solving this case. Hopefully, I've been able to help."

Troy left without any real destination in mind. B.K.'s meeting with Bill and his attorney wasn't until next week and, as far as he knew, there wasn't any additional information about the baby that Edgar Campbell and his wife supposedly adopted. Last night, when Troy filled Natalie in on their visit with Herbert, he purposely left out the part about Herbert's sexual molestation of Elana. Troy didn't think it was necessary to share that information with his wife, knowing it could possibly bring up painful memories for her.

"*Maggie hurt her*," Herbert repeated. If there was any credibility to Herbert's words, it would be revealed through Bill or Edgar and whatever connection they had to this mysterious woman named Maggie.

Chapter 24: A Straight Answer

*A*fter leaving Shauna's, Troy decided to swing by his sister's, still concerned that he hadn't heard back from her. Tracy and Al lived about fifteen minutes away from Troy's parents in a neighborhood that wasn't the best and yet could have been a lot worse. Their house was small, maybe 1,200 square feet, if that, but it was very nice. Surrounded by a wooden privacy fence, it had a brick exterior and a huge yard with a mini basketball court that Al had put up in the back for AJ, but AJ was more interested in wrestling.

Troy did not like popping up unannounced and spending time at his sister's crib was not something he did often when he was in town. The last time he came over here was when he and Al had gotten into a fight. A fight, which Troy admittedly started, but Al provoked by grabbing on his baby sister like she was some rag doll. He figured it would be safe to stop by this time of day. Tracy, a schoolteacher, was off work during the holiday break and Troy was not concerned about seeing Al since he expected his brother-in-law to be at work. Unless, of course, Al had gotten drunk last night and was too hung over to go in. That had been known to happen a time or twenty.

Troy had already rung the doorbell twice when he realized that it was after four and that Al could very well be at home, depending on his hours. As he considered turning around, the door opened. Relief fell over him when Tracy answered. "What's going on?"

"That's what I want to know. You left me urgent messages and when I tried getting ahold of you, you never called me back."

"My bad. I was freaking out about something that still isn't quite making sense to me, but I know I can sometimes overreact. Everything's fine." Sincerity was lacking in her tone as if she were trying to convince herself, in addition to him, that all was "fine."

"Is Al here?" He asked the question all the while reminding himself to stay calm, suspecting that whatever Tracy was hiding from him involved her husband. He glossed over her for bruises. There were none. *Good!*

"Naw. No one is here but me. He's working and the kids are at their friends'."

"Well…are you going to let me in or continue to treat me like a Jehovah's Witness."

She seemed to hesitate for a split-second before moving from the doorway.

Immediately, Troy was ready to leave. There was a depressing aura. The living room had all the perks one might expect in the twenty-first century—flat-screen, large sectional, and glass end tables, but there was a natural gloom that fell over the space. Maybe it was the drawn shades or the dark painted walls. Whatever the case, Troy was reminded that a house wasn't always a home. He took a seat without being invited to do so. "What's going on, Trace, for real?"

"Nothing."

The sing-song manner in which she answered made him believe her even less. Troy spent the next few minutes trying to get her to open up, even mentioning the fact that for there to be "nothing" going on, she'd obviously shared *something* with their father and if she could share it with their dad, she could share it with him. Tracy maintained her stance that she didn't want to talk, explaining that she thought she may have misconstrued some details and if that were the case, her sharing would only complicate things. Troy's interest was piqued even further, but he gave up pressing. "All right, if you say so. I'm not going to ask again." He was sure that he'd failed in his attempt not to let his frustration with her show. He would never understand why she stayed with Al any more than he would why their mom stayed with their dad. It made no sense for two beautiful women to subject themselves to verbal and physical abuse from men who should cherish them. "I love you and I'm always here for you," he added, in a softer tone.

"I know and I love you, too." Her smile was forced, but her tone was sincere. "How are things going with Elana's case?"

"Slow. It's difficult to say for sure because I'm like the third wheel in this investigation. It's hard to let someone else take charge when the case means so much to me."

"Any idea who could have taken her or where she's been until her body was found?"

"I think we've narrowed it down to two suspects."

"Who?"

Her inquiry caught Troy off guard. He wasn't used to discussing his work with his baby sister. "Since when did you become so interested in the case?"

"I've always been interested. Well, I guess not always since I was little when it happened, but the discovery of her body has everyone talking and speculating about where she's been all this time. You got any ideas?"

He toyed with how much to tell her. He'd never known Tracy

to be a gossip. Still, he did not know who her closest confidants were and did not want to risk telling her anything that could possibly get back to Bill or Edgar. "So far, there's nothing concrete to go on, but we are making progress. I'm pretty sure things have been narrowed down to one of two suspects."

The answer seemed to pacify her for the time being and she began asking how he and their father were getting along. She seemed pleasantly surprised to know that things were going well and yet there was a look on her face that Troy could not quite read. He thought about asking what was on her mind, but assumed he would not get a straight answer. They engaged in small talk for a while until they heard Al's car pull into the garage. That was Troy's cue to leave. He managed to be out the front door and back in his rental before Al ever walked into the house.

Troy went back to his parents' house only to discover it was empty. He knew Natalie and his mom had taken Nate out, but he assumed his father would be there. *Probably working on the house again.* With nothing except time to kill, Troy went for a run. No one was home by the time he returned about an hour later. Troy showered and started looking over his case notes again, also thinking about the things that had taken place in his session with Shauna. He knew there was something he was missing. He just didn't know what.

Chapter 25: Hot Topic

O n Friday, Troy managed to keep his promise and took Nate and Natalie to the Johnson Space Center. The three of them had fun and it was a welcome break for Troy, who stayed up until the wee hours of the morning reading and reread-ing notes from the case file, hoping something would jump out at him that he'd missed before. Nothing did. When B.K. called and asked if they could meet that morning to discuss Troy's session with Shauna, Troy had been tempted to postpone his outing with his family. Ultimately, he arranged to meet B.K. after taking Natalie and Nate to the airport the next day.

Now, the next day was here and Troy was trying to figure out how to break the news to his wife that he would not be returning with them.

"When are you going to start packing?" Natalie had gotten her and Nate's things together before going to bed last night. Though there were still several hours to kill before they had to be at the airport, she'd already told Troy that he could put the luggage in the car at any time. "I will be so happy to get home. The next time we come here, we're getting your mother a new mattress for this room. I *refuse* to sleep another night on that one." Seeing how she was stretching her neck while holding her hands to her lower back, Troy got behind her and began rubbing her shoulders. "Mmm.

That feels good. Oh, by the way, I forgot to tell you, that Corrine is getting Nate New Year's Eve. Instead of going to church, I thought maybe we could bring in the New Year together with a romantic candlelight dinner."

"Babe, I have a confession." He turned her around to face him, still massaging her shoulders. "I should have said something a while ago, but I honestly could not find the right time." Her concerned expression worried him. "Relax, I'm not having an affair." He kissed her forehead for reassurance, recalling how paranoid she was one time last summer that he might cheat on her after it was discovered that Aneetra's husband had committed adultery on more than one occasion.

"That didn't even cross my mind," she said unconvincingly. He had noticed her eased expression. "What's up?"

"I'm not going back with you and Nate. It's not that I don't want to, but I need to stay here and see this case through to the end."

If this scenario had been a scene in a movie, the deep tones of the *dun dun dun* music would have played and the screen would have faded to black…no, red in this case to indicate the possible blood that would be shed if Natalie were a violent person. Like a dragon spitting fire, every word out of her mouth singed his flesh as she educated him on the difference between wants and needs. According to her, he *needed* to get his priorities straight, quick, fast, and in a hurry if he truly *wanted* to return to Columbus to a happy home.

"I'm sorry, babe, I—"

"Hush! I don't want to hear it. This wasn't a mistake. You *purposely* chose to withhold this information from me. I understand that Elana's case is important to you and I probably would have been a little more supportive of you staying if you had been honest about your plans in the first place. What else are you keeping from me?"

He wanted to say "nothing," but a quick reminder of the texts he received Christmas morning from *her* kept him quiet. He made a promise to himself that when he got back to Columbus, he would tell Natalie everything about his past with her. Disclosing that information right now could be dangerous.

Natalie shared a few more unpleasant thoughts about his decision and timing before storming out of the room. The moment after Natalie left, he got a text message from *her*, almost like *she* had been a fly on the wall listening to their argument.

ThinkN of u & wanted 2 say hi. Hope all is well.

All was far from well, he thought while deleting her message.

Natalie didn't say another word to him the rest of the afternoon, but he was sure that she had plenty to say about him. Troy's suspicions were confirmed when his mom later came up to the room to scold him.

"Why'd you wait until the last minute to tell Natalie that you were stayin'?"

"Mama, I'm not trying to be rude, but you don't like me getting in the middle of things between you and Dad, so let Natalie and me handle this on our own."

"Your wife is tryin' her best to be supportive of you. Besides yesterday and on Christmas, she's barely gotten to see you. The least you could have done was communicate openly with her. I think that's what has upset her more than anything."

"It's not like she doesn't ever keep things from me." He thought about the sex of his twins. Originally, he wasn't upset that she didn't tell him, but now that his mother was attacking him, resentment began to build.

"Boy you're so bullheaded at times, I want to smack you!" Then, as usual, his mom began to adorn her speech with colorful words as she continued telling him exactly how she felt about his method of doing things.

When Troy had had enough, he grabbed Natalie's bags and headed to the car, but not before telling his mom as respectfully as he could that she needed to mind her own business.

The ride to the airport was eerily quiet. Nate, who was usually a chatterbox, had not said a word since they left Troy's parents' home. At first Troy thought he was asleep. A quick glance in the rearview mirror revealed that the youngster was simply staring out the window. It wasn't until they got to the airport that Nate spoke.

"I see an airplane!" His face lit up as though he was finally making the connection that he would be flying home. "Is 'dat plane comin' back to get us?"

"No, honey. We will be on a different one." Natalie spoke as she continued a texting conversation she had been having during the ride, which Troy assumed was with Aneetra and that he'd been the hot topic of discussion between them.

Troy hated for Natalie to leave being so angry with him. He decided to try one last-ditch effort to smooth things over as he pulled into the parking space. "Babe, I'm sorry. I should have handled things a lot differently."

"Okay," was her reply as she unbuckled her seat belt and got out of the vehicle.

Her one-word response did not reek of anger as Troy had anticipated. It was hurt and that pained him deeply. He made sure that she and Nate got checked in okay and gave her the keys to the truck so she'd be able to drive home once they landed. "I love you, Natalie," he said as they began to part ways. "I'm sorry and I promise to make this up to you somehow."

She looked up at him with those big brown eyes that screamed disappointment. "Don't make promises you won't be able to keep." She gave a slight smile and that was all the assurance Troy needed to know that, despite her being upset with him, things would be fine.

After giving her a kiss and saying goodbye to lil' man, Troy instructed her to call him when they got back to Columbus. He watched until they got through security before heading to B.K.'s office.

Chapter 26: Ill-fated Adventure

"How'd you feel things went yesterday?" B.K. sat at his desk casually dressed in jeans and a sweater.

"Okay, I guess. That was my first time ever being hypnotized, so I'm not sure. Shauna seemed pleased."

"I am, too. We now know that when Elana walked out, she didn't go too far. Both you and Elvin heard her cries coming from the front porch. You, however, provided us with one additional clue. You mentioned hearing a car door and I think whoever took Elana came to the house."

Troy could have kicked himself for not zeroing in on that piece of information. "Man, I've been investigating for a long time, yet I'm starting to feel incompetent. I recall sharing that with Shauna, but I didn't think twice about hearing the car. I assumed it was a neighbor."

"And it could have been. We also need to explore the possibility that it was her abductor. Do you remember anyone who was supposed to come by that day?"

"Nope. Well, Elvin's dad. He was actually supposed to come by the night before."

"What about your dad?"

"What about him?"

"The other day when your mom and Lilly were in my office, I

could tell that Diane was hiding something. I took her out to lunch during Lilly's session with Shauna because I wanted to see if I could get her to open up and she did. She admitted to me that your dad was supposed to pick you up from Elvin's that morning and that he never showed."

Troy guessed that his mom never shared that information with him because she knew it would only make him hate his father more at the time. "Did she tell you that his not showing was nothing unusual? My dad never followed through with what he said he would do."

"Yes, she did. She also told me that he claims not to have gotten her message, but I tracked down the guy who used to work for him and he tells a different story."

"Look, I sense where you're going and you're completely wasting your time. Besides, what are the odds that the message this guy remembers taking was on the same day as Elana's disappearance? That, in and of itself, is reasonable doubt. Whoever kidnapped Elana had to have a place to take her and my father lived with my granddad at the time. Actually, my dad was his caregiver. He would not have been able to hide an eight-year-old girl and take care of an elderly man all at the same time."

"Don't misunderstand me. I'm not accusing your father of any-thing. I'm simply trying to get all the facts. I don't mean to offend you."

"I'm not offended. My relationship with my dad is rocky at best. If I thought for a second that he was involved with Elana's disap-pearance, I'd be all over him like fleas on a cat. There was nothing odd about him not coming. It would have actually been strange if he had."

"Okay, fair enough. I stopped by Edgar's yesterday. I told him about Elana's baby and unless he could prove otherwise, I'd take my suspicions to the boys with legal authority to make an arrest."

"Wow. How'd he respond?"

"Both he and the missus were appalled at the accusation that he could have raped Elana. She made this stink about me upsetting the ambiance of their home. I'm surprised the dimwit even knew that word. Anyhow, Edgar walked me out, but this time he was more willing to help, so he says. He's supposed to be sending me confirmation of the adoption."

"What's taking so long? It can't be that hard."

"It *shouldn't* be. If he doesn't cooperate, it will make things a little more difficult."

"So, what do we do next?"

"We wait…"

Natalie sat in the Baltimore terminal ready to cry during their layover. Normally good at dealing with her toddler, she had neither the mental nor physical capacity to handle him. Nate displayed one of two characteristics when he was sleepy—extreme silliness or excessive whining—and he had chosen the latter. Nate had whined about *everything* from the minute they boarded the first plane in Texas until now.

It started when he asked to play with a specific toy that "Gigi and Grandpa" had given him for Christmas.

"It's in the suitcase, honey. Here, you can play with Mommy's iPad."

A suggestion that would have normally pacified him didn't this time. Nate cried for his toy like it was the only thing he had gotten. Natalie finally got him to settle down after threatening to throw it away if he didn't be quiet. Not her finest parenting moment. Once they got in the air, Nate began complaining that the plane wasn't moving fast enough, it was moving too fast, and later he cried because the plane had left his daddy. Then, out of nowhere, Nate started griping about his lip hurting. The same lip he busted last Saturday during ice skating, which he had not complained about all week and was nearly completely healed by now, was suddenly "hurting." Concerned that perhaps his ears were bothering him and causing such misbehavior, Natalie put extra drops in them hoping to alleviate any pressure. Nope. His ears had been fine. Nate finally asked to watch a movie on the portable DVD, but then started crying because there was no popcorn on the plane for him to eat while he watched.

Natalie knew her son had been *that* child when the stewardess came and asked if there was anything she could do to help calm him. Embarrassed, Natalie apologized to the stewardess and other passengers nearby for his behavior. There was only so much popping and pinching a mother could do before it seemed abusive and she'd done her fair share of both throughout the entire ride. Now, in the concourse, short of purchasing a sedative from the gift shop and giving it to him, Natalie hadn't a clue what to do.

While Nate hopped from chair to chair complaining that they were all too hard, Natalie put her head in her hands and cried. "I'm about to lose my mind," she confessed when she called Aneetra and filled her in on their ill-fated adventure.

"He knows better than that. Something is going on with him. Bless his heart, he doesn't know how to express himself appropriately."

Bless his heart? If anyone needed blessing right now, it wasn't Nate! Natalie went into her rage about how inconsiderate Troy's decision was and how she was so worried about having more kids. "I don't know if I can do this, Nee. I feel so incompetent right now," she sobbed as Nate continued bouncing around the concourse.

"Stop letting your hormones dictate your words. You're a good mother and more than capable of handling Nate with or without Troy's help. I know you're frustrated with Troy, and rightfully so, but remember this is a tough situation for him as well. I'm sure he feels like he's between a rock and a hard place. Hey, do you remember the name of the FBI agent who helped him with the serial killer case last summer?"

"Something Hunter. Why?"

"Maybe you can contact her and she can help somehow?"

"I'm sure I still have her card somewhere, but I don't know if I should call her. Troy doesn't like me talking about his cases with other people." Natalie's wheels turned for a few moments before she realized something. *This isn't his case.* "On second thought, it might not be a bad idea."

"If you think calling her will upset Troy, don't do it. I was only trying to offer a suggestion that could benefit both of you."

"No, I like the idea. Troy has been frustrated. I'm sure he and the investigator could use the help. I wonder why Troy didn't contact her himself, though. Maybe he already has and hasn't told me. It's not like he keeps me informed about his plans. His priority should be Nate and me."

"You are. Troy loves you and Nate more than anything. This is hard for him. You know he's probably overcome with guilt about Elana. He needs your understanding now more than your anger."

Natalie wanted to hang up the phone hearing her friend come to Troy's defense. The announcement that boarding would soon begin could not come at a more perfect time. "Good thing I have to go, otherwise, I might argue with you about always coming to Troy's defense. I'm starting to think you like him more than me."

Aneetra laughed. "I always have your best interest at heart. Sometimes you need to be reminded that you have a good man."

"Whatever he's paying you to say those things, tell him that it's not enough."

"Bye, you nut. Call me when you guys get here."

The conversation with Aneetra helped to calm Natalie's nerves. She would call the FBI lady the first chance she got. With any luck, the woman could help bring her husband home in no time. Natalie smiled at the thought while gathering her carry-on bags. Nate, on the other hand, had decided that it would be fun to jump from chair to chair. "Nathaniel Troy Evans, get down right now!" she said with a renewed sense of confidence in her parenting skills. From the quickness of Nate's response, he knew she had once again found her mommy strength. They boarded the plane with no problems and this time Nate fell asleep during the ride. When they landed, Natalie checked in with both Troy and Aneetra. Troy called her again after they had gotten home and asked if she'd gotten the picture he'd taken of her and Nate when they were napping.

"Yes. Thank you."

"Don't forget to turn on the alarm," he said.

"Don't you forget your way home."

Chapter 27: Call of Duty

*T*he next morning was Sunday and Natalie didn't attempt to go to church. For the second week in a row, she claimed Bedside Baptist. She spent the day in pajamas watching kiddy movies with her son. On New Year's Eve, Natalie woke up with a renewed sense of purpose. While Nate was still sleeping, she got up with the mission of finding the card Troy's FBI friend had left with her last summer when the lady came to visit. It took some digging, but she found it inside her desk underneath a bunch of papers.

Agent Cheryl Hunter.

Immediately, Natalie dialed her number and tried not to let disappointment set in when she got voicemail. Actually, it was bitterness that she struggled with, wondering why it was that her husband, a Columbus homicide detective, *chose* to work on a holiday in a city in which he didn't have jurisdiction and this lady with the Federal Bureau of Investigation had sense enough not to answer her phone.

"Hi, my name is Natalie Evans. You're friends with my husband, Troy, who works for the Columbus PD. You and I met last summer when you were helping him on the Bible Butcher case." Natalie paused to take a deep breath, recalling the painful fear that gripped her when the serial killer of that case targeted her family. "I'm calling because I think Troy could use your help on another case he's working. He's in Texas right now and doesn't know I'm calling you. I hope I'm not overstepping my bounds. I don't know where else to turn and...I don't know if you can help or not, but if you would please give me a call, I would really appreciate it." Natalie left both her cell and home numbers and hung up, feeling relieved and apprehensive all at the same time. What if the lady called Troy before her? Oh well, she wasn't going to worry herself about it now. *What's done is done.*

The rest of the day went pretty fast. Corrine came to get Nate as promised. Though Natalie didn't think he deserved to go to the zoo or anywhere else special after showing his butt at the airport, she could not find it in her heart to scold him any further. Besides, she'd watched movies with him all day yesterday. After Corrine and Nate left, Natalie unpacked their suitcases and spent most of the day doing laundry and cleaning the house, which had been left in disarray prior to their trip. By the time Aneetra called to see if Natalie had planned to attend Watch Night Service, she was pooped. "No, I'm going to sit this one out." Her original idea had been to plan a romantic evening for her and Troy. Even if he were there, that would not have happened considering how she felt.

"Awww, I was hoping we could bring in the New Year together since we are both without our children and our husbands."

"Girl, I'm exhausted. I'm going to sit right here and watch the *Twilight Zone* marathon. You're welcome to come over if you'd like, but I don't want you to miss church on my behalf."

"You up for a good old-fashioned slumber party?"

Sensing that her best friend did not want to be alone, Natalie said yes, feeling that she may do more slumbering than partying. Aneetra was at her house within thirty minutes and the two of them climbed in Natalie's bed like middle-school children with popcorn and sparkling grape juice.

Aneetra, who had turned forty earlier in the month, sometimes dressed older than her age. It was something that drove Natalie crazy because, although her friend wasn't supermodel gorgeous according to society's standards, Natalie thought Aneetra was beautiful, both inside and out. Sure, she had a little bit of belly hangover, but it was nothing disgusting or that a few good cardio workouts and crunches couldn't handle. Her normal size fourteen hips fluctuated between twelve and sixteen, depending on the season. It wasn't the outside that made up the bulk of Aneetra's beauty. It was her caring and loveable spirit. For the most part, there was always a smile on her dark-brown face that could radiate a room. Natalie had expected Aneetra to wear some grandma-looking gown and bonnet, but was pleasantly surprised to see how youthful her friend looked in her red-and-white Christmassy pajamas with her hair in two pig tails to the side. And she told her so.

"Thanks! I try to spice things up every now and then. Plus, I didn't want to hear your mouth."

Natalie laughed. She was always giving Aneetra unwanted fashion tips, which tended to fall on deaf ears.

When midnight hit, calls and text messages started ringing for the both of them. Though Texas was an hour behind, Troy still called Natalie anyhow. He didn't seem like himself. Natalie knew he was stressing about the case, though he did not mention specifics. He was pleased to know that Aneetra was with her. "I love you, babe."

"I love you, too." Immediately after she hung up with Troy, another call came through. "This is the FBI lady," Natalie announced to Aneetra who responded with a scowl.

"Seems a little weird that she'd call at such a late hour, don't you think?"

Natalie shrugged. It wasn't unusual for Troy to get calls in the middle of the night. It came with his line of work. "People in law enforcement don't think like the general public," she said, answering the call.

"Hello, Natalie?"

"Yes, Agent Hunter. Thank you for returning my call."

"Please call me Cheryl. I hope I didn't wake you. This is the first chance I've gotten to check my messages. Yours seemed urgent and I wanted to get back to you quickly. Tell me what's going on?"

"Actually, can we set a time to talk tomorrow? I have company right now."

"Oh." She sounded disappointed. "I suppose that would work. Would you like me to come by your house, say around noon?"

"I don't want you to go out of your way."

"It's no problem. I'll see you tomorrow."

"O-kay." By the time Natalie wished her a Happy New Year, Cheryl had hung up.

"Well?" Aneetra stared, waiting to be debriefed. Natalie filled her in. "I don't know, Nat. Something about this feels weird. Maybe I gave you bad advice by suggesting you contact her."

Natalie paused to consider the circumstances. "Naw, it's all good." She reassured both Aneetra and herself. She knew from firsthand experience that those in law enforcement often went beyond the call of duty. Cheryl, like Troy, could probably get overly zealous about her job. Everything was fine.

Chapter 28: Coincidence or Clue?

It had been so long since Natalie had seen Cheryl that she'd forgotten how petite the woman was. Natalie, who rarely seemed out of place no matter the setting, felt like a girelephant—a cross between a giraffe and elephant—next to her. Standing barely five-three, Agent Hunter could not weigh more than a solid 110 pounds. Natalie did not want to think about the lie the scale told at her last doctor appointment.

Luckily, Natalie had gotten her house together yesterday. Agent Hunter had arrived approximately a half hour early, dressed casually in a pair of slacks, sweater, and a leather jacket. Her hair bore the same boyishly short style it had when they last met. Natalie didn't remember the dimple in the middle of her chin, though. Then again, she'd been so distraught that she'd probably missed a lot back then, like the coarseness of Cheryl's voice. It had an edgy no-nonsense to it, but it didn't take away from her overall pleasant and very feminine demeanor.

"You have piqued my curiosity, so let's get right to it." Natalie filled her in on the few details she knew about the case. Cheryl admitted to having seen a glimpse or two about things on the news without giving it much thought. "Had I known Troy was involved, I would have paid more attention."

"I was hoping you would have some connections or possibly

some insight that can help expedite things. I'm asking for totally selfish reasons. The truth of the matter is that I want my husband home and I know he's not coming back until this case is solved."

"I will certainly see what I can do to help." She pulled out a pen and notepad. "Tell me everything that Troy has told you about the suspects."

Under normal circumstances, Troy would be livid if Natalie repeated anything he told her about his cases. This wasn't a normal circumstance nor was it *his* case. Besides, Cheryl was his friend and they had worked together before. All of those facts helped ease her mind as Natalie shared with Cheryl the details Troy had relayed about Elana's stepfather, uncle, and the possibility that her father could be involved.

"Any idea who this Maggie lady is that the stepfather mentioned?"

"No. I don't think Troy gave it much thought. From what he said, the guy is pretty messed up."

"Anything else?"

"Not that I can think of."

"Well, you have my number if something comes up. Meanwhile, I'll see what information I can find."

"Oh, thank you so much. I'll call Troy and tell him you're looking into this. I'm sure he'll be happy to know you're willing to help."

"No, don't you dare!" Her tone was rather sharp and for a quick second Natalie thought to tell her as much. Federal agent or not, no one was going to come into her home and talk to her crazy. Luckily, Cheryl explained herself further. "I'm sorry. I didn't mean to snap. I think it's best if I contact Troy *after* I have something to share. If this case is getting to him as much as you say, we don't want to give him false hope that I can help when we don't know for sure."

"That makes sense."

Cheryl didn't stick around for small talk. She said that she'd get started on Elana's case immediately.

"Thanks, again."

"Not a problem. Elvin, Troy, and I go way back. It's an honor to be there for my friends."

Natalie gave her a forced smile as she saw her to the door. She'd always been under the assumption that Troy and Cheryl knew each other from work. What did "way back" mean and how did Elvin fit into the equation since he wasn't in law enforcement. Ultimately, Natalie convinced herself that such details were un-important. What mattered most was that Cheryl would help solve this case and bring her husband home.

"We wait..." B.K. had said to Troy at their last meeting, but Troy felt like he needed to be doing something. Yet, there was nothing he could do. He felt useless. Maybe he should have gone back with Natalie. Then again, he'd be in Columbus wondering if he should have stayed here.

After meeting with B.K. on Saturday, Troy came back to the house and spent hours reading the same reports and trying to make sense of the same unanswered questions only to end up with the same level of frustration as before when his efforts yielded no results. The next few days weren't any better. On New Year's Eve, Troy went over to Lilly's to hang out with Elvin and his family.

It was nice to see Lilly smile. Things were starting to heat up again between her and her second husband, Jeff. They had sur-passed the "were just friends" phase. Jeff was not shy about express-ing his feelings for her. He doted on Lilly and it was nice to hear her girlish laughter in the midst of so much heartache. Troy also learned that while Elvin, Nicole, and their boys had stayed overnight in Dallas after doing some sightseeing, Jeff had kept Lilly company. He wished he hadn't walked into the living room to see Lilly slip Jeff his red fleece blanket and boxers she'd washed to take out to his truck while everyone else was in the kitchen. They both smiled sheepishly. Troy shook his head. They thought he was playfully scolding them, but he was really trying to shake the visual from his mind. Troy's only concern was memories that Jeff had been abusive to Lilly in the past. Something she'd obviously forgiven him for and something he'd seemed to deeply regret.

As the day wore on, Jeff and Elvin pulled Troy to the side and asked how the investigation was going. "It's not." Troy felt like a failure. He wished he'd looked away before seeing the disappointment on El's face.

"It's okay, man. The fact that you're trying means a lot."

"I've known B.K. for over forty years," Jeff added after Elvin walked away. "He was a heck of a cop and he's an even better private investigator. From what Elvin tells me, you are a force to be reckoned with yourself. If the two of you together can't find answers, then there are none to be found."

"I don't want to give up."

"I know you don't. You also can't drive yourself insane. It's impossible to catch every bad guy. The important thing is that you are trying. I know that, Elvin knows, and most importantly so does Lilly. No matter what, she's going to be all right. I'm going to make sure of that." He patted Troy on the back before walking away and right into an embrace from Lilly. Troy could imagine Natalie saying something corny like, "they look cute together."

When Bill showed up, Troy was so angry that he wanted to grab him by the shoulders and shake him until he revealed everything he knew about Elana's disappearance. It sickened him how Bill smiled in Lilly's and Elvin's faces all the while possibly being the cause of their heartache. Troy regretted not sharing his suspicions of Bill with Elvin beforehand. At the time, he didn't want to drive a wedge between them without proof. Now desperate for answers, he didn't care. Troy would not "wait" for Bill and his attorney to meet with B.K. He was determined to get answers now. He took hold of Bill's arm and led him aside. "We need to talk."

"A-bou-bou-bout what?"

"Don't play stupid with me. What do you know about Elana?"

"This is neither the ti-ti-time or the pa-pa-pa-place." He tried to shake free of Troy's hand, but his grip was too strong.

"Everything okay?" asked Elvin who had apparently witnessed their interaction.

"No. Your uncle refuses to talk to B.K. without his attorney, which indicates that he knows something that could incriminate him."

"Is this true, Bill?"

"It's not wh-wh-wh-what you think."

"Then why won't you talk?" Elvin took over interrogating Bill, soon drawing the attention of Lilly and the rest of the family. Cornered, Bill broke down and confessed that he had been molesting Elana for years and thought that his actions could have possibly led to her running away. It was Jeff who pulled Elvin off of Bill after Bill had gotten every blow he deserved. Right or wrong, Troy would have let Elvin get a few more hits in.

"How could you?!" cried a horrified Lilly who also lunged at him. Jeff stopped her as well, ordering Nicole to take the boys upstairs.

"I'm sa-sa-sorry," Bill sobbed, dropping to the floor.

Troy stared at him with disgust. "At Elana's service, you said that she was dumped from the back of a truck. How would you know?"

"It wa-wa-was an as-suh-suh-sumption. I did not ki-ki-kidna-nap my niece or kill her. I luh-luh-loved her."

Jeff was across the room consoling Lilly. Luckily, Troy's reflexes had been quick enough to catch Elvin before he attacked Bill again. As much as Troy wanted to take his own foot and stomp on Bill's head, he was still a sworn officer of the law. He could not witness nor participate in a potential homicide. "I got this, man," he said to El, backing him away. Bill stayed curled up like a little coward. Troy seized him by the collar and dragged him all the way out the front door, giving him clear orders to stay away from Lilly and the family forever.

Poor Elana. Troy could only imagine the pain she suffered at the hands of both Herbert and Bill. Bill sickened him more than Herbert because he was someone Elana trusted. Troy wished even more now that he'd been kinder to her. Perhaps her attempt to get his and Elvin's attention had been a cry for help. If they had been nicer, maybe she would have eventually confided in them.

Deep down, Troy knew he was overanalyzing everything. After all, they were only children, how would they have known? Still, he wanted to do everything in his power now to help rectify any mistakes of his past. Troy stayed at Lilly's a few more hours until everyone had calmed down. Afterward, he spent the rest of the evening secluded in his room at his parents' until he called Natalie to wish her a Happy New Year. An hour later, he was downstairs with his parents as the clock struck twelve for the second time that night. Both times, he received text messages from *her.* Both times he deleted them with no reply.

On New Year's Day, Troy's mom busied herself in the kitchen making black-eyed peas, cabbage, and other "good luck" foods, and his dad announced that he was going to paint the other house.

"Okay, be back by six. Tracy and 'nem are comin' over for dinner."

Troy thought about going back over to Lilly's, but ultimately decided to give them time and space to deal with Bill's betrayal. With nothing except time to kill as he *waited* on a breakthrough, Troy offered to give his dad a hand.

"Uh, sure. I could use help."

Together, they rode over to the house that was once owned by Troy's grandparents. His dad had all the painting gear of a professional, having specialized in various areas of construction over the years. Little things started coming back to Troy's remembrance such as how his father had built a shed in the back yard, or how he had single-handedly turned their five-bedroom home into four bedrooms when he converted half of a spare room into a private bathroom for him and Troy's mom. The other half was used as a playroom for Tracy. His father had done a phenomenal job at making the restructuring appear like the natural layout. The man was good at his trade. Troy was dumfounded at how his father had allowed drinking to interfere with his family, but never his work.

"And you, fathers, do not provoke your children to wrath, but bring them up in the training and admonition of the Lord." Boy, did his father fall very short of carrying out the instructions in Ephesians 6:4! He'd provoked Troy to wrath on so many occasions throughout the years, especially when he was drunk and abusive to Troy's mom. And the man had not taught him one single thing about the Lord!

Troy was about to get himself all worked up about his dad's shortcomings until another passage of scripture came to mind. *"Let all bitterness, wrath, anger, clamor, and evil speaking be put away from you, with all malice. And be kind to one another, tenderhearted, forgiving one another, even as God in Christ forgave you."* Troy, too, had many shortcomings of his own and Ephesians 4:31-32 reminded him that because God had forgiven him, he had an obligation to forgive others. If he were into making New Year's Resolutions, one of them would be to review these verses any time residual bitterness toward his father crept up. However, making such a pledge was not necessary. The Holy Spirit would remind him, like He reminded him now.

When his father asked which room he would like to paint, Troy suggested that they start in the same one. His dad initially looked even more surprised than he had when Troy offered to come with him in the first place. Then, giving a wry smile, he tossed a paint roller Troy's way and jokingly told him not to make a mess.

Troy was on the west side of the living room and his father was on the east. Back-to-back they painted while listening to the radio. Troy hummed along to familiar tunes, thinking about the things he'd learned from B.K. about the Jewish holiday, Yom Kippur. *Day of Atonement... "It was the priest's responsibility to atone for the sins of the people,"* B.K. had said. Troy had unknowingly been assuming the role of the priest by carrying the entire burden about Elana on his shoulders. He was trying to make things right and sacrificing his wife's feelings during the process. Not anymore. No matter where things stood with Elana's case, he was going home in a week. Between B.K. and the Houston P.D., he was confident that Elana's kidnapper and killer would be brought to justice. His only prayer was that it did not take long. Lilly and Elvin had waited long enough.

"This is where your grandfather slept when he was alive," Troy's dad announced as they made their way to the master bedroom. "Do you remember much about him?"

"Not really." Troy did not spend much time with his father's side of the family. Besides having the knowledge that his grandfather suffered from dementia and Alzheimer's, Troy didn't have any memories—good, bad, or indifferent—about either of his paternal grandparents.

"He was a mean old buzzard. I guess you say the same thing about me, huh?"

Troy willed his lips to remain shut and instead got in position to get back to work. Both Natalie and his mom would be proud. Heck, he was proud of himself for his great verbal restraint.

"I'm really proud of you, son. I know I have never told you that. I've never told you much of anything, but for what it's worth, I am proud."

"Thanks." Troy wasn't necessarily elated by his father's accolades. He'd made some mistakes of his own and one of them kept texting him.

I NEED 2 TALK 2U! Plz call me.

She had to be out of her mind if she thought for a minute that he would willfully open up that line of communication again. He deleted that message like he had all her others. They painted that room and then one more before deciding to call it quits.

While his dad was busy rinsing out the rollers and brushes in the bathroom, Troy decided to give himself a tour of the house. "Why are you putting so much work into remodeling when you're going to turn around and sell the place?" The carpet had been pulled up in each room and many of the walls had been stripped. All of that did not seem necessary since the new owners would probably want to add their own aesthetic touch.

"The house needed it. I've spent so much time fixing up other places that I neglected this one. I don't think there have been any major improvements to this house since you were born. Plus, if it doesn't sell, I can use it as a rental property."

All the rooms were empty except for one that had a wooden

table with a few boxes and a doll house on top. His dad had not done a good job at removing the carpet in that room as slight traces of its reddish-like fiber remained on parts of the base board. Troy walked in to get a closer look at the doll house. It stood about three feet tall and two feet wide. It had been skillfully crafted by hand. No doubt his father's work.

Troy opened one of the boxes and found various girl toys and other items—Barbie dolls, doll clothes, play jewelry, and even a few cassette tapes.

"Uh, those are your sister's old things."

The voice of his father who was standing in the doorway startled him. Troy had not heard him come down the hall.

"I figured as much." Troy had always known that Tracy and his dad were a lot closer than he and his father were, but he did not realize the extent of the time she'd spent at this house. He continued looking through the box, pulling things out one by one.

"We better get going. Your mom is expecting us for dinner."

"You want me to grab this stuff for Tracy since she's coming over?"

"Oh, uh, no, that's okay. I already asked her and she doesn't want any of it. I'm going to donate it. I hadn't gotten around to it yet."

"Wow, I didn't know Tracy was into Duran Duran." Troy cracked up as he pulled out one of the cassettes found in the box by a popular rock group in the eighties. A name carving in the wood caught his attention. "Who's Maggie?"

"I don't know." His father rushed in and started repacking the items. "Your grandfather carved that name into several pieces of furniture."

Maggie... That name was starting to bother him. Herbert had mentioned it and now the name was etched into a wooden table found at the house where his father stayed. Coincidence or clue?

"Hey, last week I tried calling you to see what was going on with Tracy. She left me several urgent voice messages. Do you know what was wrong with her?"

"Have you spoken with your sister?"

"Yes, and she didn't tell me anything, but Natalie said that Tracy was at the house talking to you and that she was upset."

"Humph. I wouldn't worry about it. I'm sure Tracy has handled whatever was bothering her. We better go before your mom starts calling," his father stated after replacing all the items in the box. He'd missed the Duran Duran cassette Troy had in his hand. Troy slipped it into his pocket.

On the way back to the house, Troy remained silent, thinking about the revelation B.K. had shared with him during their last meeting. *"[Y]our dad was supposed to pick you up from Elvin's that morning..."* Troy hoped that there was nothing more to the story than simple coincidence as he read and then deleted another message from *her.*

Chapter 29: Patches of Red

When Troy and his father arrived back at the house, his mother was still cooking.

"Give me about forty, forty-five minutes at the most and everything will be done. Your sister should be on her way soon."

Instead of following in his father's footsteps and showering, Troy wanted to look over the case file again. He was becoming increasingly irritated with the barrage of calls he'd started getting. The text messages he could ignore, but the back-to-back phone calls had crossed over into harassment.

Stop ignoreN my cails! I need 2talk 2u!!!

They had nothing to discuss. She was hanging on to a past that they'd had together over two decades ago. One she'd tried to rekindle last summer that he'd buried and had long let go. He thought they could be friends until he found himself emotionally attracted to her during a time when he and Natalie were at odds. Nothing physical took place between them, though he's certain she would not have objected. She'd been very open about her desires. Realizing that the line to adultery was easier to cross than he thought, Troy had resisted temptation by ending all communication with her only to run in to her every now and again around town. He still wasn't certain that the meetings were coincidental, but they had fared off in frequency, so he wasn't concerned. Her texts had died off as well, except for lately.

Plz call me, Troy!

He could barely delete that text message before her next one came through.

It's abt Elana's case. I have info abt Maggie.

Against his better judgment, he took the bait.

"Happy New Year!" she answered cheerfully.

"I'm not in the mood, Cheryl. What's up?"

"Gee, you don't have to sound so mean. I heard you were still in Texas and working on a case. I called a few of my FBI friends to see if I could help. How was your Christmas?"

"You said you have information about Maggie. I'm giving you three seconds to tell me what you know about her or I'm hanging up."

"You really are in a bad mood, huh? For starters, Maggie is not a she, sweetheart. It's an organization." Cheryl dropped her flirtatious tone as she laid out the facts. M.A.G.G.I.E., an underground child pornography ring, stood for Men and Girls Getting Intimate Everywhere. "The FBI has been trying to infiltrate them for years. It's an organization that has existed for decades and it's estimated that nearly a hundred thousand missing children have been abducted by members of the group nationwide. It's one of the largest child pornography operations known to date with perhaps a million or more members."

"So why haven't your people been able to shut it down?"

Cheryl explained that M.A.G.G.I.E. brought with it a lot of complications due to its size and secrecy. "You have to understand that this isn't some fly-by-night group of pervs. Members of M.A.G.G.I.E. range from low-lives to politicians and everything in between. Those on the lower end tend to get caught, but they have not been able to provide enough intel to bring the whole organization down."

"Okay, so send someone in undercover."

She sighed, her tone signaling her irritation by his questioning. "It's not that simple. Most people in child pornography rings get busted because they share pictures with undercover agents or download stuff at their jobs. It's easy for an agent to go undercover to solicit information. M.A.G.G.I.E. is different. Before one is even privy to the group's ins and outs, it's rumored that he must submit incriminating evidence of himself in a sex act with a minor child. Obviously, no agent can do this. Like I said, some members of this group have power. We're talking police officers, judges, attorneys, there's no end. It's basically human trafficking. They abduct young girls and share them. Some they kill, some they let go, some they keep. It's possible that Elana was taken by someone from this group. Even when members outgrow their fetish for young girls, many of them have families and reputations at stake, so they still won't talk."

"This is crazy. There has to be some way to stop these people instead of letting them continue to hurt young girls. Any leads on Elana's abductor?"

"No. Chances are, it's someone close to the family."

Duh? He already knew that.

"I'm afraid I don't have any more information. My contact has been in touch with the local P.D. trying to verify if there is a connection with Elana's case and M.A.G.G.I.E. I'm surprised you didn't know this since you're working closely with them."

"I'm actually working with a private investigator." Even as Troy spoke the words aloud, he wondered if this was yet another piece of information that B.K. had kept from him. "Thanks for your help. I appreciate it."

"Anytime. I'm always here for you whenever you want me."

He ignored her sexual innuendo. "Hey, how did you know I was working on this case?" He thought about the message he'd gotten from her on Christmas morning. "How'd you know I was in Texas at all?"

She giggled. "I have my ways of learning your whereabouts. I found out about the case, though, from your wife. She called me on your behalf. I take it you've never told her about us. If I were her, I wouldn't be calling the woman my husband has slept with for help."

Immediately, Troy's anger went from zero to sixty. "I told you to stay away from my wife!"

Cheryl laughed wickedly. "Relax. She's not the one I want," she said before hanging up.

Troy decided not to call Natalie while in a rage about Cheryl. He did not want to worry her. Instead he sent a text simply to say he loved her and sighed with relief when her reply came back seconds later. Now was not the time to explain his history with Cheryl. That would be one of the first things he did upon returning home.

Tracy did not show up for dinner. She called their mom to say that the kids were still with their friends and that Al wasn't feeling well, which Troy deciphered as code for he'd gotten drunk last night and was still hung over.

Troy was relieved that Tracy wasn't there though he was eager to talk to her and verify their father's story about the items that supposedly belonged to her. He would go by there in the morning. No, he changed his mind. He'd call to see if Al was at work, *then* he would go by there.

Dinner was awkward with only Troy and his parents. His mom was elated that he and his dad had spent time together. "Did you guys get a lot done?"

"Yeah. There are only two more bedrooms left to paint. I do appreciate your help, son." He smiled and Troy forced the return gesture.

His mom began talking nonstop about so many other things that Troy started to tune her out. He saw her lips moving, but he only heard B.K.'s voice. *"[Y]our dad was supposed to pick you up from Elvin's that morning…"* Then there were the patches of red carpet. Could those be a match to the red fibers that had been found on Elana's body? What about the red-haired doll he'd discovered last week in the trash can outside of his grandparents' house. Was that the Strawberry Shortcake doll that Elana had carried out with her? And what about the inscription on the wooden table? Is it possible that his father was a member of M.A.G.G.I.E.?

There was a sickening feeling in the pit of Troy's stomach. A numbing that kept him from eating much, especially the black-eyed peas his mom swore would bring good luck if only he would take a bite. "I'm not hungry."

"Seems like you would have worked up an appetite. You guys were gone a long time."

"It's been a while since I've painted. I think the fumes may have gotten to me a bit. I need some fresh air and water. You want to go for a walk?"

Troy hoped to get his mom out of the house. If what he was thinking was true, his father was a very dangerous man and Troy wanted to make sure his mom was safe.

"Yes. I think it would be fun if we all go for a walk. What do you think, Reed?"

Troy cut in before his father could answer. "Uh, I was actually hoping that you and I could go. I need some female advice about a situation with Natalie. No offense, Dad, but I doubt you know how to think like a woman."

"You're right about that. They are too emotional for me. Y'all go ahead. I'm tired anyhow. I'm going to sit back and see if I can catch a game."

"All right. Let me put on some tennis shoes and I'll meet you out front. If you and Natalie got into an argument again about you stayin' here, I'm tellin' you up front that I'm on her side."

Silence fell over the room when his mom left. Troy stared at his father trying to wrap his mind around the possibility that he could be a member of M.A.G.G.I.E.

"Is everything okay, Troy? You've been real quiet since we've left the other house."

"Where are all the guns you used to have?"

"I got rid of them years ago except for three. They are locked up in our room."

Instead of asking what kinds, Troy chose another angle. "Why didn't you come pick me up the day Elana went missing?"

He shifted uncomfortably. "I...um, I don't remember."

"But you knew you were supposed to get me, right, because you got Mama's message?"

"I, uh, it was so long ago. Why the sudden interest?"

"There's been a break in the case." Troy watched as his father's look changed from discomfort to fear.

"I'm ready." Troy's mom came bouncing back into the living room, oblivious of the tense atmosphere.

Troy hurried himself and her out the front door. "Get in," he ordered after using the key chain to unlock the doors and deactivate the car alarm.

"I thought you wanted to go for a walk."

"Get in the car!" he yelled.

Chapter 30: Many Layers

"What in the world is goin' on with you? And slow down before you get into a wreck!"

"Call Tracy and tell her we're on our way to pick her up. There's something I need to share with you both. Mama, don't look at me like that, just do it!"

She obeyed, mumbling under her breath that he was acting like a lunatic. When they got to Tracy's, Troy laid on the horn until she came outside. Like he did with their mom, Troy ordered her to get in the car. Tracy did so with little to no resistance, but only after going back inside her home to let Al know she was leaving.

"What's going on, Troy?" He ignored her, driving to a nearby residential area to park.

"Is this yours?" He tossed the Duran Duran cassette to her.

"Nuh-o."

"I didn't think so. I found this and a bunch of other girl things in a box at Dad's other house. He said they were yours and he was going to donate them because you said you didn't want them."

"He lied."

"Troy, what is this all about?" his mother pleaded.

"Why didn't you ever tell me that Dad was supposed to pick me up from Elvin's that day?"

"I see either the detective or Natalie don't know how to keep their big mouth shut! I didn't think it was necessary to tell you, seein' that you already hated your dad."

Troy would try to forget that this was yet another thing his wife had withheld from him. He had a secret of his own named Cheryl. "I think Dad is the one who kidnapped Elana."

His mom snickered. "That's ludicrous. Your father is many things, but he's not a kidnapper or a killer."

"I think Troy's right." Tracy's voice was soft, but certain as she began laying out the details that led her to the same conclusion. "You guys kept talking about how distinct her birth mark was and when I saw pictures of it in Elana's obituary, I remembered seeing it before on the lady I told you was at dad's house that time when I ran away. I asked him about her and he tried convincing me that I was mistaken. Everything happened so quickly, he said that I could not have gotten a clear look at her."

"Is that why you were calling me the other day?"

"Yeah, but I started second-guessing myself after talking to him. Then, when you came by the house and said there were suspects, I figured maybe I was wrong."

"Y'all are crazy! Your father would not do this."

"Don't you see, Mama? It all makes sense." Troy shared his entire theory, sparing them the details that he had learned about M.A.G.G.I.E. Troy's grandfather passed away when he was in high school and his grandmother way before that and yet his father had kept the house all this time. "What other reason did he have to keep the house if it weren't to have somewhere for Elana to stay? He specifically told me those things were Tracy's. Why would he lie?"

Troy checked his incoming text message. He shook his head at the contents of the message as his mother continued to defend her husband.

"He didn't have the house for Elana; he had it for his whores. I've told you that plenty of times. I don't know why he lied and I don't care. I know in my heart that your father would not do *anything* to harm a child."

"If that's true, why did I just get a text message from B.K. saying that Dad is at the police station right now making a statement?"

Troy took Tracy back home and dropped his mom off at the station. She was insistent on being by his father's side and getting to the bottom of what was going on. Troy was more concerned about the impact this would have on Elvin and Lilly and planned to meet B.K. there in order to break the news. On his way, he called Natalie to update her on the situation. Again, he left out the details about M.A.G.G.I.E.

"I'm so sorry, honey. If I thought the information Diane shared about Reed was important, I would have told you." He did not have the strength to be upset with her. "I know you're concerned about everyone else, but I'm concerned about you. How do you feel?"

"Numb." Troy didn't feel devastation or rage; he felt nothing. "And foolish." B.K. had warned him that he was too close to the situation and would miss something.

"You're not foolish. No one could have known that Reed was responsible. This is not your fault." Natalie continued giving him a pep talk all the way to Lilly's house. Troy didn't comprehend everything she was saying as his mind was preoccupied. He simply wanted to hear her voice. He would have loved to talk to Nate as well except lil' man was still with his big sister.

"Babe, I'm here. I have to go."

"Okay. I love you, honey."

"I love you, too." Despite not seeing B.K.'s vehicle, Troy got out of the car. Of all the victims' families that he'd delivered bad news to, this was by far the most dreadful. How would he look in the eye of his best friend and someone who was like a mother to him during childhood and admit that his father had been the cause of all their misery these last thirty years? The anger toward his father finally began to surface with each step Troy made to the door. He was equally upset, if not more, with his mother. She'd held the key to Elana's mystery. She'd protected that monster then and chose to do so now because, instead of coming to be with the Campbell family, she chose to be with him. Troy said a prayer asking God for strength, then knocked twice and walked in as was his custom.

Lilly and Jeff weren't quick enough in separating when the door swung open and Troy witnessed the tail end of their kiss. "I'm sorry, I—"

"Don't be. You know you're welcome any time." She blushed from embarrassment and Troy's heart pounded even faster after seeing the happiness in her eyes. He hated to take that away from her. "You okay, sweetheart?"

"I, uh, I need to talk to you and Elvin. There's been a break in Elana's case."

"*Elvin!*" Lilly yelled, grabbing hold of Jeff's hand. "Come here!"

Within seconds, Elvin ran down the stairs. "Hey, man, what's up? I didn't know you were coming by. I'm upstairs playing the game with the boys. You want to get on?"

Troy repeated the statement he'd spoken to Lilly. Elvin slowly backed up and took a seat on the other side of his mom. "There's no easy way to tell you this…um, my father was the one who kidnapped Elana and held her captive all these years." Troy explained to them how he had come to that conclusion. "He turned himself in tonight." His throat tightened as he fought back tears, standing frozen while watching Lilly cry into Jeff's arms. "I thought you guys deserved to hear it from me. I'm sorry. I didn't know until tonight."

"Don't blame yourself." Elvin was the first to speak. "It's not your fault, man. We were prepared for the possibility that someone in our family did this and after what we learned about Bill, it could have easily been him. Don't think this changes anything between us. You're still my brother."

Lilly was too emotional to talk, but she motioned for Troy to come over to her. When he did, she gave him a long hug and a kiss. "Thank you," she eventually said. "We finally have answers."

"Not so fast." They all turned around to see B.K. standing at the door. "Troy, according to your father's statement, he did not kidnap Elana. He admits to giving her a ride that day, but said that she eventually got in a car with someone else. I don't have all the details yet, but a buddy of mine said your dad has given the police permission to search your grandparents' house and that someone else has claimed ownership of the items you discovered. He's also voluntarily agreed to submit a DNA sample."

"I don't understand. He lied and said they were my sister's."

"There are many layers to this story and I think your father needs to be the one to explain them. He's still at the station, but I doubt he will be charged. Like I said, I don't have all the details, but my friend said your father is adamant that Elana got in a car with someone else."

"Does he know who?" asked Jeff.

"I'm not sure. Last I heard, he wanted to talk to his attorney before revealing any more details."

"This is so crazy. Lilly's emotions have been up and down with all these new revelations. I think she needs a break from all of this." Jeff turned to Lilly. "How about I take you away for a few days to clear your mind?"

"I don't know." She looked at Elvin. "You think that's a good idea? I don't want to leave you alone."

"Don't you worry about me; I'll be fine. I think it might do you some good to get away and rest. I'll call if we get any concrete information."

Lilly's sigh of relief was proof that she really wanted, perhaps needed, the reprieve. "I guess I better get packing. Does this mean I'll finally get to see your place?"

"Possibly," he answered coyly. "Or, maybe we'll drive until we run out of gas and see where we end up."

Lilly smiled and went upstairs.

"Thanks for everything you're doing for my mom. Actually, thank all of you. This has been a trying time and we would not be able to get through it without your support." Elvin was clearly overcome with emotion. It could be heard in his voice even if not seen by his eyes.

They men continued talking until Lilly came down. She kissed and hugged everyone goodbye. When she and Jeff left, B.K. stayed and talked with Troy and Elvin. Troy had a lot of questions about what happened with his father that either B.K. truly didn't know or didn't want to answer. Troy was baffled. He was sure that all the evidence pointed to his dad. "What do we do now?"

B.K. looked directly at Troy with a smirk as he repeated the words he was now becoming infamous for. "We wait…"

Chapter 31: Dire Circumstances

*N*atalie got off the phone with Troy and did the only thing she knew how to do for her husband at that moment. She prayed. Lately, Philippians 4:7 seemed to be a go to scripture for her during times of trouble. *"And the peace of God, which passeth all understanding shall keep your hearts and minds through Christ Jesus."* It was what she prayed over her husband, mother-in-law, and the entire Campbell family. This was a crazy situation if she'd ever seen one and everyone involved needed peace in the midst of this storm.

It was nearly one o'clock in the morning now and hours had passed since she'd last heard from Troy. She wanted to text him simply to let him know she was thinking of him, but she also wanted to give him the space to process things. She knew he'd contact her when he was ready. As much as she missed him, she would not give him any grief about coming home. Between Corrine and Aneetra, she'd have help dealing with Nate if single-parenting became too overwhelming. Diane would need Troy more than she would for the time-being.

Natalie awoke the next morning to a call from her mother-in-law. "Hey, Di."

"Have you spoken with Troy?"

"Yes. He called me last night and filled me in on things. Are you okay?"

Diane blew out a deep breath. "I can't necessarily say I'm okay, but I'm doin'. Troy didn't come back to the house last night and I'm tryin' to get in touch with him. Contrary to what he told you, Reed did not kidnap or kill Elana."

Natalie remained quiet. Troy had already informed her about how Diane was refusing to come to grips with the facts. On one hand, Natalie thought Diane was being foolish. Similar to the likes of Dottie Sandusky who refused to believe her husband, former Penn State coach, Jerry Sandusky, was guilty of child molestation despite the clear and convincing evidence, Diane seemed blinded to truth. On the other hand, Natalie could not fault any wife for standing by her man. She would do the same for Troy no matter what so-called facts others had against him. Then again, there were no suspicious circumstances to cause Natalie to question Troy's character. He never hit her like Reed had done to Diane and he never showered with young boys as Jerry Sandusky had admitted to doing. Natalie wasn't going to argue with Diane about Reed's guilt or innocence. To her mother-in-law's statement, she said nothing.

"There's a lot more to the story than Troy knows. Reed and his attorney are here and Tracy's on her way. There are some things Troy needs to hear." When Di's voice cracked, Natalie knew the situation was serious. Without any additional prompting, Diane gave Natalie a run down of the secret Reed had been keeping from her all these years and his encounter with Elana.

Natalie was relieved that he was not having an affair as she had suspected and that his relationship with Jesus had not been a front. Reed was sincere about his love for Christ and being a better person from here on out. "I'll call Troy and see if I can convince him to come over there."

"I think it would be better for him to hear everything from Reed."

"I agree. Is there anything else I can do?"

"Yes…pray."

Troy did not get any sleep last night despite being mentally and physically exhausted. He'd spent the morning ignoring phone calls from his mother and text messages from Cheryl to see how things were going. The only reason he did not turn his phone off was because he was waiting to hear from B.K. They'd compared notes last night and Troy learned, as expected, that B.K. had already known about M.A.G.G.I.E.

"I was hesitant to tell you too much because I wasn't sure about your dad's involvement. I needed to investigate some things on my own," B.K. admitted. Troy didn't harbor any hard feelings. He understood. Initially, Elvin wasn't as forgiving when B.K. finally told him about Elana having given birth. El had asked Troy if he'd known. Before Troy could answer, B.K. interjected, taking all the blame.

Eventually, Elvin came around and, for the same reasons B.K. did not tell him, Elvin would not tell Lilly. "I don't think she can handle another bombshell at the moment." The three of them talked well into the night until there were no words left to be said, only determination from all three to get down to the bottom of what had happened to Elana from August 1982 until the day her body was discovered.

Today was the day B.K. was supposed to meet with Bill and his attorney. After the fallout with Bill on New Year's Eve, neither B.K nor Troy was certain that Bill would still show. Even if he did, Troy did not want to sit in on the meeting. If the only thing Bill was going to do was ease his conscience about molesting Elana, he would be another dead end in terms of providing clues about the day she disappeared. Besides, Troy was still convinced that his father was guilty and that the only reason his dad allowed a search of the property was because he knew no further evidence could be found. He'd completely gutted the place, removing all traces of Elana's existence.

But, why would a guilty man voluntarily give up his DNA? Troy came to two conclusions: Either his father was planning to skip town during the time it would take the techs to make a comparison or he had an accomplice, perhaps another member of M.A.G.G.I.E. and the DNA found on Elana's body belonged to that person. "Hey, babe." Troy was relieved to see a call from his wife instead of his mother.

"Where are you?"

"At Lilly's. I crashed on her couch."

"Where's everyone else?"

"El, Nikki, and the boys are all upstairs still. Jeff took Lilly away for a few days so she could get a break from all this craziness."

"That's good. I need you to go to your parents' house. Your mom called me and there are some things going on that you should be aware of. Tracy and his attorney will be there as well."

"Natalie, my dad is guilty. Don't be bamboozled like my mom."

"Listen to me, Troy. Things are not how they seem. You need to go over there ASAP."

"What are you not telling me? I don't like all the secrets you've been keeping from me lately. I found out last night that you knew Dad was supposed to pick me up from over here that day."

"And I told you that I'm sorry. Now *please* go to your parents'.

It's important and I don't think it's my place to fill you in. Please go."

There was a desperation in her voice that he could not ignore. He could picture those big brown eyes pleading with him. Reluctantly, he agreed. On the way to the house, he kept talking to himself, willing himself to be calm no matter what his father said. Any progress they had made in terms of their relationship had been undone and was beyond repair now that Troy suspected his involvement in Elana's disappearance.

Tracy's car and another were in the driveway when he pulled up. Again, he prayed for strength. This time he added wisdom and restraint as he wanted to make it back to Ohio to see his family instead of being a permanent inmate in Harris County. He followed the voices into the dining room and one of the four people waiting for him stood up. *"Salome?"*

"Hello, Troy. I wish we didn't have to keep meeting under dire circumstances. I'm Reed's attorney." She held out her hand. He left her hanging. She was dressed more professionally this time.

"Elana was your friend. Why would you get involved?"

"Because…" Salome looked around the room and then back at Troy. "Reed is my father."

Chapter 32: Safe and Sound

"$\mathcal{I}$ know you have a lot of questions and there will be a time and place for them," Salome spoke matter-of-factly. "Right now, the goal is to find out what really happened to Elana and clear Reed from all suspicion. I'm the person whom Tracy saw years ago when she came over to the house. Like I told you at the wake, I have a tattoo that is similar to Elana's birthmark. Stupid idea? Maybe. At the time I was paying homage to a missing friend. The items you found in the house belonged to me. I lived there for a while with Reed, not Elana."

The weight of information overload made Troy dizzy and caused his knees to go weak. He grabbed hold of one of the dining room chairs and managed to have a seat before falling. Both Tracy and his mother had blank expressions. His father kept his head down in shame.

"Despite what you may think or feel, your father, *our* father, is not responsible for kidnapping Elana. He did see her that day and his mistake is not being forthcoming with what he knew. Reed, tell Troy everything you told me and the police at the station."

With his head still hung low, his dad began.

"I'd gotten your mother's message asking me to pick you up from Elvin's. Since I had to drop some money off to Raquel anyway—"

"That was my mom's name in case you don't remember," added Salome.

"I figured it would be no big deal to pick you up. I had some drinks while I was there. I knew your mom was aware of my relationship with Raquel and I was afraid that if I took too long getting you, she might come by and cause a scene. Raquel and I had messed around off and on since your mother and I got married. I knew Salome was my daughter and I took care of her financially, but we decided not to tell her."

"Yeah, my mom didn't want me to be burdened with the knowledge of being a love child. I found out after Elana went missing because I overheard my mom and Reed arguing. He was adamant about moving us out of that neighborhood after what had happened."

"Anyhow, Raquel tried to get me to stay and sleep off the alcohol, but I left to get you. As soon as I pulled in front of the house, Elana came up to the window with tears in her eyes."

"Troy was being mean to me. Him and my brother both, so if he asks you to buy him a push pop you can't 'cuz my mama said they had to be good to get one and they weren't being good 'cuz they were being mean to me."

Reed laughed at how eager she was to tell on the boys. She always informed him about Troy's behavior toward her whenever they saw each other at Raquel's. Elana had pegged him as Troy's father before he had known who she was, stating that she'd overheard conversations about him between her mom and Diane. Reed didn't ask for details. "I promise I won't buy him a push pop or anything else today, okay? Will that make you feel better?"

Elana nodded affirmatively. "I want a push pop and Mama is taking too long to come back. Will you take me to get one? I have some money." *She pulled eighty-five cents from her pocket to show him.*

Reed had a soft spot for little girls. He thought about his own daughters and how they oftentimes melted his heart. Elana was so darn cute the

way she pleaded with him. If he could make her day by buying her a
push pop, why not? He'd plan to stop at the convenience store for beer any-
how. He'd go now and come back to get Troy. "I'll buy it for you. Hop in."

It only took them minutes to get there. As they were headed into the
store, Reed realized that he'd left his wallet. "I forgot my money in the
car. Go in and get what you need and I'll meet you at the register."

"Okay." Elana bounced away. It was amazing how fast her tears had
dried up.

Reed got his wallet and upon entering the store, headed to the cooler
for beer. It took a while for him to decide what he wanted. Ultimately,
he bought a six-pack and went up front. There was no sign of Elana.

The small convenience store was no bigger than a 7-Eleven, so Elana
could not have gone far. Reed walked around the shop thinking that
perhaps she went in another aisle as a kid would sometimes do. Still no
Elana. The clerk was no help. He had been looking at a magazine instead
of paying attention as customers came in and out. Nervous, Reed decided
to see if she'd gone outside. He walked out the door just in time to see
Elana riding away in a cop car waving to him and holding what he
assumed was her push pop. Relieved that she was safe and sound, Reed
went back in, got his beer, and decided to go to his father's.

Troy was having a hard time understanding his dad's version of
events. "That doesn't make sense. Why didn't you come back to
Lilly's?"

"I figured Elana had gotten scared when I didn't come up front
right away and went to the officer for help and he took her home.
I knew what happened would get back to your mom. She was
always fussing about me not picking you up. I wasn't doing it that
day out of the goodness of my heart. I was actually trying to shut
her up. I knew after she'd found out about the cop taking Elana
home, I would not hear the end of it, especially since I'd been

drinking. It was a couple days before I learned that Elana had disappeared. I was scared to tell anyone what happened because I didn't want to get blamed for doing anything to her. The last I knew she was safe in the hands of law enforcement. If that officer did something to her, no one would ever believe me because I was a drunk. I couldn't risk losing everything. I had to take care of all of you, and my dad."

When Troy's father lifted his head, he didn't have to say the words "I'm sorry" out loud for Troy to hear. They were written all over his face. His bloodshot eyes and tear-stained cheeks, the sadness of his countenance, said it all. He hadn't slept either. There was a part of Troy that was still angry with him for the simple fact that he'd kept this information and Salome a secret. There was also a part that felt sorry for him and the weight he must have carried. Overall, Troy was relieved to have some kind of explanation though there were still many pieces of the puzzle still missing.

"Did you get a description of the officer?"

"No, I didn't. I've hated myself for the last thirty years for not speaking up. Maybe if I'd done so sooner or if I had even thought to follow them back to the house, none of this would ever be."

"What do you know about M.A.G.G.I.E.?"

"Nothing. I swear. Every now and again, your grandfather would randomly yell that name. Like I told you before, he also carved it into a few pieces of furniture. I think it was his conscience getting to him. I found pictures of your grandfather doing things to a little girl. Bad things. I don't know who she was and I would have turned him in, but by that time he'd started to deteriorate mentally and as horrible as those pictures were, I did not want my elderly sick father to spend his last years in prison. I was his only son and he was my responsibility. I burned them and stayed at that house to care for him until he died. The best thing I could do to protect my own children is not have you guys around him."

"Dad, M.A.G.G.I.E. is not a person." He shared with his family everything he had learned from Cheryl. "Do you think it's possible that granddad could have been involved?"

"I would like to say no simply because I'd hate to think that my father could be that cruel. Then again, I never expected to find pictures of him molesting a little girl. I guess the answer to your question is that I honestly don't know."

"If what you say about M.A.G.G.I.E. is true, that's horrible. However, that's not our concern right now and we need to leave that to the FBI." Salome was blunt. "My goal is to keep Reed out of jail. He's turned over every gun he owns and we are certain that there won't be a match to the one that killed Elana. I'm not sure how much his statement will help in the case, though. Unfortunately, the convenience store was torn down a long time ago. At least fifteen years, if not more."

Troy's mom and Tracy had been so quiet that he'd almost forgotten they were there. His mom looked as if she was trying to hold it together emotionally and Tracy looked frozen, like she was still trying to digest everything. She looked peaceful though. No longer wrestling with their father's guilt. She seemed certain that Salome had been the person she had seen at the house. With one mystery solved, a bigger one still remained.

Chapter 33: Prized Possession

Instead of waiting for B.K.'s police friend to pass along Troy's father's version of events, Troy thought it would be best to have his dad talk to B.K. directly. Together, they rode to the investigator's office. His father sobbed and apologized along the way. Troy didn't have the words to console him. He simply reminded his dad that everyone made mistakes and that it was good to have everything in the open now.

B.K. was in the lobby waiting for them when they arrived. There was no formal introduction between the two men. They said "hello" to each other and then B.K. got right to business. "By the way, I won't be meeting with Bill," he announced as they walked back to his office. "I have been informed that he went to the FBI and confessed to being a former member of M.A.G.G.I.E. He's in their custody now and will hopefully be able to help the feds bring down that organization once and for all."

Troy wasn't as optimistic. Bill was the maintenance man for an apartment complex. Based on what Cheryl had said about members of M.A.G.G.I.E., Bill wasn't powerful enough to have a significant impact in its destruction.

"I also heard from Edgar Campbell regarding the adoption," Bill continued, "Turns out, the baby is biologically his. He had an affair with someone he claims he didn't know was a minor. To cover things up, he paid the family to keep quiet and he and his wife adopted the child. I don't think she knows he's the father, which is why he was so nervous when I inquired about the adoption. Anyhow, I told him that if he could somehow corroborate the story, I would not keep pressing. Overall, Edgar has been a deadbeat father who claims he wants to do right by this last child. Now to the issue at hand." He turned his attention to Troy's father. "Thanks for coming. Let's cut to the chase. Tell me everything that you've told Troy."

Once again, his dad repeated the events of that fateful August day.

"Did you get a description of the officer?"

"No."

B.K. looked solemnly at Troy. "This doesn't give us much. Maybe I can get him in with Shauna. Otherwise, the best we can do is try to track down the clerk who was working that day. It'll be like finding a needle in a haystack, but who knows, we might get lucky."

"I'm only going to be here a few more days." Even as he spoke, Troy felt defeated. He hated leaving loose ends. "Tell me what you need from me and I'll get on it immediately. The way I see it, we have two possible theories. A, the officer took Elana back home and someone else got her or B, the officer is the one who abducted her. As much as it disgusts me, I'm inclined to believe the second theory because I would think that any cop who brings a lost girl home would want to have a word with her parents. Elana was not friendly to strangers, but she would have gone with a police officer. In those days kids were taught to trust cops and firefighters, so it doesn't surprise me that she would get in the car so easily with one."

"What if the cop was someone she knew?" B.K.'s eyes met with Troy's. Each man read the other's mind as the answer became painfully clear.

"Jeff!" they said in unison.

B.K. wasted no time calling his buddies on the force while Troy contacted Elvin. "Have you heard from Lilly?"

"No. I've called her and Jeff a couple of times to check on them, but I got their voicemails."

"Do you have any idea where they went?"

"No. I'm guessing maybe over Jeff's. I know Mama was eager to see his place for the first time. I would go by there if I knew where he lived. Is everything okay?"

"Keep trying them. If you get ahold of either of them, tell them that my dad has confessed and that Lilly needs to come to the station to identify Elana's clothing." Elvin had a lot of questions that Troy did not want to answer over the phone. "Just do it and I'll explain when I get there. I'm on my way." Blaming his father was a ploy to buy them some time and hopefully avoid tipping Jeff off.

Lilly and Jeff had been divorced by the time Troy's father had discovered that his mistress lived in the same neighborhood as Troy's best friend. Troy distinctly remembered Salome being with Elvin, Elana, and him on several occasions when Jeff gave them rides in his patrol car. His dad hadn't been aware that Lilly's ex was a police officer and somehow he'd missed or had been too drunk to recall hearing stories about the joyrides, which was why he never put two and two together.

"I'm sorry, son," his father said as Troy raced over to Lilly's. "I wish I would have gone back to the house to make sure she'd gotten home safely."

"We all could have done things differently," Troy replied. When he turned down Lilly's street, he was initially excited to see Jeff's truck outside until he remembered that Jeff and Lilly had taken Lilly's car last night. Elvin's confusion was apparent seeing Troy accompanied by his father. When Troy explained what he and B.K. believed happened, his best friend's expression turned to horror.

Troy left Elvin in the comforting arms of his wife, dropped his father off at home, got Jeff's address from B.K., and then met him at Jeff's home where the Houston P.D. were executing a search warrant.

"You can't be on the premises," an officer growled at him.

"He's with me," yelled B.K., quickly coming to Troy's defense.

"I don't care who you're with, stay out of the way," he said, giving Troy a once-over before walking away.

"They usually don't mind me lingering around as long as I don't touch anything. Many of the guys know me or know of me. Still, for legal reasons I'm not permitted inside, but I like to observe to see what's being carried out."

"Any word about Lilly or Jeff?"

"No." B.K. hung his head. "I think he knew the walls were closing in on him and that's why he wanted to get Lilly away."

"We all co-signed her leaving with him. I pray she's okay."

"How's Elvin?"

"Worried, but he's holding his own. Elvin's a strong man, but even the best of us have our breaking point. For his sake, I hope there's a happy ending to all of this somehow."

"Me, too. Normally, I don't take my cases personal, but I feel like a fool. Jeff played me. He got me on this case because he didn't think I would ever make the connection to him. And I didn't because I broke my own rule about everyone being a suspect until proven otherwise. Never once did I think Jeff would be involved. I didn't see this one coming, Troy."

"None of us did."

Like water boys sitting on the sidelines at a football game, Troy and B.K. watched as the officers did their due diligence. From the conversations taking place among those around them, Troy learned that there was a mountain of evidence inside pointing to Jeff's guilt as a member of M.A.G.G.I.E. and Elana's abductor and killer. One room had a bullet hole through the wall and Jeff had apparently done a sloppy job cleaning up the blood splatter. In addition, nude photographs were found of Elana and other girls of various ages. Jeff had a separate album for Elana filled with images from her youth to adulthood, decorated and marked with her name as a special memorabilia item. In some, she was bound and chained to a wall or bedposts. In others, she was performing lewd sexual acts. Troy didn't get a look at the photos, nor did he want to. The officers were descriptive enough during their exchanges with one another that he was able to get a clear picture. Elana was the only girl with a photo album to herself, which meant that she was probably his favorite, his prized possession and likely the one who suffered the most sexual abuse.

"I wonder if Bill knew about Jeff," Troy spoke his thoughts out loud.

"He was in FBI custody before you and your dad came to see me. I'm guessing he would have said something at that point, but who knows. Sickos like Bill and Jeff obviously don't make logical decisions."

Troy continued to ponder the possibility, ultimately dismissing the thought after the incident that took place at Lilly's on New Year's Eve. If Bill had been aware of Jeff's involvement, Troy was fairly certain that he would have said something when he turned himself in since it seemed like he's trying to right his past wrongs.

"Oh my gosh!" one officer yelled. Troy's eyes followed the direction of the scream into the garage where he could see a small item in a shoe box. It was the deteriorating corpse of a newborn, a baby girl, who had been killed by a single gunshot wound execution style, similar to Elana.

Her baby, Troy thought. As a homicide detective, he'd seen plenty of dead bodies before, even those of children, but this one knocked the wind out of him and Troy found himself grabbing hold of his knees, taking deep breaths.

"You all right?" asked B.K.

"I need to get out of here."

"Go ahead. I'll call you if I get any new information."

Troy sped out of the area, continuing to breathe slow and deep. The technique calmed his nerves. Of all the ways that Jeff could have killed that baby, shooting her in the head seemed excessively cruel and unusual, and pointed to the monstrous personality that Jeff had been good at masking from everyone around him. "God," he said aloud, "I don't understand why You allow some things to occur, but…," Troy took one more breath, "I will forever trust You."

This was a reminder to himself that, no matter how things turned out, he would not again turn his back on God. There was a time when Troy's heart had been hardened for a few years because of all the evil he'd witnessed through his job. Last summer, he'd rededicated his life to Christ and, though he was definitely a work in progress, Troy had committed to being a godly man. There was a lot he didn't get about life, but instead of turning against God, he turned to Him, reflecting on the words of Proverbs 3:5-6, *"Trust in the LORD with all thine heart; and lean not unto thine own understanding. In all thy ways acknowledge him, and he shall direct thy paths."* Now, if only the Lord would direct authorities to the whereabouts of Jeff and Lilly, all would be well.

Chapter 34: Chain of Events

Days passed with no word from Jeff or Lilly. An all-points bulletin had been issued with the license plate and description of Lilly's car. Troy had learned from B.K. about other disturbing things found in Jeff's home such as the blanket, which authorities believed had been used to wrap Elana's body before dumping it. The fibers from the fleece matched those that were found on her. It was the only red linen item discovered and Troy suspected it was the same one he'd seen Lilly giving back to Jeff the day he'd taken Natalie and Nate to the airport. Only someone with a sick and twisted mind would wrap his murder victim's body in a blanket, wash it, and then use it while staying the night with the victim's mother.

Neighbors of Jeff's were shocked to learn about the truth about the man many described as kind and caring. "He kept to himself," one woman said when interviewed by the local news, "but, he was the kind of person who would always greet you with a smile."

"I knew something was off over there," another woman stated. "His shades were always drawn and you never saw anyone but him go in and out of the house. I thought maybe he was, you know, liking the members of his same team and trying to keep it on the low." Others had various opinions of him. Some were negative, most were good. The one thing they all had in common was their disbelief that someone was held captive in their neighbor-hood for thirty years without them having any inclination.

Troy learned that there were several journals, thought to be Elana's, recovered from the premises. Elvin was eager to get his hands on those, but they needed to be retained to use as evidence if the case went to trial. Hopefully, Jeff would do the decent thing and plead guilty in order to spare Lilly and Elvin the burden of reliving Elana's kidnapping and sexual exploitations in court.

Though there were many unresolved feelings and much heal-ing that still needed to take place within Troy's own family, their issues had been set aside for the time being. Troy, his mom, dad, sister, and Salome all came together in support of a very concerned Elvin who was doing everything he could to remain optimistic. It was getting harder for everyone to do so as the days continued to pass. Cheryl's relentlessness in attempting to talk to Troy wasn't making the situation any easier. There was nothing else she could do for him and he finally resorted to blocking her number until he got back home and could properly handle things.

Upon learning the latest developments in the case, Natalie had encouraged Troy to stay as long as Elvin needed him. Nearly a week after Jeff had been fingered for the crimes, Troy was at the house with his friend when authorities came knocking.

Natalie had stopped trying to make sense of life a long time ago. As she boarded her flight headed to Texas she again prayed Philippians 4:17, asking God to grant Elvin and his family peace in the middle of this heart-breaking situation. Thanks to Aneetra and Corrine, Natalie was able to fly solo. The two of them were sharing the responsibility of caring for Nate while Natalie joined her husband in Houston. Troy didn't know she was coming, but he needed her. Even if he didn't, she needed to be there with him. If for no other reason than to let him know that she genuinely cared.

"*Natalie?*"

She looked up to see Agent Cheryl Hunter.

"I thought that was you! What a coincidence. You mind if I sit next to you?"

"No, not at all. You going to Houston as well?"

"Yeah. How could I not go to show my support after what happened? My heart goes out to Elvin for what he must be going through."

"I know. To bury his sister before Christmas and now to start off the New Year burying his mom…I can't imagine how he must be feeling." Natalie fought back tears as she recalled the pain in her husband's voice when he'd called her with the latest update. Lilly's car had been discovered off of I-45 not far from where Elana's body was found, but much deeper in the field. In an act of murder-suicide, Jeff had shot her and then killed himself the same night he and Lilly left the house. By the time Troy and the investigator had figured out he'd done it, they'd already been dead. "I wish Troy wouldn't be so hard on himself. He acts like the whole chain of events was his fault simply because when he accused his father, it set things in motion and his dad giving a statement probably spooked Jeff. I'm sorry. I'm telling you details you probably already know since you helped him with the case."

"Troy told you that?"

"No. He hasn't mentioned you at all. Thank you for not telling him that I'd contacted you. I didn't want him to be upset with me for interfering. In light of everything that has happened, I feel like I was so selfish."

Cheryl smiled. "You're welcome. And don't be too hard on

yourself. Your heart was in the right place. Is Troy picking you up from the airport?"

"No. He doesn't know I'm coming. My sister-in-law is going to get me and take me to the church."

"I'm renting a car when I get there. Why don't you ride with me?"

"Are you sure?"

"Natalie, Troy is one of my dearest friends. I've spoken to him every day since you first asked me to contact him. I know the toll this whole situation has taken on him. The least I can do is look out for his wife."

As the pilot asked the passengers to prepare for take-off, Natalie thought about Cheryl's words. Normally, she would not take so kindly to another woman telling her that she'd talked to Troy every day for the past week. Natalie hadn't even done that as there had been a couple of days when he simply wasn't in the mood to talk. She also understood that her husband would not easily ignore any business calls, especially ones from an FBI agent/friend who'd helped solve a case. The normal jealousy that she might have had over Cheryl and Troy's friendship was quickly squashed. "Thank you, Cheryl. I really appreciate you."

Chapter 35: Course of Action

*T*roy and his family stood outside the church with Elvin and other members of the Campbell family waiting to proceed inside. His parents and Tracy were both dressed in traditional black attire while Salome chose more vibrant colors, lavender and green bell bottoms with a flowery top to be exact. She seemed to use her off-duty-as-an-attorney hours to showcase the more eccentric side of her personality. It was also clear that she was good at her job as there were yet any charges to be filed against their father.

Salome seemed genuinely happy to be part of their family. Troy hadn't really had time to process the situation, but his mother and sister appeared to be doing well. He was especially proud of his mom, whom he'd expected would have cursed his father up one way and down another. When Troy asked her how she'd felt about learning of Salome after all this time, she reminded him that dwelling on the past would not do anything to strengthen their future. "Besides, my issue would not be with Salome. She had nothin' to do with it. My problem would be with Raquel and since that wench is dead, I no longer have a problem."

Troy was sure that, on some level, a psychologist would find his mother's comments disturbing. Still, he admired her resolve to make the best of the situation and enjoy whatever time she and his father had left together. He could not wait to get home to Natalie and Nate.

"Look who's coming your way," announced Tracy.

Troy's insides jumped with joy when he saw Natalie walking toward him. They knotted into a tumor when he spotted Cheryl behind her. "What are you doing here?" He was talking to Natalie, looking at Cheryl, wondering how they ended up together. He and Natalie embraced tightly as she explained that she was there to show her support and informed him of Nate's whereabouts without him asking.

"Cheryl and I happened to be on the same plane and she offered to bring me since we were both coming here so Tracy didn't have to pick me up. I'll need to get my bags out of her car when service is over."

"Well, don't I get a hug, Detective?"

Homicide had never been as strong of a thought as it was when he reached down to hug Cheryl, forcing himself to act normal. "Unless you want me to be the one to tell your wife about us, I suggest you unblock my number a-sap," she whispered viciously in his ear. She then introduced herself as his friend to Troy's parents and sisters in a sickeningly sweet manner. Afterward she thanked Natalie for keeping her company and made her way up front to speak to Elvin and his family before heading to the back of the line.

"Are you okay, honey? I hope you don't mind my being here."

Troy held her close. "Not at all. Thank you, babe. I needed you."

Atonement. That was the central message of the pastor's eulogy as he spoke about restoration, encouraging members of the Campbell family to unite in order to heal. Dysfunction had divided the family a long time ago and Bill's confession did not help rectify things. It caused an even bigger rift between the family members who stood by him and those who thought that he should be castrated and burned.

"Some things are unexplainable," said the pastor with tears streaming down his face. "Even if the perpetrator was here and we could ask him why he committed such heinous acts, nothing he said would make us feel better about the unnecessary pain that he has inflicted on this family. Elvin is a strong Christian man and it is his faith in God that is carrying him through this difficult journey. Jesus tells us in Matthew five that it rains on the unjust and the just. Sometimes, my dear brothers and sisters, when it rains, it doesn't just sprinkle, it pours. How many of you know that Jesus is a shelter in the time of a storm?"

"Amens" and "hallelujahs" flew to the pulpit.

"One of the things Elvin said to me is that though he doesn't understand this entire situation, he has peace in the midst of his pain. I can tell you that it wasn't anything I said that gave him peace. Lord knows that when I heard about what happened to Lilly, I did not have the words to say. As I prepared for today, the word atonement kept ringing in my spirit. For those who don't know, that word means to make reparations for a wrong or an injury. There's nothing we can do to make amends for what happened to Lilly or Elana. We can't even get justice through our legal system because of the cowardly way their offender chose to end things. But, what you *can* do is make sure that sin doesn't reign in your own lives. Back in the day, the priest was instructed to make yearly sacrifices in order to atone for the sins of Israel."

Troy caught B.K.'s eye and it was like they'd both relived the Yom Kippur conversation on the way to Hitchcock. The two of them had formed a bond these last several weeks and especially over the past few days as each man shared why he was burdened with guilt. Having been a friend of Jeff's for over forty years, B.K. felt that he'd been blindsided. When all was said and done, he refunded all the money that Elvin had paid to him. Troy and B.K. had to remind each other that ultimately Jeff was the only one responsible for what had happened to Elana and Lilly. They could not bear the weight of his actions on their shoulders, no matter what they could have or should have done differently.

"Hebrews ten explains how, when Jesus died on the cross, He became the final sacrifice. Yearly slaughter of animals was no longer necessary because the blood of Jesus took care of sin's debt once and for all. If you don't have a relationship with God, let today be your personal day of atonement. One day, it will rain in your life. Hopefully not in the same manner as it has rained in Elvin's, but rest assured, my dear friends, it *will* rain. If you want the peace during your storm like Elvin has during his, why don't you come now and make a decision to make Jesus your personal Lord and Savior."

There was not a dry eye in the place, including Troy's. He had set his macho image aside for a second and let the humanness of the situation settle on him and allowed the few tears that pooled in his eyes to drop. Troy leaned over to his mom. "If you want to walk up front, I'll go with you." He and his mom had not really had a conversation about salvation and he actually surprised himself by reaching out to her. The look she gave him in return indicated that if he did not change his course of action immediately, she would bless him with a speech that may very well get them both kicked out of church.

Troy kissed her on the cheek and chuckled to himself. As long as she remained resistant to changing her ways, he'd always have something to pray about.

Chapter 36: Free

The next day Troy stopped over to Lilly's to say goodbye to Elvin before he and Natalie flew back to Ohio.

"What time does your flight leave?"

"Not until seven thirty. Did Nicole and the boys make it home safely?"

"Yeah. I talked to Nik a few minutes before you got here. They're in school and she was busy working on a new catering order."

"How long do you plan to stay?"

"I don't know. The good thing about being a self-employed graphic designer is that I can work from anywhere. I'll probably leave sometime next week and come back at the end of the month. I need to figure out what to do with the house. I don't know whether to sell it or rent it. I want to do whatever Mama would want. Either way, there's some work that needs to be done on it."

"I'll text you my dad's number. I'm sure he'll do whatever you need."

Elvin smiled. "It's nice to see that something good has come from all of this. Witnessing how God is restoring and strengthening your family is amazing. You have no idea how much it blesses me."

"*You* are amazing." Troy looked at his friend with admiration, appreciative of the example he'd led of having unwavering faith. "I've learned a lot from you. More than you can ever know. Thank you."

"Is that a tear I see in your eye?" Elvin teased. "You going soft on me?"

Troy laughed. "Whatever." While he was overcome with emotion, he was not tearful. Lilly's funeral was the first time Elvin had ever seen him cry and even then, it wasn't a waterfall. Troy could have cried at Elana's service, but he was on duty at the time, scoping out the place for Elana's killer, painfully unaware that the culprit was literally right in front of him. Between the two of them, Elvin was the one unreserved when it came to showing such sentiment. "I'm not going to stay long. I came because I thought you might want these."

He handed Elvin the bag. "What are they?"

"Elana's journals. B.K. was able to get them somehow. Since Jeff is dead, they won't be needed for trial."

Elvin got one of the journals and leafed through it quickly and returned it to the bag. "Thanks, man, but will you hang on to them for me? I'm not ready to read these. If they're kept around I will be tempted and I'm sure Elana wrote some things that will be difficult to handle. I need to get a grip on my new normal before I can read about the pain my sister endured."

"I got you, man. I'll take them home with me and when you want them, let me know."

Troy and Elvin talked a little while longer. Troy hated to leave his friend alone, but his family was waiting on him. He and Natalie were going out to eat with his parents and sisters before their flight left. Troy invited Elvin.

"Naw, I'm cool, man. Thanks, anyhow. It's been a hectic few weeks. I don't want to do anything today but rest."

Troy said goodbye to his friend one last time and then left to meet up with his family.

June 12, 1989— My name is Elana Marie Campbell. Today is my fifteenth birthday. Jeff promised to give me a calendar each year so I will always know the date. I'm sad. I miss my mama and my brother. Sometimes I wonder if they remember me. Jeff says that they probably don't. He says that mama told him to bring me to his house that day and that she would pick me up later. She never came. At first, I hated her. I hated my brother and Troy, but now I know that Jeff did not tell me the truth. For my birthday, he brought home another little girl, named Karen. She's six. Jeff told her the same thing, that her mom told him to bring her here and would get her later. I know that's a lie because I heard him and some of his buddies talk about her being next. I wish I could tell her that everything will be okay, but I don't want to lie to her, too. I don't think she has been touched before like I have been by uncle Bill, Herbert, Jeff, and a bunch of Jeff's friends. I told Karen that everything they do to her will hurt at first, but eventually she will get used to it. I have.

"Maybe you should follow Elvin's lead," said Natalie who sat beside Troy on the plane. "I can tell by your face that you don't like what you're reading."

She was probably right, but Troy flipped through to another entry anyhow.

February 5, 1993—Jeff sold Karen yesterday. He said he would never do that to me because I remind him of Mama and he says that he loves her. I guess he thought that would make me feel better to hear him say. He knows I write in the journals now. He encourages it. He says that I need a healthy outlet for everything I am feeling. I don't know if I feel anymore. I think I stopped feeling a long time ago. Well, maybe not, because I feel scared for what's going to happen to Karen. Sometimes when Jeff wanted a performance, I would volunteer so Karen could get a break. She still hadn't gotten used to this lifestyle. Sometimes Jeff would let me fill in for her. Other times he was insistent that she play out his fantasies. I know Karen liked me protecting her. I don't know if she will have someone looking out for her the next place she goes.

Elana had not been consistent in chronicling her experience. Sometimes she wrote every day for a while, then other times she skipped months. There was only one entry for the entire year in 2000 and that was on January 1. Elana expressed her disappointment about the world not ending as she thought it would.

Instead of leafing through them all, Troy picked up the last of Elana's entries curious to see what her thoughts were during her final days.

July 27, 2011 —I didn't get my period. Jeff says that I'm pregnant. I hope not. I don't want him to do to my baby what he does to me.

April 7, 2012— -Having this baby is going to hurt. Jeff has been learning about childbirth so he can deliver the baby. I tried to talk him into letting me go to the hospital, but he won't. He's scared that I am going to tell someone. I told him that I wouldn't. I don't have anywhere to go if they take me away from Jeff. It's been so long since I've seen Mama. She may not want me back now. Jeff takes care of me. Like he said, I don't have anyone else. He showed me this thing called the Internet the other day and showed me information about missing children. Jeff said that they only put information about children whose parents wanted them back. Some of the kids were missing a long time and there was still things about them. There was nothing about me. Mama doesn't miss me. I still miss her.

He forwarded through the entries once again to the very last one several weeks before her death...

October 9, 2012—I think Jeff is going to kill me one day. He killed my baby. He says he didn't. He says he dropped her off at the hospital nursery, but he's lying. I heard her crying and then a big pop and after the pop she wasn't crying anymore. I will never forget that sound or how horrible I felt knowing I would never see her again. It's been months and I miss her. I didn't even get to hold her, but for a few minutes. I named her Lilly like my mom. Having Lilly and loving her taught me that there is a special connection between mothers and their children. No matter what Jeff says, Mama loves me. So what, I'm not on the stupid Internet. She loves me and she misses me. If I could talk to her, I would tell her that I'm sorry. If she asked me why I got in the car with Jeff, I would tell her everything that happened. I went outside to see if I saw Troy's dad because I needed him to pay for my push pop. Jeff pulled up, asking me what I was doing there. I told him and asked if he would buy my push pop. He gave me the money to go back in the store to get it. When I came out with his change, he said Mama asked him to get me and keep me until she came. (I heard him talking to one of his friends saying that he wanted to take me way before he did, but he never had a chance to get me alone until the day at the store.) I think he's going to kill me because he says that he is tired of keeping secrets and wants to live a normal life. I guess me and the other girls that passed through here over the years were his secrets. Jeff said that he and Mama have been talking again and he wants to marry her, but he can't with me being here and so he has to send me away. A guy came to look at me, but he didn't want to buy me. He said I was too old. I asked Jeff why I can't see Mama and he said because she doesn't want to see me. I know he's lying. Mama doesn't know I'm here. One day if she ever finds out, I hope she knows that I know she loves me. I love her, too. I don't know how he's going to kill me, if he will, but I think he will. I'm not scared of dying. It has got to be better than living locked up in a room. If he kills me, I will be free and I will get to be with Lilly.

Troy wiped his eyes hoping to catch any tears before they fell. Surprisingly, there were none. Only the silent cries from his heart, relieved that, in the end, Elana had some sense of peace.

"You okay?" Natalie reached over and gently squeezed his hand.

"Yes," he replied, putting the journal back in the bag and deciding he would not read thrugh any more entries, "Elana is finally free."

Epilogue

Two Months Later

"You're doing great babe, keep pushing." Troy sat by Natalie's side, holding her hand in the hospital delivery room. His parents and Salome were in the waiting area anxiously anticipating the new arrivals, along with Aneetra and Corrine. Tracy couldn't come because she had to teach, but she was planning a trip in the very near future. With the exception of Aneetra, who had been sworn to secrecy, Troy and Natalie had decided to keep everyone in suspense about the babies' genders.

Finally, one screaming male child was out and a few pushes later came the baby girl. Both had a healthy set of lungs. Natalie grinned from ear to ear as she held them while Troy snapped a picture. "We make beautiful children, babe."

"Don't get any more ideas, buddy. These are the last beauties we will ever make as long as I have a say in it." He laughed and joined them in the photo while the nurse took a picture. Troy and Natalie mutually agreed to give the babies names that started with E in honor of Elvin and Elana. The middle names were the same as Troy's and Natalie's.

The boy, Ean Jermaine, was seven pounds, six ounces and twenty-one inches long. The girl, Ebony Reneé, was seven pounds, two ounces and nineteen inches long. The name they had chosen fit her perfectly as it meant, "Dark beauty," and it so happened that she had a gorgeous mahogany skin tone. Ean, who was lighter than his twin, had a name that meant, "God is gracious." Neither Natalie nor Troy had been aware of the meanings when they'd originally picked the names, and upon learning the meanings they liked them even more. Natalie joked that if Ebony was light-skinned it might confuse her.

After being given the clearance, Troy headed to the lobby to get their family. His mom was relieved to hear that both babies were healthy. She'd gotten mad when Troy notified a few of his friends to tell them that Natalie had gone into delivery. She claimed that it was bad luck to notify anyone other than immediate family members until after the mother delivered. When Troy called her superstition ridiculous, she went to the gift shop and bought bubble gum, which, if chewed by at least one grandmother during delivery, would offset the curse. When Troy announced that each child safely entered the world, Salome teased his mom about having saved their lives.

Over the past couple of months, Troy had begun building a relationship with his newly discovered sister. The more Troy learned about Salome, the more he liked her. She fit right in as though she'd been part of their clan all along. She got along well with everyone and tended to liven things up a bit for their family with her hippie/afrocentric flavor and she'd been the needed glue to help repair relationships, especially between Troy and their father, whom she still called by his first name.

One by one, everyone passed the babies around. Troy took a few more photos and sent them to Tracy and Elvin. Within minutes Elvin was ringing his phone at the same time his mom was dialing Tracy.

"They are beautiful, man! We can't wait to get up there during spring break and spend some time with y'all." Elvin had always been instrumental in Troy's spiritual life and Troy admired him more and more for the way he had handled the recent tragedies. He was still faithful, still taking things one day at a time, and still not ready to read through any of Elana's journals. "What does Nate think about his baby siblings?"

"He hasn't seen them yet. He's with Sylvia and Richard." Elvin hadn't been around Nate's surrogate grandparents much, so Troy had to remind him that Sylvia was Natalie's godmother and Richard was a DA whom Troy initially knew because of their working relationship. "They are going to bring him up here later."

"You'll have to send me a picture of Nate with the twins."

"Will do."

"Give Natalie a hug for me and tell the fam I said hey. I love y'all, man."

"I love you, too, bruh."

Troy then sent pictures to a few other friends and family members in one mass text message and replies started pouring in. There was only one message that disturbed him.

Congrats on the new arrivals. They are gorgeous. Let's talk soon. Love, Cheryl.

She'd been a nuisance ever since Troy had returned from Texas. Despite the fact that he had not replied to a single one of her text messages, she was faithful in "checking in" with him every week. Concerned that he'd mistakenly included her on his distribution list, Troy double-checked. Nope. He stepped in the hall and looked around. There was no sign of her. How in the world did she know about the babies? He had not posted anything online and besides Elvin, no one else he'd sent pictures to knew Cheryl. Elvin would have never shared them with her, especially after Troy confided in him about her harassment. He'd encouraged Troy to tell Natalie, but Troy could not bring himself to involve his wife. He'd hope Cheryl would eventually get bored and move on.

"Everything all right, son?" His dad came in the hall to see about him.

"Uh, yeah. Everything is fine." Troy took a deep breath and the two men walked back into the room. Cheryl was a problem he'd have to solve on another day. Right now, he simply wanted to enjoy his family.

DISCUSSION QUESTIONS

1. At age eleven, Troy had already decided against marriage after witnessing the things that went on in the relationships of those around him. Are there factors in your childhood that influenced your view (positively or negatively) of marriage?

2. In general, the media has been accused of not giving the disappearance of minority children the same attention as that of Caucasian ones. Do you think this is true? Why or why not? Compare the cases of Natalee Holloway and Jahessye Shockley.

3. Politics can often divide friends and family members. Have you and your loved ones been divided on political issues?

4. What is your relationship with your father like?

5. What do you think of Troy's behavior at the family breakfast? Is it justified or is he being mean?

6. From where do you think superstitions originated? Why do some people so easily believe in them?

7. Given everything you know about Edgar so far up until chapter 6, do you sympathize with him? Why or why not?

8. Have you or would you ever be willing to undergo hypnosis? Why or why not?

9. Natalie recalls Troy telling her that she will make Nate "soft" by coddling too much. Do you agree or disagree?

10. In chapter 9, Diane reveals a detail about the day Elana disappeared of which Troy is unaware. Do you think this information is significant in solving Elana's mystery?

11. In chapter 10, Troy walks into a scene at his parents' home that sends him into a rage. Do you think his anger was warranted? Why or why not?

12. How do you and your spouse normally settle conflicts?

13. When Natalie talks to Diane about Jesus, Diane mentions being scared of change. Why do you think many people think that Jesus works for others, but not necessarily themselves?

14. Describe the importance of a father's role in a child's life. How do fathers help shape a child's identity?

15. Lequocious isn't really a word, but Bill uses it anyhow. Do you know the word he should have used?

16. What, if any, are some Christmas traditions that you and your family have?

17. How would you explain the definition of a superstition to a three-year-old?

18. In chapter 18, Troy thinks about his three primary suspects. Which one do you think is responsible for Elana's kidnapping and murder? Is there anyone else you would consider? Why?

19. Do you agree with B.K. and Troy that justice has been served to Herbert?

20. Did you pick up any additional clues after Troy's session with Shauna?

21. Natalie and Diane seem to have a pretty good relationship despite their differences. What is your relationship like with your mother-in-law?

22. Natalie is clearly overwhelmed by Nate's behavior in the airport. What are some techniques you use to correct the misbehavior of your children?

23. What do you think the items Troy discovered in the bedroom mean?

24. What would your response have been if you were Diane and presented with the same information Troy revealed in chapter 30?

25. Has there been a storm in your life in which you have found peace, despite turmoil or pain? Does healing eventually come as a whole or is it a continual journey?

26. What message can you take away from this story?

ABOUT THE AUTHOR

Yolonda Tonette Sanders holds two bachelors degrees from Capital University in the fields of Criminology and Political Science, and a masters degree in Sociology from Ohio State University. After working for the State of Ohio for three-and-a-half years, she took a leap of faith by resigning from her job to focus more on writing. It was a leap that she has never regretted as she became a traditionally published author and also started her own company, Yo Productions, LLC, which specializes in literary services and theatrical entertainment. Yolonda has had four novels published so far, including *Wages of Sin*, which was the first book in her *Protective Detective* series. Currently, Yolonda resides in Columbus, Ohio and is the loving wife of David, proud mother of Tre and Tia, and joyful caregiver of her mother, Wilene. Visit the author at www.yoproductions.net, www.yolonda.net, www.facebook.com/yoproductions and on Twitter @ytsanders